Los An

A severed he:
Hol

Fresh from wrapping his previous case, LAPD Detective Sam Leroy is called to the scene. Now he is tasked with identifying the victim, and finding the rest of him.

Not necessarily in that order.

Following up on the few leads they have, Leroy and his partner, Detective Ray Quinn, find themselves unravelling a complex puzzle, one which began two thousand miles from home, and which involves sex, extortion, and ultimately murder.

While Leroy follows the trail, he is feeling himself coming to the end of a relationship, and may possibly be making decisions he might later regret.

Philip Cox is married with two children and lives near London. A former Bank Manager, he pursued a career in banking and financial services until 2009, when he took a break to become a stay-at-home father. In between numerous school runs, Philip wrote *After the Rain*, which appeared in 2011. *Dark Eyes of London* and *She's Not Coming Home* followed in 2012. *Something to Die For*, which introduced the maverick LAPD detective Sam Leroy, was published in 2013. *Don't Go Out in the Dark* was published in 2014, and *Wrong Time to Die*, the second Sam Leroy story, was published in 2015. *Should Have Looked Away* followed in 2016. *The Angel* is the second story featuring reporter Jack Richardson, whom we first met in *Don't Go Out in the Dark.*

Also by Philip Cox

After the Rain
Dark Eyes of London
She's Not Coming Home
Something to Die For
Don't Go Out in the Dark
Wrong Time to Die
Should Have Looked Away
The Angel

NO PLACE TO DIE

PHILIP COX

Philip Cox has asserted his right under the Copyright, Designs and Patents Act 1988 to be identified as the author of this work.

This book is a work of fiction. Names and characters are the product of the author's imagination and any resemblance to actual persons, living or dead, is entirely coincidental.

www.philipcox.moonfruit.com

ISBN 978-1542759922

FOR ALISON, ELLA AND IONA
Toujours mes bebes

ACKNOWLEDGEMENTS

All I did was write the book! Other people helped in the process. I want to thank: Anne Poole, Sagar Chauhan, the Los Angeles Convention Center, Delta Air Lines, and the Research Departments of the LAPD, NYPD and LAFD. Also to Keith Mulvihill of ThisOldHouse.com for his insights into what happens in a house fire.

Cover photographs by Chris-Havard Berge and Jason Ralston

The author is British, but the story takes place in the United States, and most of the characters are American. So: British English or American English? The narrative is in British English, and the dialogue is mostly American English. So US readers please note that some words may be spelt differently, such as *tyres* for tires, *centre* for center.

CHAPTER ONE

ITS TINY TONGUE flicking to and fro, the gopher snake made its way slowly through the chaparral, along the dusty earth, pausing now and then to investigate the many rocky crevices and small shrubs she encountered. Twilight was approaching, and the soil still retained some of the heat from the day's sunshine.

Twilight for the gopher snake, of course, meant food. Its main diet comprised small mammals or birds, and the occasional egg. Mainly diurnal, these cold-blooded reptiles often change their activity patterns to become nocturnal during the months of intense desert heat. It was late May, and summer was beginning; early evening was slightly cooler, and this was the time its prey would emerge from their burrows and forage for food themselves. So now this snake, three feet in length, was out hunting, at the same time avoiding its own predators, such as coyotes or hawks.

Heavily bodied, the gopher snake has around sixty light to dark brown or reddish blotches on a base colour of yellow, straw, tan or cream. A dark stripe runs from in front of the eye to the angle of the jaw. The scales on its back are strongly keeled, becoming smoother on the sides.

Non-venomous, it kills its prey by constriction. However, it is often confused with a rattlesnake when alerted to danger, when it will coil up, vibrate its tail, flatten its head and hiss a warning. In fact, its genus name, *pituophis*, means 'phlegm serpent' in reference to its loud hiss.

But as with all but the most aggressive and dangerous snakes, the gopher will seek to hide from any danger rather than seek a confrontation. Through the sensitive scales on its underside, the snake can detect movement in the ground nearby, and quickly hide beneath a rock until the threat has passed.

The threat on this occasion consisted of three pairs of hiking boots. From beneath the rock, the snake watched as one pair paused not eighteen inches away from the rock. Its tail started to twitch, but relaxed when the boots withdrew. It could detect more sounds, but these seemed more distant.

The owners of the boots were three twenty-somethings, two men and a girl, hiking. One of the men, a tall, slim blond by the name of Mark, stopped walking and perched on a rock. The other man, Robbie, shorter and heavily set, paused, stretched and put his hands on his hips.

'What?' Robbie asked.

Mark tilted his head in the direction of the girl. Smaller and slighter, her pale complexion contrasted with the men's heavy tans. 'Waiting for her to catch up.'

Robbie adjusted his baseball cap and wiped his forehead. 'Come on, Jan,' he called out.

'I'm coming, I'm coming,' Jan replied breathlessly as she hurried up the slight incline to catch them up. 'I need a breather,' she panted, sitting on the small embankment.

'We can't be too long,' Mark said. 'It'll be dark soon.'

Robbie looked up sat the sky, squinted and checked his watch. 'Seven thirty almost.'

Mark consulted the pamphlet he was holding with a map. 'Says here sunset's at 7:55. Twilight till 9:30.'

'Twilight's no good for us,' Jan complained. 'We need daylight. Let's face it, guys: we're lost.'

Robbie looked down at Mark. 'Are we? You've got the map.'

Mark looked around and studied the map. He grimaced. What had started out as a straightforward hike through Bronson Canyon had not gone to plan. He looked around again.

Jan threw her arms in the air. 'Told you – we're lost!'

Still studying the map, Mark shook his head. Slowly, he replied, 'No, we're not lost…'

'Where are we, then?' Robbie asked.

'Not quite sure. Let me see -'

Jan gasped. 'Lost, then. Jeez.'

Mark ran his finger over the map. 'It should be quite easy to retrace out steps. Look, here's Franklin Avenue, where we started off, then North Canyon Drive.'

'That's where we left the car,' Robbie said. 'Hours ago.'

'No, no,' Mark replied, as his finger followed the route they had taken. At the end of North Canyon Drive there is situated the Camp Howland Parking Lot, where the three had left their rental car. 'The parking lot here,' said Mark, 'is where the unpaved road started. And we followed that to Bronson Canyon.'

'Where we explored the cave,' Robbie added.

'Don't talk to me about that bloody cave,' moaned Jan.

The cave they were referring to was Bronson Cave, not so much a cave but a fifty-foot long tunnel. It has featured in many feature films, notably *The Searchers* and *Star Trek VI – The Undiscovered Country*. The mouth was also used as the entrance to the Batcave in the 1960s *Batman* TV series.

'We should've turned back after we'd done with the cave,' Robbie said.

'Yeah, but we didn't,' Jan wailed. 'So now we're stranded here with – oh my God!'

Mark looked up. 'What is it?'

Jan stood up quickly, looking around frantically. 'I've just realised – don't they have rattlesnakes here? And mountain lions?'

Mark turned over the pamphlet he was holding and turned it over. 'Yeah, rattlesnakes, black bears, coyotes, skunks…'

Robbie grinned. 'But no crocs.'

'It's not funny, you guys,' Jan wailed. 'We're lost, it's nearly dark, and… and…'

Robbie looked around. 'Look down there, Jan. What can you see?'

She followed his gaze. 'Nothing.'

'Look. Tell me what you see.'

Puzzled, she replied, 'Just lights.'

'Yes, just lights. Lights from the city. And buildings. Although soon it'll just be lights. But we know the streets of Hollywood are down there. So we head down there.'

Mark stood up. 'Twilight lasts for another hour and a half. If we get a move on, we should get to the parking lot before it's fully dark.'

'Yeah, but the path wasn't exactly the Gore Hill Freeway. It could be dangerous in the dark.'

'So we'd better get a move on now,' Mark said abruptly as he began to head off down the hill.

Jan was about to protest some more, but stopped as Robbie put his hand on her shoulder. 'Come on,' he said quietly. They both began to follow Mark down the slope.

Mark paused as the path made a slight turn. They were on the top of a ridge. Mark looked around. Pointing behind the others, he said, 'Look up there.'

They turned and looked.

'I had no idea we were so close to it,' Robbie said.

'Now we know where we're headed.' Mark began climbing back up the slope.

What Mark had spotted was the famous Hollywood sign, its nine 45 foot letters standing proudly on the side of Mount Lee.

'There must be something up there,' Mark called out to the other two who were twenty feet behind him.

'You'd better be right,' Jan muttered.

'He probably is,' Robbie said, trying to reassure her. 'It's a tourist spot, isn't it? There's probably a cafeteria, restrooms, phone booth.'

'Yeah, it would've been helpful if we could get a phone signal up here,' Jan muttered in reply.

'Can't have everything,' Robbie said. 'Jesus, Mark; be careful.'

'I'm okay,' Mark called out. 'It's just a little steeper here.'

The three half walked, half scrambled up the steep slope, using the frequent sage brush bushes to help their climb. Mark paused again and pointed up at the sign.

'Nearly there,' he called out. 'And there's more buildings there, too.'

Robbie and Jan looked up, silently nodded, and continued their climb. It was getting darker, but they could still see the white letters of the sign, and a tall tower painted red and white and covered in communications dishes.

After five or six minutes the ground levelled off slightly. They stopped on the level.

'That's great,' Jan whined. Mark said nothing, just wiped the sweat off his forehead.

'I don't believe it,' Robbie said, shaking his head.

They were some twenty feet from the two giant Ls, but separating them from the sign was a tall fence, at least ten feet high, and topped with razor wire.

Mark began to make his way along the fence. 'There must be a gate somewhere.'

'I need a piss,' Robbie said, and disappeared behind a bush. The other two waited until he returned.

'I need to, too,' Jan said sheepishly.

Mark rubbed his face. 'Christ. We're going to be -'

Jan held up her hand. 'Don't even…'

The two men waited while Jan disappeared into the undergrowth.

Meanwhile the gopher snake had long emerged from its rock, and was continuing its search for food. Snakes do have nostrils, but their tiny tongues play an important part in hunting for food. When a snake flicks its tongue in the air, it picks up tiny chemical particles. When it brings its tongue back into its mouth, the tongue fits into a special organ on the roof of its mouth. This organ takes these particles and tells the snake what they are – dirt, plants, other animals. A predator, or prey.

This time it was prey – a two-inch desert shrew. The gopher snake moved slowly to a point twelve inches from the unsuspecting rodent, then struck. In a fraction of a second, its coils were encircling the shrew, which let out a helpless squeak, but no more. When it could feel no movement from the shrew, the snake released its coils slightly, turning to face the rodent's head, and opened its mouth, the jaws extending to take in the wider animal.

Mark and Robbie studied the perimeter fence while they waited for Jan. They both started as they heard her yell.

'What is it?' Robbie called out, as they both hurried in the direction of Jan's voice.

'There's something here,' she said.

Then she began to scream.

Having caught its prey, the gopher snake saw no need to rush its meal. Slowly, its enlarged jaws worked their way down the shrew's body, until its tail slowly disappeared down the snake's throat.

Further up the side of Mount Lee, by the time the snake had finished eating, Jan was still screaming.

CHAPTER TWO

HARRY WEBB LOOKED up from his keyboard. The little cursor flashed at him, as if to say, *come on, where's the next word?*

Harry was a screenwriter. Had been for some fifteen years now. Mainly TV, some movie work, but nothing that had hit the big screen.

Harry was also a dreamer. One day, he would hear a famous voice announcing, 'And the Academy Award for Best Screenplay goes to Harry Webb.' Cue thunderous applause.

One day.

But tonight, he was alone on his veranda working on a screenplay, looking out over the city.

Looking out over the city as his house was a stilt house on the Mulholland Highway. Stunning view when the conditions were right, but tonight they were not. He had a deadline to meet. He sat back, ran his hands through his hair and cursed.

Since he got up at seven this morning and ate his normal breakfast of raisin bran, all he had achieved was two pages. And now it was past 11PM. He habitually set himself a goal of five pages a day: today he had just achieved two after eighteen hours of staring at his keyboard.

Over the past fifteen years he had worked for a number of studios: a couple of the majors, but mainly smaller, independent, cable-only ones. The only difference he had found was the label on the bottled water in their offices.

His previous job was a two-hour pilot for a cable network, about sexual liaisons in the Senate. Nothing new there. It was taped, and the final cut sent to the network. Then they waited for The Call.

When it did come, the producer had That Voice. 'We tried our best, Harry, but the network passed on it. Another time.'

Over the last five years, Harry had been paid to write fifteen screenplays. Some do get made, most don't. His name had only appeared on one. He still fantasized about walking around sound stages, going to premiers and walking down to the stage in the Sony Theater but accepted that it would stay a fantasy.

He had gotten used to the ups and downs. Especially the downs. In this town it was useless to dwell on past failures instead of working on the Next Best Idea.

He stood up and wandered over to the edge of the veranda and looked at the horizon. In the darkness there were rivers of car headlamps. That was an advantage of living in a stilt house. To this day, he was astonished the house had stayed up so long, especially in an area prone to earthquakes, mudslides and wildfires.

About fifteen hundred of these dwellings were built between the end of WW II and the mid-1960s; city building regulations now meant that none had been built for years – nowadays they would be multi-storey mansions gouged into the landscape.

Not aesthetically pleasing, they were modest, one storey, and boxy. Not exactly a blot on the landscape, but fragile.

Fragile was the word Harry would use.

As the 1994 Northridge earthquake showed, when thirteen houses collapsed, and slid down the hillside. They were built on two or more stilts, diagonally braced by rods or cables in an X pattern, holding up the floor. Sometimes the floor was attached to the street level foundations, more often not. A bigger risk was that of fire, and a recent building code regulation required the underside of the house be enclosed or made resistant to fire for at least one hour. That was expensive, so Harry hadn't done it, and nobody had checked. So underneath Harry's house were rocks and sage brush, and an old couch.

But it was the view Harry liked most of all. His ex-wife suffered from vertigo, so never went outside. But Harry used to sit out here on the veranda, with their energetic Labrador bitch called Myrna.

But now the bitch had gone.

And taken the dog with her.

So went Harry's favourite joke, probably the only one he knew – he didn't write comedies – and which he would tell on every possible occasion.

He returned to his keyboard, and picked up the book. It was not an original screenplay that he was working on this time, but an adaptation of a best seller he had never heard of. Target audience: thirteen-year-old girls, he guessed.

Only this best seller was, in Harry's opinion, a crock of shit – 250 pages of pulp about a ghost who leaps about in time to visit his ancestors and his descendants to advise them on their lifestyle choices. How the hell could you write a good screenplay based on this crap?

He sat back and stretched. He needed some vapour. In the old days, he would have needed a cigarette, but six months back he had switched to one of those new-fangled vaporizers. Supposed to be better than his Marlboros: no coughing, no bad breath. He guessed they were okay. The vaporizers apparently contained what the guy in the store called an e-liquid, some stuff called propylene glycol, or PG. It gave off a vapour, which replaced the cigarette smoke. Harry liked the fact that he could choose different flavours: the last was cotton candy, but his preferred choice was buttered popcorn. So instead of smoking, he would be vaping.

Which he needed right now. He went back indoors, and looked around. Then rummaged around in the bedroom, then the kitchen, then the bathroom. Where had he left that damn vaporizer?

He had no idea. He swore. He didn't want to go out as he had at least three more pages to write, but he needed some vapour to get these three pages done. Harry picked up his car keys, and headed for the door.

The place Harry was headed for was his local grocery store, set five minutes' drive away in a small shopping centre off Mulholland Drive. It was at this store that Harry had been introduced to the delights of vaping.

There were four other establishments there alongside the grocery store: a laundromat, a bar, and a pizza take-out joint. The small parking lot out front had only half a dozen vehicles, so Harry could easily get a space. As he drove across the lot to the space nearest the store, he saw a man pacing anxiously back and forth. Harry thought nothing of it, and found a space, and parked. As he flicked the key fob to lock the car, he noticed the man watching him. This was a reasonably safe neighbourhood, so Harry continued to walk to the store, but remained on alert. As he approached the store the man hurried up to him, not in a threatening manner, but he was clearly distressed.

'Help, help,' he said. He had an accent, which Harry couldn't place. The guy didn't look Hispanic, or Asian, but English was clearly not his first language.

'What's up, pal?' Harry asked.

The man blurted out something Harry could not comprehend, and pointed to the row of dumpsters beyond the corner of the store. He tugged at Harry's sleeve.

'What is it, pal?' Harry asked again. 'What's the matter?'

The man pulled at the sleeve some more and gesticulated wildly at the dumpsters. Again said something in his native tongue which by now Harry had guessed was something Eastern European. Harry let the man lead him to the row of dumpsters. There were eight in total, and only one had its lid open. The man released Harry's sleeve and scampered over to the open one. He jabbed his finger inside.

Harry followed the man and peered inside. It was dark, but the lamp affixed to the side wall of the store afforded Harry the light he needed.

As he looked inside, he could feel the lasagne he had microwaved earlier try to force its way back into his throat.

'Oh, Jesus,' he said.

CHAPTER THREE

A FEW WEEKS earlier, John Thomas Hightower nestled his
ample figure into the comfort of his seat. At 224 pounds,
he was pleased to be travelling first class; had he gone
coach, this five-hour flight would be even less enjoyable.
It was just as well his firm was paying the $900 round trip
fare. Hightower, also known as 'J.T.', always insisted on
flying first class. He had to make these trips twice a year,
and felt that almost two thousand dollars was a small price
to pay to ensure his attendance at these conventions.

Hightower worked for a company specialising in rare
books, and his position as Acquisitions Executive gave

him the twice-yearly opportunity to travel to a variety of cities around the country, leaving his wife and son back at home in Jasper, Alabama.

He and his wife Maybeline had five offspring in all: two girls, now in their thirties and married with children of their own; two sons, one of whom was also married with children, and one who, much to his father's disappointment, was now living in Birmingham with a girl he met in a bar. His fifth child, a son, had just turned fifteen and still lived at home.

This particular trip was in fact the second so far this year. The first was in January and was up to Chicago, a place Hightower hated in the winter. Winters in the humid subtropical climate of Alabama are mild, and the three days in Chicago, with the ice and snow and cold, were an anathema to him. Now, in the late Spring, he had mixed feelings about this trip to Los Angeles. At home, the mercury would already be hitting the 80s, and he would be tiring of the incessant rain, so he would be feeling more comfortable physically; but the City of the Angels was anything but to Hightower. He always found it dry, dusty, dirty, too spread out.

And sinful. Hightower viewed with disdain the countless motels and bars and sex shops and hookers. On a previous trip, one evening for the want of something to do, he took a cab the length of Hollywood Boulevard, from Fairfax to Normandie, not getting out, but just out of some morbid curiosity around how the other half lived.

And now, comfortable in Seat 3B in the small first class section of the Boeing 757, Hightower was ready to begin the final leg of his journey. The first leg had been a short hop from Birmingham-Shuttlesworth to Atlanta Hartsfield-Jackson; the main part of the journey was the 4 hour 55 minute trip from ATL to LAX. As the plane sped down the runway, Hightower rested his tan felt Stetson on his lap and closed his eyes. Soon they were in the air, the aircraft banking slightly as it turned left to begin its journey across Alabama, Arkansas, Oklahoma, New Mexico, Arizona to California.

It was just after 2PM, and Hightower tried to get a brief nap, but soon the cabin crew began to make their rounds offering the first of several complementary drinks. Hightower accepted a mineral water, and glanced over at the man in Seat 3A, who ordered a double whiskey. He reciprocated the mumbled 'cheers' as his neighbour downed the bourbon in one mouthful. Another reason to disapprove of his fellow passenger, who had a goatee and long hair tied in a ponytail. Hightower guessed the guy worked in the music industry as he had out on his lap two music magazines and was constantly sending and receiving messages on a Blackberry. Then he fished an Ipad out of his carry-on case, and Hightower noticed he went straight to a record company website. The man also smelt heavily of a very sweet-smelling cologne.

Finishing his mineral water, Hightower paused as he listened to the chief steward welcoming the passengers on board Delta Airlines Flight 1755 to Los Angeles International Airport, which was due to arrive 3:32 that afternoon local time. They would be travelling at an altitude of 35900 feet, and a ground speed of 445 knots. The weather in Los Angeles was a balmy 72 degrees, and conditions were good over the flight path, so sit back and enjoy the flight.

Hightower cleared his throat and glanced across at what the man in Seat 3A was doing. He was still engrossed in one of his magazines, specifically at the page which was taken up with a large photograph of a scantily clad reality TV show star. Hightower cleared his throat again and reached into his own carry-on bag, and pulled out a Bible, King James Version. He opened it up to a page where a corner had been turned down, and found a verse he had previously underlined in pencil. Romans 3:23 – *For everyone has sinned; we all fall short of God's glorious standard.* Harrumphing again, he continued reading until he had finished all sixteen chapters of the Book of

Romans. As he read, he would look up and around, not looking at anything or anyone in particular, but thinking of his wife, his children, his grandchildren, and his church back in Jasper, some forty miles from Birmingham.

It was only three days ago that Hightower and his entire family – all three generations – except his third son were sitting in the pews at the Church of the Holy Gospel, listening to Pastor Martyn preaching – as he always seemed to – on the immorality of sex outside marriage. Hightower recalled the text on which the forty-minute sermon was based, again from the Book of Romans: *Those controlled by the sinful nature cannot please God. For if you live according to the sinful nature, you will die; but if by the Spirit you put to death the misdeeds of the body, you will live.*

He recalled feeling slightly uncomfortable listening to Pastor Martyn, and receiving a couple of awkward glances from Maybeline. Pastor Martyn had always made it no secret that he disapproved strongly of the fact that one of Hightower's children was living in sin in Birmingham, and the inference was that Hightower, as the head of the family, should have done something to stop it. But as he would say to Maybeline, what can I do? The boy had rejected all of his father's and Pastor Martyn's teachings; the only response the pastor could give was that 'your son will have to explain himself before God when his time comes.' Maybeline's response and that of his other children was, 'Let him. Pastor Martyn has a thing about sex, anyway.'

Hightower knew they were probably right, but it was the impotence and embarrassment he felt amongst the congregation which he found difficult to handle. He would say to his wife, 'All I can do is pray for him, Maybeline,' but deep down he knew that prayer was not the answer. At least the boy was living with a woman. The alternative was beyond imagination.

He did manage to doze off, despite fighting the urge to glance now and then at whatever Seat 3A was watching on his device: some movie or other. He must have slept for a couple of hours off and on, because now the cabin crews were readying the passengers for landing. They were beginning their descent into the natural bowl where the city of Los Angeles is situated. Having an aisle seat, Hightower could only sit bolt upright and get a brief glance through the window. Seat 3A was messaging, oblivious to the desert and shrubs and freeways and flat buildings below.

With a slight jolt, the 757 touched down, decelerated, and started to taxi towards Terminal 5, of which Delta had exclusive use. Being in first class, Hightower was one of the first passengers to deplane, and after thanking the steward for an enjoyable flight, he put on his Stetson and carried his bag out of the 757, along the bridge to the arrivals hall, where he awaited his suitcase.

He did not have long to wait, and, after a brief restroom stop, made his way out of the terminal building to the row of taxis where he hailed a cab to his hotel.

CHAPTER FOUR

HIGHTOWER WAS BOOKED into the Stocker on North
Alameda, across from Union Station. He checked in, and
the bellhop led him to the elevator. His room was on the
ninth floor, and much to his alarm, once the glass elevator
reached the second floor, it made the rest of its journey up
the outside of the building. Hightower involuntarily turned
towards the metal doors to avoid the view, much to the
wry amusement of the bellhop and the other two
passengers, who got out on the sixth.

Hightower tipped the bellhop a $10 bill and unpacked.
He was starting to get hungry as well as tired: after taking

a shower, he ordered a room service dinner. The food arrived thirty minutes later, and as he ate through the chicken picatta – sautéed cutlets in a citrus-caper sauce - followed by chocolate mousse, he studied the hotel brochure.

In his numerous business trips over the years, he had stayed in many different types of hotel, all with varying degrees of comfort and what was on offer, ranging from little more than motels to one step away from a Hilton. The Stocker was higher-middle range: it boasted two restaurants, two bars, a gym with sauna and two swimming pools, one indoors and one outdoors. There was also a piece on how the Stocker was built with reinforcing steel, to give added protection during an earthquake. Not something Hightower wanted to contemplate from a ninth floor room. After eating he rang Maybeline, and was asleep by ten.

The following morning, Hightower set off for the convention after a breakfast of ham and eggs in one of the hotel restaurants. The convention was based appropriately in the LA Convention Center on South Figueroa, a twenty-minute taxi ride from the hotel. The convention itself was a relatively small affair, much to Hightower's surprise, using up barely a half of the centre's 720,000 square feet of exhibition space. Nevertheless, Hightower managed to find a few items in which his firm would be interested, including a 1895 edition of Mark Twain's *Adventures of Huckleberry Finn*. Apparently, three other representatives had shown an interest in that particular book: the procedure now was for all interested parties to put their bids in sealed envelopes which would be taken back to the owner's premises in Detroit where they would be assessed. Hightower hoped that his bid of $98,000 would be accepted, as it would not do to go home from one of these events empty-handed.

The convention was due to end 6PM, but Hightower left earlier. Once the cab deposited him at the Stocker a few moments before five, he decided to take a walk around the vicinity as it was too early to eat, and he had heard Downtown LA was not a good place to be after dark.

He wandered first across the green to Union Station. Crossing over Alameda, he stood at the edge of the parking lot and looked up at the clock tower, whitewashed with a red stucco roof, its design combining Southern California's Spanish heritage with Art Deco styling, popular when the station was constructed in 1939. He reflected on how, when train travel was wreathed in glamour, this was a fitting entry point for visitors to the city. Before air travel. Before LAX.

Hightower turned and walked back across the street, heading for *El Pueblo de Los Angeles*. He had visited this national monument before on a previous visit, and remembered enjoying it, especially Olvera Street. He walked up Olvera, the oldest thoroughfare in LA, and took in the souvenir stands and shops with their sombreros, handicrafts and piñatas, turning down several offers of fresh tortillas and *pandulces*, a Mexican sweetbread. He was sure Maybeline would have liked it here, and spent hours here, but Hightower was relieved once he had reached the end of the block, and began a brisk walk back to the Stocker.

Back in his room, he read through the room service menu. He had enjoyed the chicken the night before, and read down the entrée list to see what else the hotel offered. He decided on a flat iron steak with asparagus and mashed potatoes, but as it was only 6:30 decided to make use of one of the hotel's pools before eating. He rang Maybeline to tell her about his day and let her know what time his flight got in the next day, changed into his trunks and white hotel bathrobe and, matching towel under his arm, headed to the gym and pool on the twelfth floor.

One he reached there, he was dismayed to find the pool quite busy: obviously many other business travellers chose to unwind here. Across the other side of the pool, Hightower spotted a couple of men who he had seen at the convention: wishing to avoid them, he decided to try the outdoor pool.

The outdoor pool was, in fact, one floor above, on the hotel roof. Here it was much quieter: only two other guests occupying the many sun loungers around the pool. He dropped his towel on one of the loungers and looked around. There was no bar, but there was a row of vending machines in a small covered area by the elevator doors. He sauntered over to the machines and checked what they had to offer. Only soft drinks, but plenty of choice. Hightower swiped his key card on the machine and got himself a bottle of root beer.

Back at the pool, he took a mouthful of the ice cold liquid, took off his robe and climbed into the pool. Being almost 7PM, the heat of the day's sun was fading and it was pleasantly warm; nevertheless, he found the cold water of the pool refreshing.

After swimming half a dozen lengths, he got out and returned to his lounger. He had not noticed that while he was in the pool, somebody had occupied the lounger next to his. As he sat down, the girl lying on the lounger looked up at him and smiled. He returned her smile and sat down. He took another mouthful of root beer and picked up the portion of the *Los Angeles Times* that he had brought up from his room. As he read the article – a piece on the decline of America's traditional political system – out of the corner of his eye he noticed the girl sit up on her lounger and rub sun block onto her arms and shoulders. She smiled again as her gaze met his.

'It's a bit late in the day for that,' Hightower said, feeling he ought to say something.

The girl spoke as she rubbed. 'Maybe,' she replied, 'but I burn easily and there's still an hour or so of sun left.'

Hightower nodded, even though he disagreed with her, and returned to his article.

After a few moments, the girl spoke again.

'Pardon me, sir, but can I ask you a favour?'

Hightower put down his newspaper. 'Surely.'

'I need you to rub some of this on my back, if you don't mind.'

He glanced around momentarily before replying. Sitting forward he said, 'Surely I don't mind. Where… where would you like it?'

'On my back, if that's okay with you.' She unhooked the back of her top and lay down on her front.

'That's absolutely fine.' Hightower picked up the bottle of oil and began rubbing it into the girl's back. She pushed her dark ponytailed hair to one side, rested her head to one side and closed her eyes as he rubbed. He found rubbing the oil in pleasurable; he knew he ought to stop, but thought there's no harm in just applying some sun block. He used to do it for Maybeline once, many years ago.

'There you are; all done,' he said after five minutes, wiping the excess oil onto his body.

'You're very kind,' the girl said. 'Let me buy you a drink in return,' she said, starting to lift herself off the lounger.

'No, no; you stay there,' Hightower said. He noticed the sides of her breasts as she lifted herself. 'Allow me. What would you like?'

She looked at his root beer. 'I'll take a water, please.'

'Coming up. Still or sparkling?'

'Mm?'

'The water. Do you take it still, or sparkling?'

'Oh, still.'

'Coming up,' he said again, standing up and walking back to the vending machine. As he swiped his card again, he looked back at the girl. She was lying back down on the lounger. Despite himself, he felt excited. Flattered even: here he was, a sixty-three-year old grandfather, and he was having a friendly conversation with a what? A girl no older than twenty-five. He took the bottled water back to her, thinking, what's wrong with chatting to another hotel guest?

'You're very kind, sir,' the girl said as he put the bottle on the ground next to her lounger.

'You're very welcome. Any time.'

He decided to go back into the pool again. He swam a few more lengths, each time noticing the girl on the lounger next to his. After the sixth length, he decided he had had enough and climbed out of the pool, pausing halfway up the ladder. He felt dizzy, but the dizziness passed momentarily and he climbed out. As he sat back down, he felt dizzy again. 'Oh,' he muttered, shaking his head.

The girl looked up. 'Are you okay?'

'Yes, I'm fine. I felt a bit woozy, a bit dizzy, back there. It's passed now.'

'Oh,' she said, slowly nodding her head.

'Probably the sun, and being tired from my flight yesterday. And it's time to eat.'

The girl hooked up her top and sat up. 'Where did you fly from?'

'Birmingham, Alabama. I'm here on business. Fly home tomorrow.'

'Tomorrow?' she asked.

'Yup. Catch my flight noon tomorrow.'

She nodded, as if taking in what he was saying.

'My name's John, by the way,' he said. 'John Hightower. Most people call me J.T.' He reached down to shake hands with her.

'My name's Paula,' she replied. 'Most people call me Pinky.' She paused, with a grin. 'My friends do, at any rate.'

'Why Pinky?' Hightower asked. She took a deep breath as if to reply, but he stopped her. 'You know what?' he laughed, 'I don't want to know.' He took a mouthful of root beer, paused and finished the bottle. 'What are you doing here? Where are you from?'

'I'm from the Bay Area,' she explained. 'I'm here on vacation.'

'On your own?'

Pinky laughed. 'No, I'm here with a girlfriend. Not that sort of girlfriend, by the way. She's seeing a movie.'

Hightower rubbed the bridge of his nose.

'You okay, J.T.?' Pinky asked.

'Yeah, guess so.'

'Shall we have another drink?'

'Surely, why not?' Hightower got up and bought two bottled waters. As he passed Pinky hers, he said, 'I guess I'll have water also; feeling a bit… a bit drunk.'

'Drunk?' she laughed, putting her bottle to her mouth. 'On root beer?'

Hightower laughed. 'No, probably the sun.'

Pinky put the bottle down. 'What about we finish these in your room? If you don't mind, that is.'

'In my room?' He was momentarily taken aback. 'No, I don't mind.' He stood up, put on his bathrobe, and picked up his towel. Pinky was ready, and he led her to the elevator.

'What's your room number?' she asked.

'It's… it's 9… 91… 915,' he finally replied. 'Gosh, I couldn't recall for a moment there.'

'Don't worry,' Pinky reassured him, guiding him into the elevator.

It took Hightower two attempts to swipe the key card, but eventually got the door unlocked. 'Come, in; make yourself at home,' he said to her. Pinky walked in, and over to the window.

'Wow, what a view,' she gasped, looking over the vista of the city. Hightower didn't think so, but sat down heavily on the bed. Pinky walked over to the bed and climbed onto it. She knelt on the bed behind him and pulled down his robe.

'You're just stressed,' she said, massaging his shoulders. 'That feel better?' she asked after a moment.

He twisted his head to and fro. 'My dear Pinky, that feels great.'

There was a knock on the door – three taps – and Pinky got off the bed and went to open it. Hightower leaned forward to see who it was. It was another girl, around the same age as Pinky, but she was black with frizzy hair. She stepped into the room and Pinky closed and latched the door.

'J.T., this is the friend I told you about,' she said, as they both stood in front of Hightower, each with one arm around the other. 'This is Perky.'

As the girl stood upright Hightower could see why she was called Perky.

'Perky, this is J.T.,' Pinky added. 'He's stressed, Perky.'

Perky tilted her head at an angle. 'Aw, poor baby. You sure do look stressed, honey.'

In fact, Hightower was anything but stressed. He said nothing as Perky knelt down in front of the mini-bar saying, 'Now what do we have here…?' She took out a bottle of champagne and squealed at the pop as she opened it. She untied the knot of the top she was wearing, revealing a swimsuit, not unlike Pinky's.

'Do me the honour, honey?' she asked Pinky, turning round. Pinky unhooked the top, and turned so Perky could reciprocate. Then Hightower's eyes bulged as, in turns, the two girls poured the sparkling liquid over their pert, bare breasts. He stood up, struggled to pull off his trunks, and fell over onto the bed.

'J.T., you take care,' Perky said, helping him up. 'Here, honey: you want something from the bar?'

Hightower blinked heavily. His eyes focussed on his watch. It was 7AM. He ran his hand through his hair and groaned. He had a bad headache. Suddenly he realised he was hungry. How could he be: he had had steak last night, hadn't he?

Then the implications of the time dawned on him. His flight left for Atlanta in five hours. He had a brief shower, and called to order room service breakfast, something he could eat while he packed. He needed to be in LAX by ten at the latest. He ordered ham and eggs again, and dressed quickly. He was halfway through packing his suitcase when there was a knock at the door. He had just come out of the bathroom, so reached out to open the door while he continued packing.

'I'm very impressed, son,' he said to the young Asian man, smartly dressed in a dark suit and white shirt and tie, who stepped into the room. 'I only called to order five minutes ago.'

The young man said nothing, just quietly closed the door. Hightower stopped and looked at him quizzically. 'Breakfast?'

The man smiled. 'No, Mr Hightower, I haven't brought your breakfast. I'm not even from the hotel.'

Hightower frowned, puzzled. 'So who in tarnation are you? What do you want?'

The man smiled. 'Mr Hightower, I won't keep you long. I have something to sell you.'

Hightower laughed. 'To sell me? Son, what are you trying to sell me? The convention was yesterday. You telling me you traced me here to my hotel to sell me… what? A first edition?'

The man smiled again, gently shaking his head. 'No, Mr Hightower, not a first edition.' He laid a letter-sized brown envelope on the dressing table. 'Insurance.'

CHAPTER FIVE

OVER THE YEARS, there have been many studies, in many countries, into sleep patterns, in both children and adults. All coming to more or less the same conclusions.

A study commissioned by Michigan State University found that in the normal adult there are two main stages of sleep, alternating at roughly ninety minute intervals. There is rapid eye movement or REM sleep when the brain is active, and the body is paralyzed, except for eye movement, middle ear ossicle movements, and respiration. In non-rapid eye movement sleep, the brain is less active, but the body can move.

When a normal individual first falls asleep, they enter a stage of sleep drowsiness, then gradually move to stages of deep sleep. After a while, they then revert to the drowsy stage and the cycle begins again.

LAPD Detective Sam Leroy was in non-rapid eye movement sleep, in deep sleep, when his phone gave off its high-pitched bleeping sound, four times. Even though the little Nokia was by the side of his bed, two feet from his head, his only reaction was a grunt, and some slight movement.

Ten minutes later, it rang. Leroy had always eschewed the more fanciful ring tones favoured by some of his fellow officers: first line of a favourite song, or a movie theme. His was a plain vanilla ring, sounding just like a landline. He began to stir, as by nature the phone's ring was louder than a notification bleep.

It rang six times before it stopped. Or was it eight? By the time Leroy was conscious enough to reach out, the phone had stopped ringing.

He picked up the phone and checked the display. The little digital clock read 5:37AM.

'You have to be kidding,' he addressed the phone, rubbing his face with his other hand.

5:37 - now it was 5:38 – meant that he had gotten exactly 4 hours 38 minutes sleep. No, less than that as he arrived back home at one. He figured he was asleep by 1:15, so that was 4 hours 25 minutes sleep.

The reason for his late arrival home was a case he and his partner Detective Ray Quinn had wrapped the night before. A homicide for sure, but a case more complex than the norm. The norm was that the victim was slain either in the course of a robbery, or by a member of their family, or somebody with whom they were or had been in as relationship.

The Kelton case, as it had become known, was more complicated. Particularly as Kelton was neither the name of the victim nor of the perpetrator.

Marv Kelton was a celebrity. Not on the A list, or even the B list, but some kind of celebrity nevertheless. He had had a brief acting career, mainly daytime soaps, but for the past two or three years he had hosted a game show programme on a kids' TV channel. The sort of thing where two teams of kids, ages 7 to 13 or 14, compete to answer general knowledge or specialty questions, and have to go through some kind of obstacle course to win some crappy prize. Sort of Jeopardy meets Celebrity Squares meets God knows what.

Two seasons into the show, a couple of allegations around Kelton began to surface. First rumours, gossip, nothing specific, then the parents of a ten-year-old girl made more specific allegations. Something along the lines of Kelton used to invite certain kids into his dressing room after the shows had been taped for a soda and a cookie. The allegation was that, alone with the girl, he touched her and got her to touch him. Just as a game. Once this allegation began to surface, other parents came forward. No physical evidence, even after the kids concerned were examined. It was just the kids' word against Kelton's. The police were called, and the department concerned, the Child Protection Section of the LAPD Juvenile Division, preferred charges; however, the District Attorney, after questioning the children concerned, decided there was insufficient evidence to proceed. His main reason was that the children's stories were not consistent, and it was unlikely that any jury would convict.

So Kelton was not charged. Declared innocent. He gave a couple of press conferences to restate his innocence, and to say he felt no ill-will toward the children concerned. And that he looked forward to the next season. There were the normal media rumblings on the lines of there's no smoke without fire, and a brief but unsuccessful campaign to have his star removed from its place on Hollywood Boulevard. This campaign began to gain momentum, until a representative of the Hollywood Chamber of Commerce made a statement to the effect that once a star has been added to the Walk, it is considered a part of the fabric of the area. Therefore, never has a star been removed. In any case, Marv Kelton was never charged, and is, therefore, innocent of any wrongdoing.

The network president made a statement that they had always been confident of Kelton's innocence, and they looked forward to working with him in the next and subsequent seasons.

A couple of months later, the show was quietly cancelled.

Everything went quiet for another few months, and then Kelton began to get threats. Calls from untraceable cell phones, graffiti on the outside of his Beverly Hills house. Then, in the middle of the night, somebody defecated on his star on the Walk of Fame.

Then his bodyguard was shot dead. Not in the line of duty, but by accident. By coincidence, Kelton and his bodyguard, Enrique Valli, were of similar appearance. Same height and build, same hair colour, same heavily tanned face.

Valli, however was not shot defending his employer, but in a bar down in Culver City, which is how Leroy was involved, rather than a detective from the Hollywood Division. It must have been Valli's day off, and as he was sitting at the bar, a man walked right up to him and shot him through the head. The killer made no attempt to resist arrest, just kept saying, 'That's for my boy.' He was mortified when he was told he got the wrong target.

Leroy and Quinn made the arrest just before five that afternoon. Rather than holding the parent in a cell until the next day and processing him during their normal shift hours, Leroy decided they would get him charged, arraigned, and finish the paperwork before they went home. That way they could start their next shift with a clear desk. Well, as clear as possible: he really felt the Kelton case should have been assigned to a different division, and wanted it done and dusted.

Therefore, he wished Quinn good night at 12:30 and got indoors at 1AM.

And now it was 5:40AM and his lieutenant was ringing him already.

Leroy blinked a few times before the phone rang again. This time he answered.

'Yes, Lieutenant.'

'Sam, it's Perez. You awake? Sorry, dumb question. Sorry to wake you, I should have said.'

'No, it's okay,' Leroy replied drowsily. 'What's up? It's before six; are you at your desk?'

'I'm on my way in, but I need you and Quinn. You two have a DB up off Mulholland. The local guys are already up there, SID also.'

'Off Mulholland? But why Ray and me?'

'Because the Captain says so. And he says so because the Deputy Chief says so. He feels there might be a connection with that Kelton case.'

'Lieutenant, that's a bit -'

'I know, Sam. I'm sorry. And I know you and Quinn couldn't have gotten much sleep. Just go up and take a look, yeah?'

Leroy rubbed his face again. He was beginning to wake up. 'Sure, Lieutenant. No problem. Do we know anything about the vic?'

'All I know is there's a DB in a dumpster off Mulholland, and everybody above my pay grade has asked for you.'

'Swell. I'll call Quinn now.'

'Sam, there is one thing about the body you ought to know.'

'What's that?'

'It wasn't intact.'

CHAPTER SIX

IT WAS 6:45 when Leroy finally arrived at the Mulholland
Shopping Center, a rather grand name, so he thought as he
pulled into the parking lot, for such a tiny collection of
joints.

He was attending the scene alone: after hanging up on
Lieutenant Perez, he dialled his partner, Detective Ray
Quinn, whose wife answered.

'Oh, Sam,' Holly had said almost in her sleep, 'surely
you don't need Ray already. He's only just gotten off to
sleep.'

Leroy was about to reply as he heard Quinn's voice in the background and then Holly replying, her hand over the phone. Then Quinn came on himself.

'Hey, Sam, what is it?'

'Sorry to disturb, Ray; we've had a call.'

'But we've only just -'

'Listen, Ray. I'm just calling to tell you I've gone to the scene. I can do this part solo. The scene's apparently full of SID and the local guys.'

'What's the call about?'

'According to Perez, there's a DB in a dumpster in some mall off Mulholland Drive.'

'Up there? So why did he call us?'

Leroy took a deep breath. 'Again, according to Perez, everybody from the Captain thru the Chief of Detectives right up to the First Lady thinks it has to do with the Kelton case. And have said we need to get first dibs.'

'How can it be connected?'

'I have no idea, and Perez, who's half asleep himself, says he's just following orders. One other thing he told me is that the guy in the dumpster is missing his head. If it is a guy, that is.'

'Ah.'

'You got it, but let me tell you something: I'll go check this one out, but if I smell a terrorist angle here, it's going over to the Feds before Perez gets his second cup of coffee.'

'Sure. Man, the head.'

'So, I'm going up to the scene now, and I'll meet you back at the Desk later.'

So Leroy had arrived at the scene alone. As soon as he had hung up on Perez earlier, he took a two-minute shower, threw on a black zip fleece jacket over a white tee and black pants, matching shoes. No time to shave, so he was also wearing three days' stubble. The little parking lot was probably busier than it had been in ages. Three black and white sets of wheels: two Dodge Chargers and one Utility, which the Scientific Investigation Division was probably using, were straddling five spaces. A white Ford Transit which Leroy recognised as belonging to the Coroner's Office was parked outside the laundromat, its offside wheels parked upon the sidewalk. He could see two figures sitting in the van. One was smoking.

Leroy parked neatly in one of the remaining three spaces. Slamming his car door shut he paused and looked around. There were four premises here: *Mount Olympus Cleaners*, *Joe's Bar*, *Pizza the Hills*, and *All Niter*, a 24-hour grocery store. Adjacent to the grocery store was a row of eight dumpsters, presumably two for each store, one for recycling and the other for general trash. The dumpsters, with a ten-foot perimeter, were bordered by a stretch of yellow tape, endorsed in black CRIME SCENE - DO NOT CROSS. Three uniformed officers were standing around the area, and two figures in blue jumpsuits were milling around the dumpster. Leroy opened his trunk, took out, unwrapped, and put on his own jumpsuit, also blue, but with LAPD in white on the back.

Sunrise at that time of year is just before six, and it was light by now. From his car, Leroy could look down the hill in the direction of the city. The cloud was low; a precursor to the *June gloom* which was common in late spring to early summer. Brought on by the Catalina eddy weather system, it had arrived early this year. *May grey* would have been more appropriate. In the distance, rising above the smog Leroy could make out the high-rise buildings Downtown: the 73-floor US Bank Tower, once the highest building on the West Coast until it was supplanted in 2016 by the Wilshire Grand Center, also 73 floors, but some 81 feet higher.

Suited up, Leroy turned and walked towards the dumpster. A uniformed officer recognised him and walked over.

'Detective Leroy?' the officer asked.

Leroy nodded. 'Sam Leroy.'

'Cruz. Peter Cruz.'

'Is that the dumpster?' Leroy asked as they walked over to the scene. Cruz held the tape as Leroy ducked under.

'U-huh,' Cruz replied leading him over to the only open container. One of the forensic team was taking photographs, inside and outside the bin, as Leroy peered in.

The first thing he noticed was the smell, a mixture of rotting food and piss. The bin was full of black plastic trash bags, several of which had been torn with some of the contents, paper, plastic, and food, spilling out. Lying in with the bags, was the body.

With no head.

It seems to be a man's. He was wearing a pair of sneakers, jeans and a check shirt.

Leroy looked over to Cruz. 'When was this called in?'

'Just after midnight. A guy who was visiting the grocery store for some smokes.'

Leroy looked around. 'Where is he?'

'We took a prelim statement and let him go. I have his address. Says he's a screenwriter.'

'Do we know what he was doing in the dumpster? Putting the body in there?'

'I don't think so, Detective. He didn't actually find it. He said he called in here for cigarettes when another guy who couldn't speak English stopped him and took him over here.'

'Another guy. And he's gone home, too?'

Cruz nodded.

Leroy looked at Cruz again. 'Tell me: The screenwriter call this in just after midnight, right?'

Cruz nodded again.

'Which means you guys arrived around 12:30, yes?'

Another nod.

'So, why is it that I got my call some five hours later?'

Cruz shook his head. 'Sorry Detective, I can't answer that. We were just told to wait here until you arrived. My sergeant said it he was told that it might be connected with a killing in Hollywood, and the team dealing with that would be coming.'

'Dullshit,' Leroy said, taking one more look inside.

'Detective?'

'Forget it. Not your fault.' Leroy looked over to the forensic team member. 'So what have you found so far?'

'Very little at this time. We need to take the body out of the dumpster.'

'It was called in nearly seven hours ago. Why is he still in there?'

'We were waiting for you to arrive before we moved the body.'

'Jeez. Okay, get the body out of there. Put him down here for now.' Leroy stood to one side as the two SIDs and two patrolmen, one each limb, lifted the body out of the dumpster and laid it on the sidewalk in front. Leroy knelt down and took another look.

He could see that *rigor mortis* had started to set in, as the body was in a grotesque semi-foetal position. The clothing had grubby marks on it, probably from the stuff in the dumpster, as there were traces of papers and food on the clothing. It appeared to be a man's body. He could see there was some soiling on the blue jeans, around the groin area. The blue and green checked shirt was partly tucked into the jeans, partly loose. Two of the buttons were undone. The shirt collar and shoulders were stained black, and the neck was covered in a black treacly layer. Leroy looked briefly at the neck where the head had been removed: he could see it was a straight, clean cut, and could make out the top of the spinal cord under another layer of dried, congealed blood.

Leroy checked the man's shirt and pants pockets for identification, but they were all empty.

'No ID,' he said to anyone who was listening. 'The pockets are empty. No wallet, no papers, no keys, not even a snotty Kleenex. Is that the ME's transport?' he asked Cruz, looking over at the Transit.

Cruz looked over too. By now, the men in the van had seen the body being lifted out, and one of them was walking over.

'They said they would wait for you.'

'Christ,' Leroy muttered, shaking his head.

The ME, whom Leroy did not recognise, stopped at the body and looked down. 'You've gotten him out, then?'

Leroy looked up at him. 'Where's Hobson?'

'He doesn't start till eight. I pulled the graveyard shift.'

'He's all yours,' Leroy said, stepping back. He dove under the yellow tape, and returned to his car, climbing out of his jumpsuit and replacing it in the trunk. As he slammed the trunk shut, he could see the ME fussing around the body. While he was waiting, Leroy wandered, hands in his pockets, down to the intersection with Mulholland Drive. Rush hour was beginning in earnest, although in the background he could still hear the steady sound of traffic down from the Hollywood Freeway and Cahuenga Boulevard. On the corner of the cross street was a plaque announcing *Laurel Hill* in a dark green, ornate font. In the opposite direction to the city and the freeways, the ground rose in a gentle hill, covered in shrubs and cypress trees.

He turned back and walked into the grocery store. Picked himself a bagel with turkey and gave it to the girl behind the till.

She spoke robotically. 'That'll be two dollars forty, plus tax.'

Leroy paid and asked her, 'How long have you been working?'

She stared at him blankly. ''bout six months. Why?'

He shook his head and showed her his badge. 'No, I mean when did you come on shift?'

'Six.'

'Were you working last night?'

'No, I do six thru two.'

Leroy nodded over to the television monitor behind the till. There were four images on the screen, three of inside the store and one of the parking lot. 'Is that stuff recorded?'

'Don't know; I mean, I guess so. You'd have to ask Mr Chin.'

Leroy nodded, and took his change. 'Okay, I'll get him later.'

He took a couple of bites from his bagel and pulled a face. It was as tough as the pot roast his grandmother used to give him when he was a boy. He swallowed and took one more bite, tossing the rest into a trashcan. The bagel must have been yesterday's stock: just as well he wasn't that hungry.

He noticed the ME standing up and looking around, clearly for him. He wiped his mouth and walked over to the yellow taped area.

'Detective,' the ME said, standing hands on hips.

'What's the time of death?' Leroy asked. 'Approximately.'

'That's difficult to establish in this case,' the ME replied slowly.

'How so?' Leroy asked.

The ME cleared his throat. 'Well, as you know, if the body is warm, then death occurred only a few hours previously.'

'U-huh,' Leroy replied, looking around again.

'And if it's kind of cold and clammy, then death occurred between eighteen and twenty-four hours before.'

Nodding, Leroy raised his eyebrows as if expecting more information.

'Unfortunately,' the ME continued, 'in this case the body was kept unnaturally warm by the rotting garbage.'

'Great,' Leroy sighed. 'Best guess, then.'

'There'd been some decomposition. Not much, but the body was lying in a pile of rotting food.' The ME looked back at the dumpsters. 'I thought they were supposed to recycle their trash.'

Getting the guy back on track, Leroy said, 'I noticed there was a degree of *rigor mortis*.'

'Yes, that's right. Now that will begin two to four hours after death -'

'I know.'

'And is normally completed eight to twelve *post mortem*.'

'Age, race?'

The ME took a deep breath. 'Male, Caucasian; I'd guess, somewhere in his thirties. Where's his head, by the way?'

Leroy shook his head. 'That has to be located. It's not in the dumpster, at any rate.'

'That won't help with identification.'

'No, but when you get him back to the lab, you can take some samples. Then we can see if he's a match on CODIS. If not, then unless we find the head, we'll have to go through CCTV and hope somebody reports him missing. What about the cause of death?'

'I can't say right now. Back in the lab we'll check for foreign DNA, also for any signs of sexual assault. But none of the marks on his body indicate cause of death. No entry or exit wounds, I mean.'

Leroy and the ME ducked under the tape as the two SID investigators began taking photographs of the body.

'Obviously,' Leroy said, 'if he was killed by a blow or gunshot wound to the head, we won't know anything about it until we locate it.'

'Sure,' the ME agreed. 'The blood tests will show up if he was poisoned. Or sedated.' He tapped the side of his own neck. 'The cut… well, that appears to be very clean. A very clean cut. Done with a very sharp knife.'

'Like a hunting knife?'

'Possibly, but I can't identify at this stage any serrations.'

Leroy looked over at the body and shook his head. 'Why cut his head off?' he asked, himself more than the ME.

'That's your job. As I said, there's no obvious entry or exit wound on the body. Also the cut is extremely clean.

That would suggest he was already dead when he was decapitated.'

'How so?'

'If he was alive - and conscious - he would have struggled, so the cut wouldn't have been as clean as this one. Of course, he could have been severely restrained, or drugged. But if you look at the neck and shirt…' He started to lead Leroy back to the corpse.

'No, it's okay; I've taken a look.'

'Okay,' the ME said, standing still again. 'You see the blood stains on his neck and shirt. The top of the shirt. The blood's just run down from the wound; almost trickled down, like from a leaky pipe. If he was alive when he was decapitated, the blood would have spurted out. Like a fountain.' He made a gesture with his hands to illustrate a fountain. 'So,' he explained, 'my preliminary findings are that he has been dead over twelve hours, died probably from a head wound, and decapitated for whatever reason *post mortem*. I doubt he was killed here. Was there much blood on the trash?'

Leroy shook his head. 'No, there's not. Therefore, he's unlikely to have been killed here.' He looked down at the corpse. 'No, just dumped here.'

The ME said, 'I'm done here. We'll take the body back to the lab. I'll let you have my full report by tonight.'

CHAPTER SEVEN

IT WAS ALMOST nine and Leroy and Quinn were both sitting outside Harry Webb's stilt house. Quinn had arrived ten minutes earlier, pulling up directly behind Leroy's car, which was stationed on the same side of the street as Webb's, but three houses down.

'I thought you might need this,' Quinn said, as he passed Leroy a *Dunkin Donuts* bag. 'Strong and black with a donut.'

'Gee, thanks,' Leroy said, peering into the bag, 'but I think a can of *Monster* might be what I really need.'

'How much sleep you get?' Quinn asked.

Leroy shook his head. 'About three hours, I guess. I'll catch up this afternoon.' He leaned back and dropped the paper bag on the back seat. 'You ever heard of this guy?'

'Nah. I googled him before I set off for here. He's not done much – a few TV shows, pilots that never made it to a full season.'

'Movies?'

'Just TV. Not even network shows, just cable.'

'Am I off base,' Leroy asked, 'in thinking there might be a connection with Kelton?'

'Apart from the fact that they both live in the same town? Yes, I think you're off base, Sam.'

'How old is he? Married, divorced?'

Quinn recollected. 'Forty-six. Divorced five years ago. No mention in the article of any significant other.'

Leroy made to get out of the car, pausing as another vehicle passed by. 'Let's hope he's in.'

'We should have called ahead,' said Quinn as they walked towards the house. 'Would have saved a wasted journey.'

'Let's just see,' Leroy replied. They climbed the wooden staircase and walked along a weed-strewn path through a small front yard which had not been attended to in ages. Weeds and tufts of grass littered the earth, all around the two large cactus plants.

Leroy opened the screen door. The front door was a heavy wooden door, stained dark. There was no obvious bell or knocker, so Leroy banged hard on the wood. For a while there was no reply: they glanced at each other. Leroy knocked again, and this time they could hear coughing from inside, coming closer to the door. It opened slightly and Harry Webb peered around the door. He was very short, no more than five feet and had to look right up to Leroy, who was holding out his badge.

'Detectives Leroy and Quinn, LAPD. Harry Webb?'

'Yeah, hold on.' The door closed while Webb released the safety chain and opened the door. 'I was kind of expecting you guys. Come on in.'

Leroy and Quinn followed Webb through the house to the lounge, which had French doors opening onto a veranda. The lounge was one of those places clearly occupied by a solitary man. Not untidy as such, but cluttered with books. No 'female touch'. From the veranda one had a view right down into the city. The Hollywood Freeway was flowing slowly in both directions. There was a small table and chair on the veranda. On the table was a packet of Marlboros, a glass of what could have been water, a notebook and pen, and an open laptop. Quinn began to veer towards the table until Webb steered him back indoors.

'Here, take a seat,' Webb said, indicating the bulky brown leather couch. Leroy and Quinn sat on the couch and Webb joined them on the matching chair opposite, coughing as he sat down. 'Where did I...?' he muttered, looking around. He got up and stepped over to the table on the veranda. Taking a cigarette, he returned to the chair, reached over for a lighter, and lit the Marlboro. 'You don't mind...?' he asked.

Leroy and Quinn shook their heads. 'Your house,' Leroy said.

Webb nodded, took a drag, and coughed again. He was short, had close cropped grey hair, and his face was wrinkly, the result of too many years' sun and nicotine. He looked at Leroy. 'Leroy,' he said. 'I got a good memory for names. You,' – he wagged his finger as he spoke – 'were the detective on that Marv Kelton case, weren't you?'

'Well remembered,' Leroy said.

'Like I told you, I got a good memory for names. Pity the bastard got off. I always felt there was something not quite right about the guy. Then when I read about someone taking a dump on his star down there...' His sentence was punctuated by chuckling and coughing. 'Did they ever take away the star, by the way? I read there was some kind of campaign running.'

'No, it hasn't been removed,' Quinn replied.

Leroy added, 'The Chamber of Commerce says it's part of the fabric of the street now.'

'Yes, yes,' Webb said. 'I remember reading that now. Something about stars never being removed. That's bullshit, of course.'

'Mm?' Leroy said.

Webb took another drag and sat back in the chair. 'You ever heard of an actor called David Manners?'

Leroy wondered where this was all going. 'No, I haven't.'

Webb waved a dismissive hand. 'He was a B movie actor back in the thirties. Did a few horror pictures for Universal. A faggot, of course.' He paused. 'No offence.'

Almost in unison, Leroy and Quinn replied, 'None taken.'

'Well, anyway, he made a few crappy pictures, then just dropped out. Just gave it all up. Became some sort of hermit, I gather. And you know what? His star just quietly disappeared. Got taken away. No fuss, no announcement. Just – poof. Gone. Now ain't that fascinating? And then you have Jackie Chan's star. Now that had to be moved someplace else 'cause some wise-ass decided to put it in front of the Chinese Theater.'

Leroy sat forward. As interesting as Harry Webb's history of Hollywood was, he had questions to ask and was almost falling asleep. 'Riveting. So we don't detain you any longer than's necessary, sir, can you just tell me about last night?'

Webb squeezed what was left of the cigarette into an ashtray. 'Not much to say, really. I was out there working on a piece I'm doing - an adaptation of a book, a shitty book between you guys and me – and I needed a smoke. Not one of these; I'd begun to use those e-cigarettes, you know, and I couldn't find the vaporizer. So I decided to drive down to the store and get another. It was Chin down at the store who'd gotten me into the vapour ones.

'So, I got into the car and drove down to the store. I'd just gotten out of the car when some weirdo ran up to me.

Well, not exactly ran; just leaping around like he'd messed his shorts.' Webb began to laugh, then coughed. 'Maybe he had. He didn't speak English - well, nothing I could understand, anyway – but I could tell he wanted me to look inside one of the dumpsters. I looked in and saw what was in there.'

'And what did you see?'

'And what did I see? I saw that poor bastard lying in with the trash. Missing his head.'

'You could see that clearly? It was night.'

'There's a street light behind the dumpsters. I could see well enough.'

'What time was this, approximately?'

Webb gave a theatrical shrug. 'Around midnight?'

Leroy asked, 'Did you touch anything?'

'You mean did I touch the poor guy? No way. Or the dumpster. I didn't bother to check his pulse, if you see what I mean. Have you found his head, by the way?'

'Not yet. What did you do then?'

'I ran into Chin's and called him. Oh, I took the foreign guy with me; he was still wailing and calling out Christ knows what. Then I called 911. I used the booth down there as I'd left my cell here. Then I waited for you guys to show up. Chin gave the other guy a drink - sold him a drink, I mean – to calm him down. I bought a packet of smokes. *Real* smokes this time - no cockamamie vapour. You talked to the foreign guy yet?'

'Not yet. He's our next port of call.'

'You're going to need a translator. You want to go to… I forget the name of the outfit, but they got offices on Sawtelle Boulevard. Tell them Harry Webb sent you.'

Leroy stood up, followed by Quinn. 'I'll be sure to do that. Thanks for your time and co-operation, Mr Webb.'

Webb started to lead them to the door. 'Always pleased to help out LA's Finest.'

As he held the door open for them, Quinn turned round. 'And good luck with the script, sir.'

'Thanks.' With that, Webb closed the door and fastened the chain. Leroy and Quinn took the wooden staircase back down to their cars.

As they paused by their vehicles, Leroy checked his phone. 'Well, nothing yet from Perez about the interpreter.' He yawned. 'Let's both go back to the Desk. I'll try to grab some sleep there or in the back room at Martha's. If the translator materializes then there's no reason why you can't speak to' – he looked down at the notes – 'Evald Mets solo.'

Some one hundred feet above, Harry Webb was looking out of his bedroom window. He watched as Quinn and Leroy got back into their respective cars. He watched their cars pull away, negotiate the twists and turns of his street until they were out of view. Then he returned to his little table on the veranda, took another mouthful of vodka and tonic and lit another *real* cigarette.

CHAPTER EIGHT

LEROY WAS DESTINED not to catch up on sleep that day. No sooner had he joined the 405, then Lieutenant Perez called him.

'Sam, I just got off the horn from the ALS: they can provide a translator late morning.'

'Late morning? Lieutenant, that's cutting things a bit close.'

'Yeah, I know, but I had to request someone who specialises in East European languages, and you got him from eleven till one. After 1PM, the cost to the Department goes up.'

'Okay, so that'll give us two hours with Mets. That should be enough.'

'No, Sam. That two-hour window includes his travel time to and from Mets's place. I'm guessing you're going to see him there.'

'Planned on doing that, yes. So that gives me around an hour. That should be enough. Who is the translator anyway? Anybody we've used before?'

'Don't think so. The guy's called Miller. Charlie Miller. They say his specialty is Eastern European languages, so he'll be okay with Estonian.

'I've checked out Mets's address. It's just off Reseda Boulevard. Now there's a coffee shop I know on Reseda, Reseda and Oxnard; I've arranged for him to meet you two there 11:30.'

'Okay, Lieutenant. I'm heading south on the 405 right now, so I'll call Ray and we can meet up there.'

'Quinn not with you?'

'Nah, he's in his own car. I did the Mulholland scene solo, as we'd both been up until 1AM. We met up at Webb's place.'

'And there was me thinking you two were partners. You know, doing things together, travelling together in the same car, not a convoy.'

'We are, Lieutenant. We don't normally travel about separately, you know that. But then we don't normally finish one shift at 1AM, and start the next five hours later.'

'Okay, okay. Go interview Mets now, then team up in the same vehicle asap, okay? You're supposed to be partners – and all you're doing is driving gas costs up. Keep the interview as short as you can, then he can get back to his office by one.'

Leroy hung up on Perez and called Quinn, who was further down the 405. They arrived at just after eleven, both parking right outside the coffee shop.

It looked just like a Starbuck's but wasn't: a pretty generic place – you ordered from a vast range of esoteric drinks at the counter, declined an overpriced pastry, and waited at the end of the counter for the barista to make the drink. Quinn ordered a latte; Leroy a Strong Americano with sugar. They sat down in plain sight in a booth where they had a view of the door.

Quinn sipped his latte. 'What do you think about Webb, then?'

'I believe him. I took a dislike to the guy, but I think he's telling the truth. It all seems believable, plausible. Before I left the scene, I looked through the CCTV footage from the grocery store.'

'Anything of interest?'

Leroy shook his head. 'Not yet. Only one of the cameras had a POV of outside the store, and that was in the doorway.'

'Not where the body was found?'

'Not as yet. There were other cameras about, but all of the other places were still closed. Maybe after we've done here, we could go back up there - the other places are a pizza joint, a laundromat and a bar, so should be open by then – and take a look at their cameras.'

'Traffic cameras?'

'Possibly, possibly, but we need to know what we're looking for first.' Leroy looked at his watch. 'It's twenty-five after now. He's late.'

They watched the people coming in, looking for a possible translator. The coffee shop seemed to have a brisk trade: no real lines at the counter, just one or two customers coming in as one or two went out.

Two twenty-somethings, both with headphones and wearing baggy tee-shirts and baseball caps on backwards.

An old guy in a raincoat, looking incongruous in the spring sunshine.

A middle-aged man in a white polo shirt and red pants.

'Do you think that's him?' Quinn asked.

'Maybe,' replied Leroy. 'He looks kind of translatory. Not sure about the red pants, though.'

However, the man in red pants picked up his coffee, being passed in the doorway by two younger guys, both wearing suits and chatting on their cell phones.

A couple, the man wearing a blue jumper and matching jeans. The girl wore a white blouse with a black miniskirt. He held the door open for her.

A woman with a double stroller. She was having difficulty negotiating the coffee shop doorway: Quinn stood to help her, but was beaten to it by the man in blue. The woman thanked him, and he passed her on his way out to the street.

Quinn turned back and returned to his seat. Just as he sat down, the woman in the white blouse stepped over.

'Detectives Leroy and Quinn?' she asked. 'I'm sorry I'm late. I'm Charlie Miller.'

CHAPTER NINE

SHE SAT DOWN.

'I still haven't got used to the traffic over here,' she said, slightly flustered.

The first thing Leroy and Quinn noticed was her British accent. Then her shiny, dark hair, tied into a ponytail. Then, the long firm legs emerging from the tight miniskirt. As she sat down, she put her tiny black bag and reflective Raybans on the table.

'Don't worry about the time,' Leroy reassured her after they had gone through the introductions. 'We get caught out as well, sometimes. But we do need to go right away. My Lieutenant says we only have you till 12.30.'

'Don't worry about that,' she replied. 'It's not your fault I was late.'

Leroy stood up to leave, the others following.

'Where did you park?' Quinn asked.

'Across the street, round the corner. There's a little car park there.'

'Leave your car there for now,' Leroy said, holding the door open for her. 'The address is only a couple of blocks away and Detective Quinn will drive.'

They climbed into Quinn's car. He waited for a gap in traffic and made a one-eighty to head north up Reseda.

Leroy turned round in his seat to face Charlie. 'So – is it Charlotte or something?'

'Yes,' she smiled. 'Charlotte, but my friends - well, pretty much everybody - call me Charlie.'

'And you're British?' Quinn asked.

She laughed. 'You guessed. Yes, I'm from London.'

'What part?' asked Leroy. 'I've been there a couple of times.'

'South London,' she replied. 'Place called Wimbledon. Have you heard of it?'

'Wimbledon, as in tennis?'

'Yes, that's the place.'

'Do you play tennis?' Quinn asked.

'Hate it,' she replied. 'I'm more into racing.'

'Horses?'

She laughed again. 'No! Formula One.'

'Really?' Leroy said surprised.

'Mm. Anything fast on four wheels, in fact.'

Leroy smiled. He liked the way she pronounced the word *fast*. Getting the conversation back on track he asked, 'The guy we're going to see speaks very little or no English. Only Estonian. You can translate Estonian?'

'Absolutely. I specialise in former soviet bloc languages: Estonian, Lithuanian, Latvian, Belarusian; and, of course, Russian.'

Leroy nodded, approvingly. 'That's very impressive.'

'At school I found I had a natural affinity for languages. That's how I got my work visa.'

'How long are you here for, then?'

'Until the end of next year.'

'Here's Jovan,' said Quinn. They had arrived at their destination.

Jovan Street was a dead-end. A collection of single-storey houses, some whitewashed, some painted a mushroom colour. All had lawns out front, with a plethora of different coloured herbie-curbies. At the dead end part of the street, the road widened, and the houses were now two-storey with integral garages.

'He can't live here, surely,' said Quinn, turning the car round at the end of the street.

'The address,' said Leroy, 'was for an apartment building. Pull over here.'

Leroy had noticed a man of retirement age out front of one of the houses mowing the grass. As he got out and walked across the grass, the man stopped and looked up.

'Can I help you, son?' the man asked.

Leroy showed him his badge and then the sheet of paper with Mets's address.

The senior pointed back up the street. 'Jovan goes back that way. I'm not sure, but I'm guessing the place you want is at the other end of the street. There's some apartment building along there, over the cross street. Over Etwanda, I think it is.'

Leroy thanked the man, and returned to the car. The guy paused to watch Leroy, Quinn and Charlie head up the street, then returned to his lawn.

His directions were correct, as once over the cross street, the houses turned to apartment buildings, occupied by clearly less affluent residents. They found the place they were looking for, and pulled in.

The building itself resembled a motel: in fact, the style of the construction and the amount of parking space suggested it might have originally been one, and sold off in a previous time to be privately developed. A heavily built man with a silver grey beard and shoulder length hair was tending to an enormous motorcycle, its chrome gleaming in the bright sunshine. He watched as the three visitors approached the building, looking for apartment 217.

They took the small flight of stairs to the second level, walked along the balcony to the door. Leroy knocked and after a few seconds a little man, middle-aged, opened the door.

Leroy held out his badge once more. 'Evald Mets?' he asked.

Mets muttered something, nervously nodding his head. Leroy nodded to Charlie. She looked down at the little man and spoke to him in his native tongue. Mets gained a relieved expression on his face and took a step back, allowing them access.

'I just said you were from the police, and wanted to ask him a few questions and he had nothing to worry about,' she said by way of explanation to Leroy as they stepped inside the apartment.

From the size of the place it could have well been a former motel room: a small stove, cupboard, sink and refrigerator had been installed in one corner. A woman, presumably Mrs Mets, was at the stove; three young children were sat on the floor watching a cartoon on television.

In Estonian, Charlie explained to Mr and Mrs Mets who they were, what Leroy and Quinn wanted to ask, and that she was from the American Language Service and would be translating.

'I speak a little English,' Mrs Mets said. 'He speaks little.'

Mets nodded his head eagerly.

Mrs Mets turned the TV volume down and Leroy began asking Mets the questions he had, with Charlie translating. Immediately Mrs Mets explained that her husband worked as a chef in a restaurant on Reseda

Boulevard, and that he needed to leave for work very soon, otherwise he would be fired.

'If we need to, we'll explain to his employer that he was helping us out, and if they try anything, they'll have the LAPD to deal with,' Leroy said. Charlie translated, and Mrs and Mrs Mets seemed reassured. Leroy then got on with the questions.

Mets said he had been visiting a friend in that locality. He had two bags of garbage in his car. He was only allowed four bags of garbage to be collected each week, so he called in at that shopping center on his way home to put the bags in the dumpster. As he opened the lid, he saw the body there, and then noticed the head was missing. Mets got slightly hysterical as he related the part about the missing head. He was running into the shop to raise the alarm when he saw the other man arrive. As he spoke very little English, he took the other man to show him the body.

'Okay,' Leroy said slowly. This was nothing new. He took the name and address of the friend Mets said he had visited, then stood to leave. 'Thank you for your time, Mr Mets,' he said. 'Can we give you a ride to your restaurant?' Mets declined the offer.

Leroy, Quinn and Charlie made their way downstairs to Quinn's car. As they pulled away, they saw Mets on foot, scurrying down the street.

'What a strange little guy,' Quinn muttered.

'Yeah,' Leroy replied thoughtfully. He swung round to Charlie. 'Thank you for your help today, Ms Miller.'

'Charlie.'

'Charlie. We'll drop you back at your car.'

As Quinn turned into Reseda, once more they saw Mets half walking, half running down the street. Leroy was surprised at how quickly he had gotten there, but noticed there were alleyways between the buildings; Mets must have taken a short cut.

Quinn pulled up at the parking lot where Charlie had left her car.

'Thanks once again,' Leroy said as she got out.

She reached into her bag and pulled out a business card. 'Here,' she said, slipping the card in between Leroy's fingers, 'my number's on there. Call me if you need any more help, or advice.' She paused a beat. 'Or anything.'

Quinn looked into the rear view mirror watching Charlie walk back to her car.

'Very nice,' he said.

'Ray, you're a married man,' Leroy chided him.

Quinn chuckled. 'But you haven't gone off liquor just because Martha's is open all day. In any case, you're almost a married man.'

'Er, not quite.'

'Mm?'

'Joanna and I are, you know, kind of taking a break right now.'

'Shit, Sam; I didn't know. What...?'

'Long story, another time. Get us back to the coffee shop.'

As they turned back into Reseda, they noticed Mets going into what they guessed was his place of work: an Eastern European restaurant. Quinn pulled up behind Leroy's car. 'So what now?' he asked. The CCTV at that mall?'

'I reckon so. We'll go there first, then check out this friend of Mets. Did you read the address? It's in Burbank. That's an odd place for a friend of a little immigrant who can't speak English to live. Look at the route he would have had to take: Burbank to Tarzana via Mulholland Drive?'

'If he can't speak English, how's he going to be able to drive? Quinn asked.

'If he can't speak English, he'll have to speak Spanish, or he'll never get a licence,' Leroy said. 'And I can't see him speaking Spanish, can you?'

'No way.'

Leroy continued, 'There's something not right about that little guy. Even if he does have a friend up in Burbank -?'

'How did he get up there?'

'Yes, how?'

'But why show Webb the body? If he did have something to do with it, why raise the alarm?

'I know. We're missing something here. In any case, Burbank to Tarzana via Mulholland Drive: that's a long detour just to dump some garbage.'

CHAPTER TEN

LEROY NEEDED THE restroom, so went back inside the coffee shop. While he was inside, Quinn started the car and did a one-eighty so he was facing north up Reseda Boulevard. He waited for Leroy to come back out onto the street and called out, 'See you at Burbank, then.'

Leroy waved and got into his own car, doing his own one-eighty. Quinn was moving slowly in the number one lane for Leroy to catch up. Once Leroy was in the lane, both cars set off.

As they took Reseda north, Leroy noticed the restaurant where Evald Mets was working as a chef. It was called the

Europa, and according to the signage, specialised in eastern European cuisine.

Leroy was reflecting how, in better times, Joanna might have been interested when something else caught his eye. Further up, close to the intersection with Victory Boulevard, scampering along the sidewalk was Mets himself.

Leroy flashed Quinn and switched on his siren. Quinn saw, and they both pulled over. Mets had heard the *whoop* of the siren and paused, looking over as Leroy and Quinn pulled over to him. As they got out of their cars, Mets stood looking around and moving from one foot to another, as if he was figuring out whether to wait or run.

'Mr Mets,' Leroy called out as they walked up to him. 'Where are you going?'

Mets's mouth opened and shut a few times while he searched for the right words. 'I go… I go deliver a letter for my boss.'

'Very far?' Quinn asked.

'No, not far. Just along here.' He pointed up Reseda.

'And you don't drive?' Quinn asked.

Mets shook his head.

'How did you get up to Burbank, then?'

'Burbank?'

'Your friend in Denny Avenue. You visited him last night.'

'Oh, yes. My friend – he give me ride there.'

'And back home here?'

'Yes, back home here.'

'But why did your friend make that detour along Mulholland Avenue? You know, where you found the body?'

Mets squinted his eyes. 'Sorry, I no… I no under -'

'It's nothing. We were concerned,' Leroy explained untruthfully, 'that you might have gotten into trouble with your boss for being late for work on account of us.'

Mets shook his head. 'No, no trouble. Everything okay.'

'Glad to hear that,' said Leroy. 'But just call us if there is, okay?'

'I will, I will,' Mets replied, nodding his head eagerly. 'Everything okay.' He was keen to get away.

'You have a good day now, sir.' Leroy turned and he and Quinn left Mets and headed back to their cars. 'Let's see where he goes,' Leroy said as they crossed the street. Back in his car, Leroy took out a pair of binoculars from the glove compartment. Quinn joined him in the passenger seat.

On this corner of Reseda and Victory, there is a small group of shops: a 7/11, a Thai restaurant, and a Western Union. Leroy watched as Mets crossed the modest parking lot.

'Well, he didn't park a car here,' Leroy said, passing the binoculars to Quinn. 'Where can he be going? He works as a chef in a restaurant. It's lunchtime. Why isn't he cooking?'

'He's crossing over,' Quinn observed. Mets was waiting at a crosswalk to cross over Victory Boulevard. After a minute or so the red man standing changed to a green man walking and Mets and three other pedestrians crossed.

'Maybe he's checking out the opposition,' Leroy remarked.

Quinn put down the binoculars. 'How so?'

'Look what's over there.'

Quinn looked again. 'Oh yes.' On the opposite corner was a McDonalds, a large red-brick building with a line of cars waiting for drive-thru.

'He's headed for the parking lot,' Quinn said. 'Look.' He passed the binoculars back to Leroy.

'Yeah… shit!' Leroy said, as a large white truck appeared from the right, blocking his view. He put the binoculars down impatiently and waited until the truck cleared the crossing. However, once it had turned left and headed down Reseda presumably towards the freeway, an orange and grey bus took its place on the other side of the street.

'We've lost him now,' Quinn said.

'We'll see about that.' Leroy dropped the binoculars, started the engine and pulled out into the traffic, earning a blast on the horn from a van driver who had had to apply his brakes noisily. Quinn leaned out of the passenger window, showing his badge. Leroy turned right onto Victory Boulevard, then left across the traffic into the McDonalds parking lot. He drove round the lot twice, but there was no sign of Mets. As they waited for a gap in traffic to leave the parking lot, Quinn pointed to a bus stop a few yards east along Victory. The orange and grey bus was in the distance.

'Think he got on there?'

Leroy shrugged. 'Who knows? We can catch him later. Let's get up to this pal he said he was visiting over in Burbank.'

'His command of the English language seemed to have improved,' Quinn said.

'It seemed to. I don't know.' Leroy looked around. 'If he doesn't drive, where could he have gone? I think I'd like to talk to him again, but we'll need to get Charlie back.' He paused a beat. 'If he doesn't speak English that good, he couldn't drive.'

'You mean, he couldn't get a licence. Unless he's fluent in Spanish. We said that.'

Leroy paused a moment in thought, brought out of his reverie by the car behind. 'Come on, Ray; let's go see his pal.'

Leroy waited while Quinn ran back to his car, then they both headed east along Victory Boulevard for the next five or six miles. Once they reached North Hollywood, they turned south onto Vineland which more or less took them right to Denny Avenue, where Mets's friend lived.

The street they were headed for comprised a row of large immodest two storey houses, some with small yards out front, some with larger expanses of grass. Some with neat white picket fences, some with generic chain link fences, some with more ornate iron railings.

The house they sought, number 2544, was one of the places with a larger yard, cropped grass, and cactus-type plants on each corner. The yard was bordered by a brick wall around two feet high, topped with iron railings, painted black with gold-painted arrows topping the rails. There was no gate, just a gap in the wall and a gravel path, winding unnecessarily leading to the front porch. On the porch were two chairs, a bench and a table. White metal bars were over the windows, which had white wooden shutters closed, keeping the outside world out of the house.

As Leroy looked around, Quinn knocked hard on the front door. A few moments later, a small, Hispanic woman opened the door.

'Yes please?'

Leroy held out his badge and introduced himself and Quinn. 'Is Mr Dudinsky at home? Mr Andrey Dudinsky?'

The little Mexican woman shook her head. 'No, he not at home.'

Leroy sighed, more than a little frustrated. 'Is there a Mrs Dudinsky?'

She shook her head. 'He not married.'

'You're the housekeeper, I guess?'

'Yes, I am.'

'And there's nobody else in?'

She shook her head again.

'Is Mr Dudinsky at work?'

'Yes, he at work.'

Leroy asked, 'We need to talk to him. Where does he work?'

'He work at Europa Restaurant, on Reseda Boulevard. He manager there.'

CHAPTER ELEVEN

BACK ON THE sidewalk, Leroy head-butted the roof of his car three or four times.

'Son of a bitch,' he said. 'We've come all the way up here and the bastard was at the restaurant all along.' He looked over at Quinn. 'Tell me, does Mets really not understand what's going on, or is he just plain stupid? Or is he cleverer than he's making out, and jerking us off?' Leroy tapped the roof of his car, opened the passenger door and took out a notepad and pen.

'What is it?' Quinn asked, going over to him.

'Look,' Leroy indicated. He was drawing a kind of map on the notepad. It was triangular, an inverted pyramid. Leroy spoke as he drew. 'Everything seems to be around these three locations. First, Laurel Canyon, and the dumpster. Then Tarzana, where Evald Mets, the guy who apparently found the body *here*,' – he tapped the paper – 'lives and works. Then we have his *friend*, who is actually his boss, a guy by the name of Andrey Dudinsky, living up here in Burbank. Three quite disparate places, but not too difficult to get to from either of the others. From Reseda and Victory all you have to do is what we did, or you could get down to the Ventura Freeway, make a left somewhere along *here*, and you're where we are now. How long did the journey take us - thirty minutes?'

'Yeah, about that.'

'It would take about the same taking the 101, I guess. Maybe longer in the rush hour. From here, you'd have to take one of the north/south streets, Vineland maybe, down to - I forget the name of the road - to Mulholland Drive and Laurel Canyon. That's… again, thirty minutes, maybe a tad less.

'Then from the mall, you could head up Laurel Canyon Boulevard, through Studio City here,' - another tap – 'back onto the 101. Head west and you're back in Tarzana. Thirty minutes again?'

'I know that route,' Quinn said. 'More like twenty.'

'Right, so it's not exactly a huge detour to make a journey from here to *there* – an hour?'

'But why?' asked Quinn. 'There'd be plenty of places on that route to get rid of a body. Why go all the way down there?'

Leroy leaned back on his car and folded his arms. 'Right now, I've no idea.'

Quinn asked, 'Isn't there a park down in Laurel Canyon?'

'There is,' Leroy replied. 'It's a dog park. You know, where dog owners take their pooches off their leashes so they can run about and hump each other.'

'Why not dump the body there, then?'

'Because it's bound to be found. If you buried a DB there, you can take book a dog would dig it up. No, in a dumpster the chances are it would remain undiscovered for days, maybe longer. Maybe not at all if it was concealed in a large pile of garbage bags. They'd all go to a landfill site, or an incinerator.'

'So there must be a reason why whoever dumped the body went to that location.'

'Sure, but Mets and his boss could have nothing to do with the body. On the other hand, there's still the question of what Mets was actually doing there.'

Leroy tapped his car roof. 'Come on, Ray; let's get down to the mall.'

Leroy's estimate of journey time was quite accurate: his and Quinn's cars arrived at the shopping centre some twenty-two minutes after they left Burbank.

'One more look,' Leroy called out, striding over to the dumpsters. He lifted up the lid and looked inside. Shut the lid and walked around the row of bins. Crouched down and ran his hand over the pavement. He shook his head briefly and stood up, brushing the front of his pants.

'The SID guys would have gone over things here with a fine toothed comb,' Quinn said.

Leroy nodded. 'Yeah. On the way here I rang Caltrans. There are no traffic cameras on the intersection over there, so that's a dead end. We'll just have to hope the CCTV here gives us something. I've already checked out the cameras in the grocery store. When I was here earlier, everywhere else was shut. They're all open now. Come on, let's go to the cleaners.'

The Mount Olympus Cleaners Inc had no security camera at all. Just a burglar alarm. Blank there; although as the manageress pointed out, people don't normally hold up laundromats. It was the same with the pizza delivery unit.

It was a different story at the bar. Joe, the manager and proprietor of the appropriately named *Joe's Bar*, proudly and enthusiastically showed them the five cameras which were installed in the bar. Three were inside, with varying points of view, one was out back, and the other was in front, with a view of the entrance porch.

'I'm guessing this is all recorded,' Leroy said to Joe, as the three men stood around the television monitor in the small office behind the bar. It was a quiet time of the day, and there were only half a dozen customers.

'It sure is.' Joe ran his hand along a shelf on which there was a row of neatly stacked discs. 'One disc for each day, running 24/7.'

'You have four images on the screen here,' Quinn said. 'Is that what would be on the disc?'

Joe replied, 'Naturally, officer.'

'We'll need to borrow the disc for yesterday,' Leroy said. 'When's the cut-off time? When does one disc end and the next begin?'

'10AM, when I get in.'

'Okay,' Leroy said. 'So I'd need discs for yesterday, and the day before. And the day before that, just to be sure. Will that be okay?'

'Surely.' Joe took the last three discs off the shelf. 'Here you are, Detective.'

'Are the views static?' Quinn asked. 'Just as we're seeing here?'

'No. Every so often the cameras move: not very much, just an arc of around forty-five degrees.'

'So,' Leroy said, pointing out into the bar, 'the camera you have with a point of view of the door – is it always the door, just a different view?'

'Kind of,' Joe replied. 'It pans from over by this side of the lot, from the street, over to the other side of here.'

'The other side of the parking lot?' Leroy asked eagerly.

'Certainly, yes.'
'Including that row of dumpsters?'
Joe nodded.

CHAPTER TWELVE

'NOW FOR THIS wise-guy Dudinsky,' Leroy called out to Quinn as he backed out of his parking space.

'What about the discs?' Quinn asked.

'We'll see Dudinsky first, also Mets again, then we'll head back to base and get the cameras checked out. We might also hear something from the ME by then.'

'See you back in Tarzana, then.' Quinn climbed into his own car and followed Leroy out of the lot.

Leroy's journey time estimate was somewhat off-key this time: rather than the thirty minutes he had estimated, the journey took fifty. They both parked outside the

Europa restaurant, Leroy by the kerbside as he was the first to arrive, Quinn being forced to double park.

The restaurant was not particularly big, just one unit on the street. It had a white fascia with the name of the business in green, this being matched by the canopy. Three sets of tables for two were positioned on the sidewalk, each with a menu slotted into a wooden base, each empty. It was not possible to see inside owing to the wooden venetian blind, but this may have been to keep out the bright light from the sun, which was shining directly onto that side of the street, getting lower all the time. The restaurant was open, and Leroy and Quinn stepped in.

Inside was larger than the shopfront suggested. There were half a dozen tables for two, five booths on one side, and a variety of other sized tables, some for four, some for six. Two booths and half a dozen tables were occupied. Large sepia photographs of men, women and children dressed in traditional east European costume adorned the walls. Accordion music was playing quietly from a loudspeaker.

On seeing Leroy and Quinn enter, a man dressed in a dinner jacket walked around from behind the small bar and walked over, carrying two large laminated menus. 'A table for two, gentlemen?' he asked, with a slight accent.

They each showed their badges and introduced themselves. 'We need to speak to Andrey Dudinsky. Is he on the premises?'

The smile on the maitre d's face froze. 'I'll just check, sir. Would you wait here, please?'

Leroy nodded, and the maitre d' stepped through a curtained doorway. After a few moments he returned and went straight over to one of the booths. A much younger man, early thirties and in shirtsleeves, followed him.

'Would you come this way, please?' the man asked, also with the trace of an accent. Leroy and Quinn followed him through the curtain and into an office. To get to the office they had to walk down a short corridor, past the restrooms and the kitchen. Emanating from the kitchen was a lot of heat and a strong smell of cabbage being cooked. As they passed by Leroy looked in to see if he could see Evald Mets, but could not.

'Please sit down,' the man said once they were inside the office.

'Are you Andrey Dudinsky?' Leroy asked as he sat down.

'Well, yes and no,' Dudinsky replied. No accent this time.

'Excuse me?' said Leroy.

Dudinsky rubbed his forehead and sat down. 'My name is actually Andrew Dudley. When I opened this place, I felt that using a non-American name would make the place sound more authentic. Andrey Dudinsky seemed the nearest equivalent to Andrew Dudley. It's Russian.'

'So you're American?'

'Sacramento.'

'What about the rest of your employees?' Quinn asked.

'They're all genuine. Genuine Europeans, I should say. All legal.'

'We're not here for the INS,' Leroy said. 'What about Evald Mets? Is he a chef here?'

'Yes, he is.'

'He's Latvian?'

'No, Estonian. From near Tallin, I think.'

Leroy nodded.

'How long has he worked here?'

'Couple of years, I guess.'

'Is he a good chef?'

Dudley shrugged. 'Average, I guess. I've had no complaints. Why?'

Leroy ignored the question. 'Is he working today? I didn't see him as we went past the kitchen.'

'He should be. He was. Turned up late this morning. Started work preparing lunches, then said he felt ill, so the Chef said to go home.'

'The Chef? I thought Mets was the chef.'

Dudley smiled. 'Evald's more of a kitchen assistant here. We have a chef, who runs the kitchen, and another kitchen assistant. And Evald. It's quite a small kitchen, so we don't exactly follow the Brigade system.'

'What's that?' Quinn asked.

Leroy looked over to him. 'It's a kind of hifalutin level of ranks in the kitchen industry.' He looked at Dudley. 'Am I right?'

Dudley pulled a face and nodded. 'It's kind of a hierarchy, yes.'

Leroy said, 'We were down here earlier and saw Mets hurrying up Reseda Boulevard. He said he was running an errand for his boss. Would that be you?'

Dudley shook his head. 'Not at all. He said he was sick.'

Leroy said, 'He lives off one of the cross-streets, correct?'

'Er – I think so.'

'But we saw him go as far as Victory Boulevard when he… when we lost him. So you've no idea where he was going?'

'No, I'm sorry. Is Evald in some kind of trouble?'

'Did Evald visit you at home last night?'

'At my house?'

'U-huh. At your house.'

'Not at all.' Dudley gave a little snigger. 'I'm the manager here; he's a kitchen assistant. There'd be no reason for him to go to my house. Did he say that?'

Leroy nodded. 'Said he had to take you some paperwork, receipts or something.'

Dudley shook his head. 'No, he didn't visit.'

Leroy asked, 'And you were in last night?'

'Yes. We don't open Mondays, so I wasn't here.'

'Were you alone? We met a housekeeper, Mexican is she?'

Dudley seemed surprised. 'Carmen, yes. She's Mexican, here quite legally, also. You went to my house?'

'Came directly from there. Carmen said you were here.'

Dudley seemed less ebullient now. 'Yes, I was alone. I was out playing golf in the afternoon, got home around six, watched TV until eleven, when I went to bed. Alone.'

'Just so I'm clear,' Leroy said, sitting forward, 'Mets works here in the kitchen, went sick, and didn't visit you last night. Do I have everything right?'

'Pretty much. Why are you looking for Evald?'

'Just routine. Mr Dudley, here's my card: when Mets returns here - and I realise it might not be today – I'd like you to call me, yes?'

'But don't tell him,' Quinn added.

Leroy's phone bleeped. He paused a beat then said, 'Thank you very much for your time, sir. I appreciate it.'

'You're welcome, Mr... Leroy. And please come by one evening or lunch time. We offer a delicious Ukranian *borsch* - soup – for only $5.99; one of our newly-introduced entrées is a mouth-watering Russian salad: sliced cucumber, onions -'

'Maybe,' Leroy said, standing up. 'Thanks again.'

Dudley led Leroy and Quinn through the restaurant, leaving them on the sidewalk. 'Jerk,' Leroy muttered once they were alone. 'Andrey Dudinsky my ass.'

Quinn laughed as Leroy took out his phone and checked his messages. 'That might have been the ME. I hope he has some news.' He read the text message, then put the phone back in his pocket. 'Come on.'

'Was that Hobson, then?'

Leroy spoke as they walked back to their cars. 'No, that was Perez. They just found the missing head.'

CHAPTER THIRTEEN

A MILE FROM the scene, along Mount Lee Drive, Leroy encountered the police road block. Mount Lee Drive is not exactly the busiest road in Los Angeles, and the two patrolmen were standing by the edge of the road looking out over the city. One of them was smoking and quickly tossed his cigarette away as Leroy's car approached. Leroy slowed to a halt, wound down the window and held out his badge.

'Head right along here, Detective,' said one patrolman while the other pulled the barrier aside. 'They're all by the comms centre.'

'Sure,' Leroy replied. 'My partner's a mile or so behind.'

As he passed through the barrier, he leaned out and said to the patrolman who had been smoking, 'You need to be careful about smoking up here. You could cause a brush fire.'

Embarrassed, the officer muttered something and as Leroy pulled away, he could see in his rear view mirror a frantic search for the missing butt.

The last intersection Leroy had seen was with the aptly named Tyrolean Drive: whilst not exactly as mountainous as its Austrian namesake, the roads were comparatively narrow, and Mount Lee Drive took a slow, meandering route, clinging along the side of Mount Lee itself, to its end at the City of Los Angeles Central Communication Facility.

The Facility is perched on Mount Lee just above the HOLLYWOOD sign, and comprises a couple of small whitewashed buildings and a white and red tower hosting dozens of eclectic communications dishes. The facility provides communication services for the City's numerous authorities such as the police, fire department, emergency and otherwise.

Leroy followed Mount Lee Drive through several 180 degree turns, the final one leading to the slight incline which leads up to the facility, just above the rear of the sign. Just past the back of the massive D, through the open gate, joining the other three vehicles parked. As he got out of the car, Leroy could hear an engine throbbing, the generator required to power the crime scene lights.

'Where is everybody?' Leroy called out to the officer, who called back, 'Down below the sign. The gates are open. Security's switched off.'

Leroy waved his thanks and headed down the hillside. He noticed Quinn's car arrive, and indicated for his partner to follow.

The world-famous and iconic sign stands on the side of Mount Lee, 45 feet tall and 350 feet wide. From a distance it looks wavy because of the contours of the land, but in actual fact the letters are nearly level. The original purpose of the sign was not to advertise Hollywood, but to promote *Hollywoodland*, the real-estate development owned by Harry Chandler, the then publisher of the *Los Angeles Times*. Built in 1923, the sign was built to advertise the 500-plus homes for sale as part of Chandler's development. Eventually, the sign fell into disrepair and in 1949 was taken over by the Hollywood Chamber of Commerce, which removed the last four letters and kept the sign as a landmark.

In 1932 the sign was the location of the suicide - the only recorded suicide here - of the actress Lillian (Peg) Entwhistle. After RKO studios refused to renew her contract, she made her way through the thick brush, climbed to the top of the H, and jumped.

Since then, there has always been some kind of security around the sign: nowadays more sophisticated than merely fences. The LAPD has installed motion detectors and CCTV; the perimeter fence is tall, topped with razor wire; there are infrared lights and cameras, and there are even monitoring microphones and motion sensors. Any movement within the perimeter triggers an alarm. The penalty for intrusion is now a thousand dollars.

All this was switched off this afternoon as Leroy, followed quickly by Quinn, arrived at the actual scene, fifty feet down the hillside. Leroy could see the usual attendees at such a scene, which was normally the end of somebody's life. There was no yellow crime scene tape here; it was hardly a major thoroughfare. Dr Russell Hobson, one of the chief MEs, and an old friend of Leroy's, was in attendance. He saw his friend arrive and turned towards him.

'Hey, Sam; I heard you had an interest in this one.'

'Yeah,' Leroy said, scampering down the last few feet of the hill. 'We picked up the rest of him earlier in the day.'

'We don't know that yet. Who's to say it's the same person?'

'Jesus.'

'You two want to see?' Hobson asked.

'Okay. Lead the way.'

Hobson led Leroy and Quinn along a pathway - the ground had levelled off beneath the sign - and through some bushes. 'There you go,' he said, breezily.

It was indeed a severed head.

Resting at a forty-five-degree angle against a rock and tuft of brush, it seemed to be staring up at the sign. It was a man's, not youthful but not old, with short, unkempt brown hair. The hair on the side of the head, just above the temple, was matted with a thick black residue. Part of the left cheek and around the left eye had been gnawed at. There were still some ants crawling around the wounds and the neck. Quinn coughed. Where the head had been severed, the cut was clean, as with the corresponding body.

If this was the same man.

'What can you tell me, Russ?' Leroy asked.

'Some of it is hypothesis at this time, but you can see the cut on the neck is very clean. Done with a very sharp cutting implement.'

'Same as the torso,' Quinn observed.

'Hunting knife, maybe?' said Leroy.

Hobson shrugged. 'Maybe. That's something we'll check. The decapitation wasn't the cause of death. Look at the expression on the face: no sign of pain, or anguish or stress. I would say having your head cut off would be painful, wouldn't you?'

'Unless it was done real quick,' Quinn said, 'like with a sword.'

'True,' Hobson conceded, 'but look at the side of the head. That's probably the exit wound: there's no GSR, no sign of heat.'

'So he was killed by a shot to the head?' Leroy said.

'Looks like it. Quick, and clean.'

'Done here?'

'Who's to say? I guess you'll need to search, but there's no sign of any casing or anything around here. But the decapitation took place here.'

'How can you tell?' asked Leroy.

'Look down there. Can you see?'

Leroy crouched down and sure enough, around the base of the neck, the soil was slightly darker. He looked up at Hobson. 'Like a dried up pool of blood.'

Hobson nodded. 'Right. Now, normally any blood would be soaked up by the soil, as it's started to do here. See? It's soaked in some, you know, but enough for us to take a sample.'

'Lucky,' Quinn remarked, kneeling down to look.

'Yes, it is,' Hobson said. 'The ground here is so dry. When was the last time it rained here?'

'Winter?' asked Leroy.

'Yes. I checked: the last precipitation here was February 22nd. And that was half an inch. So there's not really anywhere for the blood to go. Very fast, at any rate.'

'Time of death?' Leroy asked.

'Too early to say. There's been quite a bit of degradation as you'd expect. One of our first tasks is to check it belongs to the body you found. Then take it from there.'

'Thanks, Russ.' Leroy turned to the uniformed officer behind Quinn. 'Who found it?'

'Three kids. Backpackers. Australians.'

Quinn asked, 'What were they doing up here? Making out?'

'They said,' the officer replied, 'they had gotten lost. Out hiking. Saw the sign and thought there'd be something up here: a restroom, maybe a cafeteria.'

Leroy laughed. 'A cafeteria? You're joking.'

'That's what they told me, Detective. Apparently the girl needed to take a whiz, dove into here and found it.'

Leroy shook his head disbelief. 'Where are they now?'

The officer indicated back up the hill. 'Up there, waiting for you guys. Either in the office there or in one of the cars.'

'Let's go talk to them,' Leroy said.

'You done with the head?' Hobson asked.

'Yeah, I guess. For now.'

'In that case, I'll get it back to the lab. See if we get a match.'

'Christ, I hope so. Come on, Ray. Let's talk to these kids.'

They clambered back up the hill, passing the blue suited scientific investigation division officers making their way down.

'I'd hurry,' Leroy said to them. 'They need to get the head back to the lab before any evidence is compromised more. And check the scene for cartridge shells.'

When they got back to the facility Leroy asked where the backpackers were. All three were sitting in the back of one of the patrol cars.

Leroy opened the rear door and leaned on the roof. Quinn crouched in front. They introduced themselves, and the backpackers did the same.

The two men introduced themselves as Mark Smith and Robbie Lee, both from Sydney, Australia. The girl, who had a blanket wrapped round her shoulders said her name was Jan White, from Newcastle. The two men were sitting next to each other, the girl by the window.

'Newcastle?' Quinn asked, thinking of the one in England.

'Newcastle, Australia,' Jan White replied. '150 k's north of Sydney.'

'You guys here on vacation?'

'Yeah,' said Mark Smith. 'Due to fly back home day after tomorrow.'

'What were you doing up here?'

'Getting lost,' Jan grumbled.

'Obviously,' Leroy said. 'Where were you headed?'

Robbie Lee answered this time. 'We were heading back to Canyon Drive. We had our car parked down there.'

'Bronson Cave,' Jan said. 'The guys wanted to check out Bronson Cave.'

'And you got lost?' said Leroy.

'I had a map -' Mark began to say.

'Yeah, right. Upside down,' Jan muttered, staring out of the window.

Mark continued, 'Well, anyway, the map didn't correspond with the terrain here…'

'So we could see the Hollywood sign,' Robbie cut in, 'and used that as our frame of reference.'

'They thought there'd be something up here by the sign,' Jan said.

'Like a cafeteria or something?' Leroy said, looking down with a grin at Quinn.

'Yeah,' said Robbie, 'at least a dunny - a restroom – and a phone box. None of us could get a signal up here.'

'Yes, that's quite ironic,' Leroy said. 'Here is the most sophisticated communications centre in Southern California, but it's not a cell phone tower. Reception always is patchy up here.'

'So we found out,' Jan grumbled.

Leroy asked, 'So, you all needed the bathroom?'

'She did,' Mark replied, looking out of the car window.

Leroy looked at Jan.

'Yes, I did. I needed to go. The bushes were all I could find. I went in there, just as I was… you know, squatting, I saw it.'

'That must have been a shock for you,' Leroy said.

'No kidding it was.'

'Did you touch it?'

'No way. I just ran.'

'Screamed a lot,' said Mark.

Jan flashed Mark an angry glare but said nothing.

Robbie continued. 'We all ran. We found a gate in the fence, but it was locked. We made our way round the fence, up the side of the hill. When we did make it to the top, a cop car was there already.'

'This place is heavily alarmed. You would have tripped one.' Leroy straightened up and looked around. The sun was beginning to set, the sky above the Pacific beginning to turn a purplish red. 'Where are you kids staying?' he asked them.

'We have an apartment on Highland Avenue,' Robbie told him. 'Just down from the Hollywood Bowl.'

'Okay. One of the officers will take you back to the Camp Howland Parking Lot – I'm guessing that's where you left your transportation?'

Robbie and Mark nodded.

'I'd suggest you stick to the sidewalks till you fly home.'

'Don't worry, we will,' Jan said.

'We'll be in contact once more before you go,' Leroy told them, 'just to check if there's anything else you might have remembered, and to take formal statements.' He called over to the patrolman whose car they were using and arranged for their ride back to their car. He and Quinn watched as they headed back down Mount Lee Drive.

'What now?' Quinn asked.

'It's twilight now. There's nothing much for us to do here. Russell's taking the head back to the lab, and we should get the prelim report on the body any time.'

'Let's hope they are a match.'

'God, I hope so. Let's call it a day. I need to sleep like right now. We'll pick things up in the morning.'

With that, they both returned to their respective cars and slowly made their way out of the facility, through the twists and turns of Mount Lee Drive, to the now darkened streets below.

CHAPTER FOURTEEN

IT WAS AN hour later when Leroy finally reached home, home being his apartment in a small building in a side street in Venice. It was a warm evening, the sky was clear, and the streets were busy with people walking one way to the Promenade, and the other to one of the many restaurants on Main Street.

He parked his car in his usual spot in the space in front of his building. He inhaled deeply, taking in the sea air. He lived not far from the beach, and late at night when the streets were quiet, he could hear the waves crashing against the sea wall. Tonight he was sure he could hear the music and sounds from Santa Monica Pier, less than two miles away.

Up on his floor, as he stepped along the corridor to his apartment, he noticed a light under the door. He was too tired to remember whether he had left a light on or not that morning. Cautiously, one hand on his service weapon, he put the key in the lock. The door was already unlocked; he turned the handle and opened it.

'So there you are.'

On the couch, sitting on one cushion and her legs curled up on another, was Joanna Moore, Leroy's girlfriend. A fourth grade school teacher, Leroy had begun seeing her a few years back after meeting her in the line of duty. She also lived in Venice, alone: by some unspoken agreement, they had each retained their own apartments, allowing each other to have their own space, but at the same time spend evenings in together. Being a teacher, she kept more or less regular hours; Leroy did not. He had not seen her for four days: in their early days together, they saw each other, or at least spoke, every day; of late it had been less frequent.

She had two piles of school books on the floor: one pile for assignments she had marked, the other for unmarked work. As she greeted him, she laid down the book she was reading.

'Hey there.' Leroy tossed his keys onto a table and flopped down on the other end of the couch. 'Wasn't expecting you. How long have you been here?'

She looked up at the clock. 'Since just before six. I didn't feel like staring at my own four walls another night, and I wanted to make sure you were still alive.'

'Say what?'

'I'd not heard from you since the weekend. I tried to call you a couple of times, but you never picked up.'

He ran his one hand over his face and yawned. 'Sorry. It's been crazy the last couple of days. I've not had time to scratch my ass, let alone check my messages.'

Joanna nodded over to the kitchen. 'I brought some food over.'

'Great,' Leroy said, not particularly enthusiastically.

'Nothing special: just some Chinese stuff we can heat up.'

He blinked heavily. 'Cool, thanks.'

'I had some bad news today,' Joanna said.

He blinked again and looked at her. 'Oh, what?'

'Meryl West – you remember me talking about her?'

'No.'

'She used to work in the languages department. About the same age as me; no, a little older, maybe.'

Leroy said nothing.

'She took extended sick leave about eighteen months ago when she was diagnosed with breast cancer. She had chemotherapy, and it looked as if it had gone. They were talking about her coming back to work, part-time.'

Leroy sat forward. 'Perez called me about five thirty this morning about a body found in a dumpster off Mulholland. No head. I've just come back from the Hollywood sign where they found the head.'

'Sam, I'm talking. Meryl West.'

He flopped back down. 'Sorry, miles away. Carry on.'

She huffcd. 'Well, we heard today that the cancer had returned, more aggressive this time, and she died at the weekend.'

Leroy looked over at her, reached out and held her foot. 'Sorry to hear that.'

'She wasn't that old. Married with kids.'

Leroy said nothing: he stared into space, slowly shaking his head.

Joanna huffed again. 'The funeral's on Friday. Some of us are going.'

He stood up, stretched. 'Have you eaten?' he asked.

'I did already. I wasn't sure when you'd be back.'

She got up and followed him into the kitchen. 'Why were you up in Hollywood, anyway?'

Leroy put the food into the microwave and pressed the button. 'We were working on that case where some TV host's bodyguard got offed by mistake.'

'The one where the guy was accused of -?'

'That's the one. We wrapped that about one this morning. Perez called me four hours later as the powers that be think that the body found in the dumpster might be connected to this case.'

'Why do they think that?'

He put up his hands. 'Why do they think anything? Because the body was found near Hollywood? You tell me.'

'Are they connected?'

The microwave pinged and he took out the food. 'No, of course not. But now we've started on this one, we'll see it through to its conclusion.' He took the tray of food over to the couch and sat down, apologetically tripping over one of Joanna's pile of books. He lay on the couch.

Joanna followed him over to the couch and sat astride him. He moved slightly underneath her. She leaned forward and began to unbutton his shirt.

'How much sleep did you say you got last night?' she asked.

'Three or four.'

'You must be tired. Sam, if I go to Meryl's funeral Friday, would you be able... Sam? Sam?'

It was gone 11PM when Leroy's bladder woke him. He lifted himself off the couch. There was cold Chinese food next to the couch, and Joanna's books had gone. The apartment was quiet and empty.

'Shit,' he said aloud, lying back down again.

CHAPTER FIFTEEN

NEXT MORNING, LEROY and Quinn were both at their desks at Police HQ on Butler and Iowa.

Leroy arrived first, and began his day by updating Lieutenant Perez with the progress they had made so far. Perez and Leroy were once partners, and when the position of Lieutenant came up, both applied for the job. Perez got it, mainly because as the previous captain told Leroy, 'he kisses ass better than you.' They never had been friends in the true sense of the word, and their working relationship now was always cordial and professional, but deep down,

Perez always suspected that Leroy resented being overlooked.

Which he didn't.

'Do you think this John Doe's linked to the Kelton case?' Perez asked. 'You know, it wasn't my idea, getting you involved. This is Hollywood Division's turf. Not that they're complaining.'

'My gut feeling's that they're not. Kelton's bodyguard was shot in a bar in plain sight. Period. This one seems to have been shot in the head, which was then cut off.'

Perez grimaced. 'Anything to indicate a terrorist angle here? You know, the head being cut off?' He made a hand gesture across his throat as he spoke.

'Unlikely. He was already dead when they did it. My theory is, and I was thinking it through on the way in this morning, that this is a botched attempt to dismember the body to help hide the remains. Only something stopped them, or disturbed them.'

'Really?'

'Think about it. We've had cases before where killers have cut up a DB and distributed the body parts around. An arm, a leg, or even a torso, are easier to hide than an intact corpse. And if you're going to cut up a body, where are you likely to start?'

Perez nodded. 'The head.'

'So we really need to get the guy identified.'

The lieutenant seemed to lose interest at this point. His desk phone rang. 'Well, keep me in the loop,' he said, picking up.

When Leroy got back to his desk Quinn was already at his, watching something on his screen. He looked up as Leroy arrived.

Quinn asked, 'I've been wondering: all that high-tech kit up there protecting the sign – why didn't it pick him up, or the guys who killed him or dumped him?'

'It only has a particular range. You get too close to the sign, or the perimeter fence, and bells start to go off down in Hollywood Station. But remember, the head was found some way down the side of Mount Lee, beyond the range of the infrared cameras and CCTV and microphones. Bummer, really. Might have made things easier for us.' He pointed at Quinn's screen. 'Is that what I think it is?'

Quinn nodded. 'Yes, it's the CCTV footage we got yesterday from the bar.'

Leroy sat down to watch as Quinn held a key down to get the footage to the time Harry Webb said he arrived.

'I'll give Hobson a call,' Leroy said, his eyes still fixed on the screen.

Hobson answered almost immediately.

'Morning, Sam. I had the feeling you'd be calling.'

'Any news for me, Russ?'

'The head does match the body, to begin with.'

'It matches?' Leroy repeated, for Quinn's benefit. 'And?'

'The COD was a gunshot wound to the head, as I suggested yesterday. There were entry and exit wounds. Have they found the bullet yet?'

'No, not as yet. I know they've combed the immediate vicinity of the scene yesterday, but we don't know if he was killed up there.'

'Well, the head was certainly cut off there. We found traces of soil on... well, on the neck of the torso. Obviously transferred there from the knife.'

'It was a knife, then?'

'Yes. Six-inch blade, no serrations.'

'Hunting knife, then?'

'Looks that way, yes. Also, it looks from the diameter of the wound and passage through the head that the bullet was something like a .44.'

'Any DNA matches?'

'Give me a break, Sam; you know the score with that. We've taken a sample, and it's going in with the next batch. So we're talking about five to ten days. Maybe two weeks.'

'Two weeks?'

'Yup. Unless your lieutenant feels it's urgent and authorises a fast track.'

'He's not going to do that.'

'So it's one to two weeks. And I also need to manage your expectations regarding the DNA. It could well have been degraded. Remember he was lying in the brush and in the garbage. The test might come back rodent.'

'I'll bear that in mind. Can you mail me over a mug shot? Then we can begin searching existing records. He may have a record; he may have been reported missing.'

'Will do. On its way. He was Caucasian, around thirty, I'd say. Dirt on the fingernails, which doesn't match the soil up by the sign. So he may not have been killed there. We're checking the dirt, though.'

'Great,' Leroy sighed. 'Anything else?'

'No wedding band.'

'Great. He had no ID on him, either.'

'Apparently not. Couple of other things: there was a scar on his upper left leg – quite old, but it looks like he may have been knifed there some time in the past. He also had a tattoo: *Jolene*, on his right arm.'

'Jolene? Wife, sweetheart? Somebody who's missing him?' He nodded at Quinn, who had sat up, no longer looking at his screen.

'Or he could have been a Dolly Parton fan. And he ate not long before he died. Fried chicken.'

'Fried chicken?'

'And French fries. And apple pie and ice cream.'

'You know how many places in LA serve fried chicken, fries and apple pie?'

'One or two, I'd guess.'

'Right, absolutely. Anything else?'

'No, that's all I have for you for now. Sorry it's not much. His mug shot's gone over, so better luck with that.'

Leroy ended the call, and turned back to Quinn. 'You heard all that? When we've done here, we'll start comparing his face with our records, CODIS, the DMV.

Might have to look out of State for a DMV match. You found anything here?'

'I've located when Harry Webb met up with Mets.'

'Who I'd still like to talk to again,' Leroy said, leaning over Quinn. 'There's Webb. He was pretty much on the button with the time.'

'And there's Mets,' Quinn said, putting his index finger on the screen.

They watched Mets pull a reluctant Webb over to the dumpster, saw Webb look inside, then feel his pockets, then run off camera.

'That's when he ran to a phone booth,' said Leroy. 'He said he left his cell phone at home. He was checking his pockets for it.' He stood up. 'Okay. So far, so good. Now let's rewind, slowly. Maybe we can get a POV of the dumpster line.'

They watched the screen as the picture rewound. The camera moved from the dumpsters, across the parking lot, then back to the dumpsters. Leroy exhaled loudly as it moved across the lot, breathing in again when it returned.

The time and date stamp showed 10:56PM when the view was again of the dumpsters.

'Look,' Leroy said, putting his hand on Quinn's shoulder. 'Freeze it.'

'It's a pick-up,' Quinn said quietly, his face inches away from the frozen picture. He pressed a key and the picture continued reversing, frame by frame.

'There they are,' whispered Leroy, as they saw two figures get out of the pick-up. They ran round to the back of the vehicle, and appeared to be lifting something out. Then they disappeared into the shadows.

Quinn forwarded the picture a few frames to get their faces. 'It's so dark, and one's wearing a hood, the other some kind of hat.'

Leroy squinted at the picture, then shook his head. 'There's nothing there to enhance. Let's take a look at the licence plate.'

It was still not clear. Then they saw the reverse lights illuminate.

'Yes, we'll be able to make out the plate number,' Leroy said.

Then the camera moved.

CHAPTER SIXTEEN

WILLIAM KIRK SAT back in his first class seat as the
Boeing 757 touched down with a bump. After a few
moments the voice of the senior crew member came over
the loudspeaker thanking passengers for travelling on
Delta Flight 1755 from Atlanta to Los Angeles. In spite of
her requests to the contrary, the passengers in Kirk's
compartment stood up, reaching for the overhead lockers
in the normal race to see who could get off the aircraft
first.

Kirk was in no particular hurry.

The flight arrived some twenty minutes late, and so it was almost 4PM when they finally reached the Terminal 5 gate. Kirk took his turn in disembarking and followed the other first class passengers down the corridor to the exit. He had no check-in baggage, just a small case which he was able to wheel direct to the exit. Once he reached the street, he briskly wheeled his case over to the row of yellow cabs and took one to his hotel. On arrival, he was greeted by a smiling receptionist wearing a name badge which declared his name was Matthew.

'Welcome to the Stocker Hotel, Downtown Los Angeles,' Matthew smiled. 'We hope you have a pleasant stay with us.'

Kirk checked in and was handed the key card to room 867. He looked down at the card and handed it back to the receptionist.

'I requested a room on the ninth floor,' he said. 'It has to be the ninth.'

The receptionist looked down at his screen. 'I'm sorry, sir, but I can't see anything on your booking about a floor request. I'll just check availability of ninth floor rooms.' He tapped a few keys and looked up at Kirk. 'I'm very sorry, Mr Kirk, but there are no rooms available on nine.'

Things were not going as planned. Making no attempt to keep his voice low, Kirk said, 'That's not good enough. I need to speak to your supervisor. Where is he?'

The receptionist's eyes darted back and forth, checking that other guests were not listening. 'Please wait here, sir. I'll fetch the Duty Manager.'

Kirk waited, leaning on the desk, tapping his fingers on the polished surface. Momentarily, a woman appeared at the desk. She appeared in her mid-thirties, was heavily but smartly made up, her long dark hair plaited at the back. She wore dark pants and waistcoat, over a white blouse. Above her left breast was the same hotel employee badge the receptionist was wearing, with *Katherine Huth, Duty Manager* embossed in black.

She introduced herself and asked Kirk how she could help.

Kirk explained about the floor. 'I'm superstitious, you see. Nine is my... my lucky number. If I go to stay anywhere, I always have to stay on the ninth floor. That's why I always request a ninth floor room when I book.'

She looked at him momentarily, her expression not changing. Then she pressed a couple of keys on the keyboard. 'You booked online, sir?'

'That's right.'

Katherine Huth stared at the screen a few seconds. 'No, there isn't anything on the booking about a ninth floor room, sir. Let me check what we have.'

Kirk nodded over to the receptionist, who was now checking in an elderly couple. 'We do have some limited availability on the ninth,' she said slowly, 'but they are higher specification rooms than the one you have right now.' She looked up at him. 'I can arrange an upgrade if you wish, but that will cost another $195 per night of your stay.' She looked down at the screen. 'Although I think we can reduce that to $100 a night, as there's clearly been some kind of error.'

Kirk grinned at her. 'That would be satisfactory. My company's paying, in any case. They know about my lucky number.'

'Quite,' she said, her face still betraying no emotion. Kirk handed the Room 827 key card to her, which she swiped again, and passed it back, with a new envelope on which was printed 918. 'Here you are, sir. I apologise for any misunderstanding. I hope you enjoy your stay here at the Stocker Downtown.'

'Thank you.' Kirk took the updated key card and turned around. A bellhop was almost two feet behind him, holding his hand out for Kirk's bag. Kirk was led to the elevator and then up to the ninth floor. He had not realised that the elevator ran on the outside of the building and, not being afraid of heights, gazed intently at the streets and buildings below as the car sped up the side of the hotel.

Once in the room, Kirk passed the bellhop a $20 tip, telling the boy it was okay when he said how generous Kirk was being.

Once alone in his room, Kirk checked the facilities here and the room service menu, not that he had any intention of availing himself of room service.

As he had had an early start that morning and had only eaten chips and nuts on the flight, Kirk decided to eat. Before going to one of the hotel restaurants, he called in at one of the bars. He ordered a beer, and remained on the bar stool as he drank. It was still early, and there were only a few other people there with him: two business men working on laptops and one man and his secretary. Kirk only guessed she was his secretary; she was obviously not his wife.

Once in the restaurant, Kirk ordered the day's specialty, which was spicy paella, with jalapeno sausage and shrimps. He returned to the bar after eating: it was still quiet. The man and his secretary were still there, but left shortly after Kirk arrived. Two separate groups of businessmen were sitting around tables, and two twenty-something girls were laughing with the bartender. One of the girls left shortly afterwards after taking a phone call.

Kirk finished his beer and went back upstairs to watch some TV and go to bed.

The next morning, dressed in a business suit and tie, Kirk went back down to the same restaurant and ordered breakfast: grits with bacon, scrambled eggs, toast and coffee. Having eaten, he went, with his attaché case, over to reception. The Duty Manager from the previous night, Katherine Huth, was on duty. Kirk asked her to call him a taxi to the Conference Center; after checking he was happy with his ninth floor room, she ordered one.

The taxi deposited Kirk outside the main entrance to the LACC, and after passing the driver a twenty, Kirk ran up the steps to the main door and went inside.

There are five halls at the Exhibition Center; today only two were in use. In the South Hall was a bridal gown convention, and the Kentia was hosting the International Drone Expo. The latter interested Kirk most, so he went to take a look. He had no invitation or ticket, of course, so was unable to gain admission; however, he was able to take a complimentary copy of *Drone Pilot* magazine and walked, still looking business-like, to the Customer Services Desk. He asked the man behind the desk the way to book space at the LACC, as his company was considering an event. The man said the sales managers were out at present, so would *sir* like to leave his details, then one of the managers would get back in touch. Kirk complied and asked directions to the cafeteria.

The man directed Kirk to the cafeteria on the second floor. It was little more than a Starbucks kiosk and a handful of stainless steel tables and chairs, but Kirk bought himself a latte and chocolate croissant and sat down. He flicked through the magazine he had picked up: there was little of interest here, but he noticed on the vacant table next to him was a copy of that day's *Times*, so he leaned over and took that.

After reading the newspaper front page to back, he still had time to kill. It was far too early to return to the hotel, so decided to take a walk around. He had one more look around the LACC, then decided to walk over to the Staples Center. There was nothing there of interest to him; just somewhere to go and to see.

His route eventually took him as far as 7th Street, and he paused outside a movie theatre on 7th and Figuero Streets, appropriately named FigAt7th. So he spent the next two hours watching a movie.

*****

Kirk returned to the hotel just after four. He noticed that a group of three young men in suits had also returned to the Stocker, each talking animatedly into their phones. He recognised them as going into the Drone Expo that morning, so was comfortable that he had returned at a feasible time. He felt hot and sweaty so went up to his room for a shower.

It was almost five after his shower, so he took the elevator down to the foyer, and stepped outside. It was too early to eat, so Kirk decided to look around the vicinity. His first stop was Union Station. He crossed over Alameda with dozens of commuters, strolled through the small gardens separating the two halves of the parking lot, and stepped in to the station lobby. Walking past the rows of long wooden benches and the coffee shop and kiosk, Kirk made his way to the bank of luggage storage lockers. He fished a key out his pocket, looked up and down the lockers for the corresponding number, opened the locker, and took out the contents of the locker. With the small package under his arm, he strode back to the hotel.

It was approaching 6PM, but still warm and sunny. Thankful for this, Kirk felt it was time for him to take a swim. He returned to his room, stored the package, and changed for the pool. Donning the fluffy white hotel bathrobe, and clutching the matching white towel under his arm, he headed back for the elevator.

On arrival at the roof-top pool, he paused under the covered section where the elevators were. He could hear the rumble of the traffic below, punctuated by regular blasts of car horns. Then a different type of horn, this time from one of the locomotives over at Union Station. There was a siren in the distance.

Kirk walked over to one of the many white loungers around the pool. Only three were actually occupied, so it was easy for Kirk to choose one. He draped his robe over the head rest, and sat down, legs outstretched. The three loungers that were occupied were occupied by two middle-aged women, and one man. Kirk guessed they were business people, as Downtown LA is hardly a place for tourists to stay. He then noticed a fourth person, a man who was swimming lengths of the pool. After a while, one of the women climbed in the pool, but swam separately from the man.

Kirk lay back to enjoy the sun; after ten minutes, both the man and the woman got out of the pool and returned to their loungers. Kirk decided to swim a while, so climbed in and did half a dozen lengths. After swimming he held on to the steel step handrail and looked around while standing in the six feet of water. He ran his hand over his face and brushed his dark hair back. As he looked around, squinting slightly in the sun, he noticed a girl arrive. She was in a swimsuit and carried a towel. Kirk watched as she walked past and selected a lounger, away from the four others' and Kirk's. Kirk waited a few minutes and nonchalantly swam a couple of lengths, happening to pause two thirds of the way along the pool, where she was sitting. Again, he trod water as if taking a breather, but trying to make eye contact with her. He was unsuccessful, partly because of the sunglasses she was wearing, and also she was totally taken up with the iPod she had set up, its thin earphones around her head. Kirk could just about make out the beat of whatever she was listening to.

Kirk decided to get out of the pool. As he did so, a young man appeared, dressed in trunks and carrying a hotel towel under his arm. The man headed straight for the young woman, leaned down to kiss her on the lips, then sat down on the lounger next to her. She looked up at him, they had a brief conversation, and returned to lying on her back, listening to her music. He did the same.

Kirk sighed. He had had enough, so he left the poolside and returned to his ninth floor room to change back. Inviting as it was, Kirk eschewed the room service menu and went down to one of the hotel restaurants. He ordered steak, medium rare, French fries, and succotash. The restaurant was half-empty, and he dined unmolested.

After eating, he made his way to the other bar, where he ordered a Jim Beam and coke. As he had done the evening before, he sat on the barstool, nursing his drink, exchanging words now and again with the bartender. As he sat there, several guests came and went. Two men at the other end of the bar were having a heated and slightly drunken discussion about politics: one was a Democrat, the other clearly a card-carrying Republican. Two guests behind him were each having cell phone conversations: the first was a business call; the second was not. The second man was talking to his wife, telling her how much he loved and missed her and the children. As soon as he finished the call he returned to the booth he was sharing with a redhead in a short red dress.

Then Kirk smelt perfume. It was not a brand he recognised. He looked up and saw a very attractive girl making herself comfortable two stools away. She would have been around twenty-five, a figure to die for, heavy dark hair down to just below her shoulders. She was wearing a black cocktail dress and black pantyhose. She ordered a Long Island Iced Tea. Kirk watched the bartender mix the drink: the vodka, the gin, the rum and the tequila, then returned to his own glass.

'Cheers,' Kirk said, holding his own glass up as she put hers to her lips. She muttered something, took a sip and put the glass on the counter to fumble about her little matching black bag. She took out a small packet of Kools, and continued to fumble. Kirk continued to watch her out of the corner of his eye. Eventually she took a cigarette out and turned to him.

'Excuse me, do you have a light?'

Kirk did not smoke, but always carried a lighter for occasions such as this. Shielding the flame with the palms of his hands, he lit the menthol cigarette.

As they made eye contact, Kirk had one thought.

It's showtime.

CHAPTER SEVENTEEN

SHE SAT BACK on the stool and took a deep drag from the cigarette. Pursed her lips and blew out a thin jet of menthol smoke. After a moment she held out the packet to Kirk; he declined.

'Trying to give them up,' he said disarmingly.

She nodded and put the pack back into her bag. Took another drag.

'You here on business? she asked.

Kirk nodded, taking a sip of his whiskey and coke. 'I'm here for the expo.'

'What's that?'

He sat back and took a deep breath. 'At the LACC – the Conference Center. The International Drone Expo.'

'Drone?' she asked. 'You mean…?' She waved one hand around in a circular motion.

'Yup. My company manufactures the batteries that go in the little suckers.'

'Cool,' she said, nodding her head, pretending to be impressed.

'Yeah. I should say propane fuel cells, to be exact. We manufacture the D245XR solid oxide cell.'

'Wow.'

'Yeah, it's cool,' he agreed, nodding his head, reflecting on how useful the *Drone Pilot* magazine had been.

'Where you from?' she asked.

'Atlanta, Georgia. You?'

'Bay Area.'

'Vacation?' Kirk resisted the temptation to ask if she was there alone.

'Kind of. I'm here with a girlfriend.' She paused. 'A girl *friend*, not a girlfriend, if you see what I mean.'

Kirk nodded.

'She's kind of an actress up there, came here for a couple of auditions.'

'And you came with her for kind of moral support?'

The girl nodded. 'Yup.'

Kirk offered his hand. 'I'm Bill, by the way.'

'Paula.'

They shook hands.

'You got family in San Fran?' Kirk asked.

Paula blew out more smoke. My mom does. Lives with some guy near the Presidio.'

'Not your old man?'

She shook her head. 'He left us when I was a kid. Haven't seen him since.'

'Siblings?'

'What?'

'Brothers or sisters?'

She shook her head again. 'Just lil' old me. What about you, Bill from Atlanta? You got a wife and kids back home?'

Kirk nodded enthusiastically. 'I sure do. Married ten years. Three kids. You want to see a picture?'

Paula nodded while stubbing out her Kool. Kirk dove into his wallet and picked out a photograph of a woman and three children. 'Here,' he said, pointing at the figures in the picture, 'that's Emeline, my wife; that's Tracey-Anne – she's eleven now; that's Bill Junior – he's eight; that's Darlene, who's five.'

'Nice,' Paula said.

Kirk put the picture back. 'Thanks.'

'Wait a minute,' Paula said.

'What?'

'Your eldest girl, she's eleven?'

'Yeah,' said Kirk slowly.

'And you guys have been married ten years?'

'Yeah... now I see what you mean. Yeah, we were together a while before we got married.'

'That must have been kind of uncomfortable for you; you know, having a kid and not being married. In Atlanta, I mean.'

Kirk paused a beat. 'A little. Jeez, it was so long ago, I can hardly recall. Yeah, Emeline's parents kept insisting.' He looked around. 'Your friend's late.'

'Guess she has to wait till the auditions are over.'

'Where is the audition?'

She shrugged. 'Somewhere in Hollywood, I guess.' She nodded down to his empty glass. 'You want another?'

'Don't mind if I do, thanks.'

'What was it?'

'Jim Beam and coke.'

Paula indicated over to the bartender.

'Hold on,' Kirk said. 'I've had two already. I'll just have mineral water.'

'No, have something stronger. Have one more.'

'I need a clear head. No, you're right; I'll have another. But make it a vodka and lemonade this time.'

Paula frowned. 'Bill, you shouldn't mix drinks.'

He held up his hands. 'Okay, you win. Thanks.'

The bartender poured Kirk another whiskey and coke. Kirk took it and asked if she was having another.

'Not yet,' she replied holding her hand over her glass. 'I'm pacing myself; it could be a long night if my friend's audition goes well.'

Kirk laughed. 'Yeah, could be.' He got off his stool. 'Just the men's room. Back in a minute.'

'Sure, Bill. I'll still be here.'

Kirk headed over to the restrooms. There was a single door with a circular window which led to a small passage where the doors to the men's and women's rooms were. Kirk stopped in the passage and peered round to look through the circular window. He could see Paula still sitting at the bar with their drinks. She was on her phone, and had moved to the seat next to his. She briefly turned round to face the restroom door: Kirk ducked down and went into the men's room.

He returned after a couple of minutes. Paula had lit another cigarette and was staring behind the bar. 'Hey,' she said as he got back.

'You found your lighter?' Kirk remarked.

'Mm? Oh, yes. It was in my purse after all.'

Kirk picked up his drink and took in about half. He noticed the coke was still bubbling. 'That's good,' he said, sounding contented.

She looked at him and smiled. 'So, Bill,' she asked. 'What are you into?'

He took another mouthful. 'What am I into? What do you mean: interests, hobbies?' He lowered his voice and leaned towards her. 'Or do you mean *sexually*?'

She shrugged. 'Whatever.'

He swayed slightly on the stool. 'Well, I like... drones,' he said, laughing.

She laughed too, putting her hand on his upper leg. 'I guessed you might.'

'I'm not sure what else I like. Most stuff, I guess.' He picked up his glass and stared into it. 'I think I've had too many Jim Beams,' he said, downing the contents. He looked over at her. 'What was your name again?' he said, laughing.

She smiled, another drag. 'Paula.' Now it was her turn to lower her voice. 'But my friends call me Pinky.' She leaned closer to him. 'Bill, do you want to know why they call me Pinky?'

He turned to face her and, with mock seriousness, said, 'Yes, that would be interesting.'

She got off her stool and took his arm. 'Not here. Let's go to your room. What number is it?'

'Nine… nine…'

'What room number, Bill?'

He took out his card. 'Here you are: 918.'

Paula took the card and helped him walk to the elevator.

'I'm feeling a little woozy,' he slurred. 'Shouldn't have had that third one. Or was it the fourth?'

The elevator arrived and Paula guided him in. Kirk lcancd against the elevator wall as they ascended, the lights of Downtown LA receding as they climbed. Paula fiddled with her phone, looking up at Kirk and smiling.

She led him down the corridor to 918 and slid the card into the lock. The light flashed green and Paula opened the door, helping Kirk inside. She led him over to the bed and sat him down.

He sat up slightly. 'Are you going to show me why they call you Pinky?' he asked, trying to put his hand on her dress.

She took his hand away and kissed him on the forehead. 'Presently, lover. All good things come to those who wait.'

Then there was a knock on the door. Paula kicked off her shoes and opened it.

CHAPTER EIGHTEEN

PAULA OPENED THE door wide and another girl was standing there. About the same age and build as Paula, she was black and had frizzy hair. She wore a similar cocktail dress to Paula, but hers was red. Kirk noticed her long, black, shiny bare legs.

She sashayed into the room, kissing Paula on the lips as she passed her. Paula shut the door.

'Bill,' Paula said, 'this is my friend.'

'From the audition?' Kirk asked.

'That's right, honey,' the other girl purred, stroking his hair. 'My name's Perky.'

Kirk's eyes focussed on the outline of Perky's nipples through her dress. 'I see why they call you Perky.'

Perky looked at Pinky and stroked her face. 'Mm, you have a naughty one here.'

Pinky looked down at Kirk. 'Naughty boy. I told you to wait.' She crouched down and opened the mini-bar, taking out a bottle of champagne.

Kirk said to Perky, 'She's going to show me why she's called Pinky.'

Perky looked over at Pinky and kissed her on the lips again, looking back at Kirk. Then the two girls embraced, in a full, passionate kiss. As they embraced, they each unzipped the other's dresses, so when they ended their embrace, both garments fell to the floor. Now they both stood in front of Kirk, Pinky wearing black lacy panties and black stockings, and Perky in plain red ones, with a little black Aquarius symbol on the side.

Perky opened the champagne: with a loud pop, the cork shot across the room and hit the wall behind Kirk. The two girls giggled, then turned to face each other. Perky then began to pour the champagne over Pinky's naked chest. Putting the bottle down, she put her face between Pinky's breasts and began greedily licking up the sparkling drink. Pinky raised her face to the ceiling and began to moan, caressing Perky's hair.

Kirk, meanwhile, had ripped off his shirt and pants and was now on the bed just in his shorts. The two girls paused and looked over at him amusedly while he fought to remove the shorts. Now he was naked on the bed, swaying around in a drunken fashion, watching as Pinky's mouth went down onto one of Perky's breasts.

On his knees, balancing on the bed, Kirk manoeuvred himself over to the edge. He reached out to the two girls, but Perky's arm flashed out and pushed him away. Off balance, and unable to coordinate his movements, Kirk tumbled back down onto the bed.

'Patience, honey,' Pinky called out. 'I told you: you have to be patient.'

Nodding eagerly, Kirk crawled back so he was sitting upright leaning on the headboard. Now he sat back, heavy-eyed, watching the two girls. By now, Pinky had taken off her panties and Perky was on her knees. The champagne had run down onto her stomach and Perky was licking it off, getting lower and lower.

Kirk was fighting to contain himself.

Then he lost the fight.

Then he passed out.

CHAPTER NINETEEN

KIRK AWOKE, HIS head throbbing.

He rubbed his face. It was morning – 7:25 to be exact. Daylight was filtering into the room through the gap between the heavy drapes.

Kirk stood up, still shaky. He padded over to the window, and opened the drapes, squinting as the morning sunshine flooded in.

He looked down. He was naked. He rubbed his face and scratched his head, trying to recall. He made himself some strong coffee and took a long shower, alternating between very hot and freezing cold. Once out of the shower, he made more coffee and dressed.

Checked under the bed, and switched on the television

Sat on the bed, watching *Good Morning, America*.

It would not be long now.

Kirk was right: it was not long. At just after 9AM, there was a knock on the door. A quiet, polite, conservative two taps. If it was somebody from the hotel such as room service or housekeeping, it would be three taps, and a voice would quietly call out.

No voice this time. Just two taps.

Kirk muted the television and went over to the door. Through the spyhole he could make out a figure. It was a man, dressed in open necked shirt and jacket. He was of Asian descent, dark hair neatly gelled back. Probably two days' designer stubble.

Kirk unlocked and opened the door.

The man gave him pleasant smile. 'Mr Kirk?'

'Yes, I am he. Come on in.'

The man thanked Kirk politely as he stepped into the room, closing the door behind him. He was carrying a small brown leather zip-up briefcase under his arm.

'You this morning's duty manager?' Kirk asked. 'I saw your Ms Huth yesterday.'

Another Asian smile. 'No, sir. I am not the duty manager. I am here on another matter.'

'Oh, yes?' Kirk enquired, finishing his coffee.

'I've come to sell you something, Mr Kirk.' As he spoke, he unzipped the briefcase.

'Sell me something?' Kirk slapped his temple. 'Sorry, I get it: you're from the LACC. I'd forgotten I'd left my details with you guys.'

'No, Mr Kirk. I am not from the LACC. I'm here to sell you something else.' As he spoke, he passed Kirk a brown envelope he had taken out of the briefcase. 'Insurance.'

'Insurance?' Kirk snatched the envelope and tore it open. Gasped as he saw the contents.

The envelope contained five colour photographs, six by four. Kirk flicked through them: they were photographs of him and the two girls from last night. On the first, Kirk was sitting against the end of the bed with Perky sitting astride him. Kirk's eyes were closed and he had a languid grin on his face. On the next, Pinky was sitting up and Kirk's face was buried in her crotch. On the third, Pinky was lying on the bed with Kirk on top. And so on.

Kirk looked up at the man. 'Wha…?'

The man smiled again. 'It looks as though you and the girls had a fun evening. But, I'm not sure if Evelyn… is that your wife's name?'

'Emeline.'

'Emeline. Not sure if she'd see it the same way. Or what about the kids? How would they feel if they saw Daddy munching pussy instead of selling drones?'

Kirk made a lunge. 'You son of a -'

The Asian put out a hand to stop him. 'Now, now, Mr Kirk. Let's be civilised.'

'You said insurance. How much do you want?'

The Asian tapped his chin with the corner of the envelope. 'Let's see. How about two thousand now, while you're in LA, then another two every month?'

'Two grand a month? Are you crazy?'

'Look at your beautiful family, Mr Kirk. Or may I call you Bill? Isn't two thousand worth making sure you don't lose them? It's only five hundred dollars a week. That's what? Seventy bucks a day? Same as a trip to Disneyland.'

Kirk rubbed his face and sighed. He flicked through the photographs again. His hands were shaking. 'All right, all right. Two grand a month. And I get to keep these?'

'Free of charge. Introductory offer.'

'What about the negatives?'

The Asian laughed. 'Negatives? Bill, you're still living in the 20th century. It's all digital now, man; where have you been?'

Kirk said nothing, just flicked through photographs again.

'No, they are screenshots from the movie.'

'Movie?'

'Sure. Just twenty minutes or so. You don't want that, or these stills showing up on YouTube or Facebook or… Need I go on?'

'All right, I get the picture.' Kirk looked around the room, panicked. 'I don't have two thousand here.'

'Of course you don't.'

'Well, how do I get it to you?'

'Give me your cell phone number. I'll call you later to give you instructions. Give you time to get to an ATM.'

'Okay.' Kirk scribbled down a number on a sheet of hotel notepaper.

'Thank you, Bill.' The Asian looked at the number and slipped the note into his coat pocket. 'By the way, when I call you, it will be from a pre-paid cell phone. No GPS. So don't bother trying to be clever calling the police. Just think of Evelyn and the kids, and how much your family means to you.'

'Emeline.'

'Whatever.' The Asian patted his coat pocket. 'I'll be in touch, Bill. Have a nice day, now.' He turned round at the door. 'My name's Lee, by the way. Mr Lee. And remember: discretion is essential.' With that, he left the room, quietly closing the door behind him.

Kirk stood still for a few moments, then stepped over to the door. Peered out into the corridor, both ways. Then went back into the room. He switched the kettle on for more coffee and dialled room service. Ordered grits, eggs, bacon and toast, with filter coffee. He picked up the photographs and flicked through them again. Held two of them up at an angle, grinning. Keeping the television on mute he lay down on the bed, clasping his hands behind his head. He smiled and started singing softly.

Alabama, Alabama
So far from you have I roamed.

Alabama, Alabama
Now I'm soon comin' home.

CHAPTER TWENTY

IT WAS JUST before midday when Lee rang Kirk. Kirk let it ring five times, then picked up.

'Bill Kirk.'

'This is Mr Lee, Bill.'

'I guessed it would be you.'

'I feared for a moment you weren't going to pick up. What were you doing?'

'I was in the bathroom. You're calling with your delivery instructions?'

'That is correct. You have the money?'

'Not yet. I was waiting for you to call first. I'm going to the bank later.'

'Good decision, Bill.'

'Let's not prolong this call. Where and when?'

'Let me see. Your hotel is across the street from Union Station, yes?'

'Yup.'

'Go over there at 5:30. You will see that in the main part of the depot there are rows of wooden benches, after the restaurant tables and across from the kiosk.'

'I know, yes.'

'I shall meet you there, back row of seats if possible, just before the entrance to the tracks. I shall have with me a black backpack. You will need to have something similar with the money inside. We can then discretely exchange bags.'

'And that's it? You're going to check the cash in plain sight?'

'I don't think there's a need to; do you, Bill? Just think of your family.'

'All right. Two grand in a black backpack, 5:30 at Union Station.'

'You got it. Have a good day, Bill.'

With that Lee hung up. Kirk pursed his lips and tapped his chin with the phone. About five hours to go. He leapt off the bed and put on his shoes. Checked under the bed once more, made a visual check of the room, and left. As he walked through the lobby he saw that Ms Katherine Huth was on duty: they made eye contact and he gave her a cheery wave. She looked up and gave him a reluctant smile.

Kirk was sure that one of the stores in the lobby would have a black backpack on their shelves, but they were bound to be expensive. Even though ultimately he would not be paying, he saw no reason to get ripped off. As he left the hotel, he turned to the left and headed towards Olvera Street. He had been here once or twice before and knew he would be able to find what he was after at one of the shops there. They would not exactly be Wal-Mart, but a lot cheaper than the boutique in the hotel.

And he was correct. Olvera Street is full of stands and stores, catering for tourists, offering all kinds of memorabilia and souvenirs, all with a Mexican theme. At the second store, for $8.50 plus tax, he found exactly what he was looking for. Telling the little Mexican woman no change was needed, he swung the backpack over his shoulder and headed out.

It was one o'clock now, and Kirk was feeling hungry. He looked around and saw a restaurant across the street. He wandered over and checked the menu outside *La Noche Buena*. He was not a fan of Mexican food, but noticed they did offer genuine American fare also. That was good: also good was the fact that the little restaurant was almost empty, a plus point as far as Kirk was concerned as he hated eating in crowded places.

An hour later, and Kirk emerged after having consumed fried chicken, French fries and coleslaw, followed by apple pie and coconut ice cream. He checked his watch. Time to get back to the hotel now and prepare. His reservation was for four nights: if he was really lucky and this evening went as well as he hoped, he would not need to go through the bother of extending his stay in LA.

In his previous job, Kirk always made a point of arriving at a conference or a meeting at least an hour before the event began, to get a good parking spot, to look over the venue, and get familiar with his surroundings. Today was no exception. At 4:40 he was ready. With the black backpack on the bed, he knelt down and felt underneath the king-sized divan. A brown box was fixed to the slats underneath the bed. Kirk unpeeled the grey duct tape and pulled the box out, opening it on the bed.

In the box was a small handgun – a Heckler & Koch Compact 45. Kirk lifted it out and felt its weight. The box also contained a suppressor and a box of 9mm cartridges. Kirk loaded the weapon and fitted the silencer and tested the weight again, aiming at his own reflection in the bathroom mirror.

Not perfect, but manageable. He took the brown leather holster out of his suitcase and put it on, followed by his coat. Slipped the loaded HK into the holster and the suppressor into his pocket.

4:52PM.

Showtime.

CHAPTER TWENTY-ONE

KIRK TOOK THE elevator down and walked through the lobby to the main doors. He looked out for Ms Huth, for no special reason other than curiosity, but it looked as if she was off duty now.

He crossed over North Alameda and walked through the little parking lot in front of the station. Kirk looked up at the white tower with the red stucco pointed roof: the clock on the tower indicated just before five.

Once through the doors, Kirk paused and looked around. He couldn't see Lee, but there was no reason why the little weasel couldn't be here early too.

The benches in question were at the end of the main hall, on one side, facing outwards. Kirk walked past the circular white clothed tables of the *Traxx* diner on one side, and the newspaper and magazine kiosk on the other. As Lee had said, the benches were just before the entrance to the subways which lead to the tracks and the MTA lines. Kirk paused and looked around once more, checking the passengers who were browsing at the kiosk. No Lee.

Kirk turned back and walked out of the building. He stopped at the edge of the parking lot, and sat down on the edge of the low whitewashed wall bordering the neatly maintained flower beds. Here he could remain partially out of plain sight, yet have a view of the main doors so he could see when Lee arrived. He was uncertain if there were any other entrances or exits, but this was the main one, and he only had one pair of eyes, anyway.

Now 5:08PM, and rush hour was getting under way. There was a steady flow of commuters heading into the station, and every so often, Kirk could hear a locomotive horn, loud and imperious, unlike the frequent car horns he could hear all the time.

Kirk waited.

It was now 5:31 and Kirk had not seen Lee arrive. The Asian may have been in the crowds of commuters arriving, and it occurred to Kirk that he may have actually arrived on the MTA. Whatever, it was time for Kirk to go back inside.

As he reached the row of benches, Kirk could see Lee sitting on the back bench, right at the end. Lee was not wearing the coat he had on earlier, just an open-necked shirt. The bench was empty save Lee and three women right at the other end. Lee sat up as he saw Kirk arrive. He did not slide along the bench as Kirk stood in front, so Kirk brushed past and sat down next to him.

'You're a few minutes late, Bill,' Lee said, looking directly ahead.

'Sorry.' Kirk shuffled around in his seat. 'I lost track of time. Excuse the pun.' He held the backpack between his legs, as Lee was doing with his

'The money is in there?' Lee asked, nodding down to Kirk's bag.

'Maybe.'

'Excuse me, Bill?'

'I've brought you something else.' As he spoke, Kirk casually pushed his coat back to reveal the holster and the HK. Lee glanced down, reacted briefly, then regained his composure and looked ahead again.

'You're being very foolish, Bill. Just think how your wife and your children would feel if they should see what you were doing last night.'

Kirk leaned to the left, so his left arm was touching Lee's right. 'Let me let you into a little secret, Mr Lee. I can't keep calling you Mr Lee, can I? What's your name?'

Lee paused before replying. 'Chong.'

'Chong,' Kirk repeated. 'Chong. Chong. Chong.' He kept repeating the name, as if practising pronouncing it. Lee was becoming irritated, but tried to hide his irritation. 'You see, *Chong*,' Kirk continued, 'the woman and the kids in that picture I showed the girl won't really give a rat's ass what I was up to last night.'

'I don't understand you,' Lee said.

Kirk chuckled. 'How did she do it? Rohypnol?'

'She did use Flunitrazepam, yes.'

'Rohypnol to you and me. And that was why she almost pissed her pants when I said I wanted a mineral water or a vodka, wasn't it? Rohypnol these days has a blue dye which would show in a clear liquid, but not in whiskey and coke.'

Lee straightened up. 'What do you want, Bill?'

Kirk ignored the question. 'And I'm guessing once I was out, the girls - with you helping, maybe – manhandled me into those positions?'

Lee asked again, 'What do you want, Bill? Surely you're not going to shoot me in the middle of Union Station.'

Kirk patted the HK. 'I have a silencer. Nobody's going to hear a thing. It's rush hour, remember? Well, *you* want me not to call the police, right? *I* want you to tell me who's running your outfit, and to refund the money you've extorted from my friend John Thomas Hightower.'

'Hightower?'

'Big fat guy from Birmingham, Alabama. He was here a couple of weeks ago.'

Lee nodded. 'Yes, I remember. You and he are friends?'

'Well, more the friend of a friend of a friend. So, first, give me the name of who you're working for.'

Lee said nothing.

Kirk's hand moved slowly down to the HK.

Lee gave Kirk the name.

'Excellent. Well done. Now, I want you to call your boss, and say I want Hightower's money returned.'

'When?'

'Call your boss now. Say we'll come and get Hightower's money. I'm told he's paid you four grand so far.'

Lee took out his phone and began to dial. Kirk reached out and stopped him.

'Wait,' Kirk said. 'Let's just go over there. Go see your boss.'

Lee said nothing. Just nodded acquiescence.

'Come on, then.' Kirk stood and took Lee's arm as the Asian stood as well. 'You parked out front?'

Lee shook his head. 'Gateway Center. Other side of here.'

'Which way, then?'

'This way. Follow me, please.'

Kirk was amazed how, even at gunpoint, Lee remained as polite as he was in the hotel room. Lee took Kirk past the subways to the tracks and along a corridor. As they passed the escalator down to the Gold Line, the passage became a bridge over the railroad tracks, after which the bridge connected with the parking garage.

'Which floor?' Kirk asked.

'Up one floor, Bill.'

On entering the garage, they took the elevator up one floor. Now covering Lee with the unholstered HK, Kirk asked, 'Which car is yours?'

'The silver one over there.'

Lee led Kirk over to a silver Ford Mustang V6, its roof folded down. It had either been freshly valeted, or was new. Kirk could smell the leather.

'Very nice, Chong,' Kirk said. 'But you can probably afford it.'

'Thank you, Bill,' Lee said politely as he climbed in. Still covering the Asian, Kirk climbed in the front passenger seat. Both men threw their backpacks into the back.

'Remember,' Kirk said as he pointed the HK at Lee, 'no tricks.'

'No tricks, Bill. I give you my word.'

As Lee turned on the ignition and noisily revved the engine, its sound echoing around the parking level, Kirk became aware of another smell as well as that of fresh leather.

A sweet smell.

Then William Kirk could smell nothing.

CHAPTER TWENTY-TWO

DELROY SWITCHED OFF the Honda CB1000R and kicked down the stand. Once the throbbing of the 1140cc engine had stopped, the air was silent, and still. The sky was clear and the moon was bright – not a full moon, but as near as damn it. Looking up at the night sky, Delroy could see dozens and dozens of stars of varying brightness. He could see the flashing lights from two aircraft, one of which seemed to be reducing height and heading towards LAX; the other in the other direction, probably having taken off over the ocean, then making a one-eighty to head eastwards He could also make out a helicopter, flying much lower, heading across the city.

In one direction, he could see nothing. He knew there was nothing anyway; just mountainside. In the other direction, looking down, he could see hundreds and hundreds of streetlights, across and down, like a gigantic chequer board. Somewhere down there, was his house, with his brother, his mom, and his nana.

Amongst those white streetlights were lines upon lines of white vehicle lights and red vehicle lights, slowly crossing the chequer board. Some of these lights were travelling parallel with the streetlights; others were moving across the board at an angle. Delroy guessed these were the freeways.

As the moon was bright, Delroy did not need to provide his own illumination, either a flashlight or the Honda's headlamp. Both carried extra risk.

He unhooked his backpack and checked the contents. All there: three aerosols of paint. One black, one yellow, one red.

Returning the cans to his backpack, Delroy set off. Walking across the empty blacktop, he headed for the building. He looked it up and down and whistled. This would be some coup. All he wanted was to be appreciated for who he was; to be *noticed*. His older brother always got the glory; he was just *the kid Delroy*.

Just the kid.

Now they'd see.

At school he was no good at drawing, no good at painting. But Delroy was *artistic*.

He was an artist, looking for his canvas. And after circling the perimeter of the building, stumbling sometimes, he had found it.

He took out his three cans, and shook the first, the yellow.

Cans of aerosol paint contain two things: paint and propellant. The propellant is liquefied gas. At normal temperature, it is a gas, forced into the can at high pressure, causing it to liquefy. Pressing on the nozzle releases the pressure and some of the propellant reverts to gas. The gas then shoots the paint out. When a can is shaken, it rattles. This is the sound of a metal ball bearing mixing the paint and propellant. Delroy and his contemporaries felt the rattling sounded cool, and was even cooler being done to music.

When the rattling stopped, indicating the paint and propellant were adequately mixed, Delroy pulled at his left sleeve, and held the excess material over his nose and mouth.

Then he began work.

On his way up the mountainside, he thought about what type of message he should leave. When he was twelve, he was just tagging, which was literally kids' stuff – just putting your name really with one colour. Basic stuff, though with the advantage that it was quick. You could leave your tag and be gone before the cops or security guards got there. Some of his older friends had graduated to *heaven*; that is, leaving your mark on somewhere very hard to reach, like a railroad bridge or a freeway sign.

No, Delroy wanted to leave his mark in his own way: not too simple, yet not dangerous for the artist. He wanted to impress those about him, but not to reveal his identity to the wrong people.

He knew what he would paint. He would leave what was known as a throw-up: an outline and a fill. The normal bubble font. Not that Delroy knew what a font was.

He began the word.

A large, bubble-font of the letter H. Then an O. Then an L. Then another L.

Then Delroy froze.

Was that the sound of a car? Surely not. Not at this time of night.

He listened intently. It was, and it was coming nearer.

Then Delroy could make out headlights. Not coming in a straight line, but weaving to the right first, then the left, then the right, as one would expect travelling up a mountain road.

Too close for comfort now. Not bothering to pick up his bag or the paint cans, Delroy hit the deck. Where he had landed was open ground: in this bright moonlight, he could easily be seen here in plain sight. He took a deep breath and sprinted twenty, thirty, yards down the hill to where there was more brush, and cover. There he lay, his stomach and face pressed against the sand and rock. He was breathing heavily, partly as a result of the sprint, partly as he was terrified.

The pair of headlights had stopped. So had the engine. Closer up, he could tell it was not a car; something slightly larger, like a pick-up truck. He could hear the sound of doors slamming, then of voices. Men's voices, but Delroy could not make out what they were saying.

The voices - Delroy could make out only two – travelled down the side of the hill. Delroy clung to the ground hard.

More talking. The voices appeared raised. Now the two men were shouting. Delroy could hear some other indistinguishable sounds, and then the voices were coming up the hill again.

Clinging to the deck, Delroy held his breath as two pairs of feet passed not six feet away from his head. They were walking quickly, but not in a straight line. As if they were carrying something.

Now Delroy was shaking with fear. He could feel something warm and wet between his legs, then soaking through the upper part of his jeans. 'Shit,' he whispered through clenched teeth.

As the voices got further away, Delroy could make out one of them saying something like, 'I know another place.' The conversation continued further up the hill before the doors slammed again. The engine fired up. By the engine sounds and the way the headlights moved, Delroy could see the vehicle was turning round, before the sound and red tail lights, weaving right and left again, disappeared from view.

It was a full five minutes before Delroy plucked up the courage to get up from his hiding place.

CHAPTER TWENTY-THREE

'GODAMMIT! I DON'T believe it,' Leroy groaned as the camera moved, its point of view tracing across the parking lot. He rested his hand on Quinn's shoulder. 'See if it pans back in time.'

They waited, but by the time the screen showed the dumpsters, the truck had gone.

'Take it back to the truck.'

'Okay.' Quinn reversed the footage and froze the picture. 'It looks like a Dodge,' he said.

'Yeah?'

'Yeah. Holly's old man has one. Years old, though; this one looks newer; you know, shinier.'

Leroy stared at the screen, saying nothing.

'What about the tyres?' Quinn asked. 'SID would have taken pictures of the scene, or we could go back and take a look ourselves.'

Leroy rubbed his chin. 'You mean, see if we can identify the tracks, match that to a make of tyre and try to get a make of vehicle that way?'

'Sure. Why not?'

'Couldn't hurt, I guess.' Leroy sat down at his own desk and logged on. 'Let's hope they've uploaded the report,' he said as he pressed a few keys and waited. It had been uploaded: saying nothing, Leroy speed-read the report. He shook his head. 'That's a no go. It was hard, dry pavement, no skid marks. Some tyre marks, but no identifiable impression, marks from many vehicles.' He logged out, and returned to Quinn's screen. 'Nice idea, though.' He stared back at the screen. 'The licence plate is the answer.'

Quinn zoomed in on the back of the truck, but close up the image was out of focus. He looked up at Leroy. 'Would that guy you know at the FBI be able to help?'

'Calloway? Maybe; I'd rather we didn't ask him unless we had to.'

'But Sam; he'd -'

Leroy patted his hand on Quinn's shoulder again. 'Probably. But maybe Sudeep could. I wonder if he's about.' As he spoke, Leroy wandered off into the corridor.

Sudeep Khan was a fellow officer. After leaving college with two or three degrees, he went to work for Microsoft in their Sacramento office, from where four years ago he was recruited by the LAPD to support the cybercrimes division. He had forgotten more about IT than Leroy could ever learn.

While Leroy was away, Quinn kept zooming in and out, trying to read the plate number. Eventually he took a magnifying glass out of his desk drawer and held that up to the screen.

'Very high-tech,' Leroy said as he returned, alone. 'I'm guessing it didn't work?'

'No.' Quinn shrugged and tossed the glass back in the drawer. 'No Sudeep?'

Leroy shook his head. 'He's in court this morning. I've left a message for him; hopefully he'll be back this afternoon.'

'So, we keep on with this?'

Leroy tapped the top of Quinn's screen. 'Not for now. Let's wait for Sudeep. Let's go talk to Mets again; at least try to. One more attempt before we park him for now.'

'Restaurant or home?' Quinn asked later, as they approached Reseda and Victory.

Leroy checked his watch. 'Restaurant first. It'll be lunchtime soon, so he's more likely to be there. Anyway, it'll be good for that prick Dudley to feel some more heat.'

They parked outside the *Europa* restaurant. It had not yet opened for lunchtime, but through the window they could see the staff preparing things. Leroy banged on the glass and held up his badge. After a little what looked like panicky conversation, one of the waiters let them in.

'Is Mr Dudley in?' Leroy asked.

The waiter at first didn't understand who Leroy was referring to. 'Ah, Mr Dudinsky?' he eventually replied.

'Whoever. Your manager. Is he in? I want to see him.'

'Yes, yes, come this way, please.'

The waiter led Leroy and Quinn through the restaurant. Dudley met them at the door leading to the restrooms, kitchen and his office. 'Detectives,' Dudley said with a hint of sarcasm, 'how can I help you today?'

As he replied, Leroy looked beyond Dudley's shoulder. 'In actual fact, sir, it's Mets we want to see. Is he in?'

Dudley shook his head. 'I'm afraid not. He hasn't shown up for work today. Yet,' he added.

'Was he working last night?'

'Hold on, please.' Dudley turned to one of the waiters and spoke to him in another language. Neither Leroy nor Quinn could understand, but the word *Evald* was in there somewhere. The waiter replied, shaking his head, and waving his hands in the air.

Dudley turned back to Leroy. 'I was attending a reception in Bel-Air last night, so was not here; but I understand Evald did not show up then, either.'

'Do you know why? Did he call in sick?'

'No, he didn't. After the lunchtime rush, I had planned on calling in on him. He doesn't live far from here, as it happens. Shall I tell him you called?'

Leroy turned to go. 'Don't worry, sir; we're headed up there now. I'll tell him you're concerned about him, shall I?'

Dudley opened his mouth to reply, but Leroy and Quinn were already walking out. They returned to their car and headed back up Reseda, soon making a left into Jovan Street. They left the car out front, parked next to the gleaming motorcycle. There was no sign of the owner this time, though.

'My folks had a neighbour once,' Quinn said as they walked past the Harley. 'He had a set of wheels like that. Was always out front cleaning and polishing it. It was always spotless, always gleaming, so's you could use it to shave into.'

'Yeah?' Leroy asked, as they climbed up the stairs, only half-interested.

'Thing is,' Quinn went on, 'we never, ever, saw him ride it. Never.'

Leroy smiled and knocked on the door to apartment 217. They could hear a television playing inside. Then somebody turned the volume down and a second later the door opened. It was Mrs Mets.

Leroy held up his badge and asked if Mr Mets was in.

Mrs Mets ushered them inside and closed the door. 'No, my husband is not here,' she said in her broken English. As she spoke she looked down at two young children who were sat on the floor watching Tom and Jerry on the television.

'Oh. He's not at work. Where is he?'

'He… he's gone missing.'

'Missing? Since when?'

'Since he went to work yesterday. After he spoke to you.'

Leroy said, 'After we spoke to him yesterday, he went to work. His boss said he sent Evald out on an errand. Do you know anything about that?'

She shook her head.

'Have you reported him missing?'

She shook her head again.

'You ought to.'

'He has done this before. He always comes back after a few days. I think he visits another woman. Anyway,' she added, looking up at Leroy, 'don't I have to wait 48 hours or something?'

Leroy shook his head. 'That's a fallacy. You've gotten that from the TV. You can report a missing person as soon as they go missing. Here.' As he spoke, he gave her one of his business cards after writing down a number on the back. 'This is the number of our Missing Persons Unit. You ought to give them a call.'

She took the card, nodding.

'When he does get back,' Leroy added, 'please tell him we need to talk to him. He's not in any trouble; I just need to ask him one or two more questions.'

With that, and with one more glance down at Tom and Jerry, Leroy and Quinn let themselves out. Back in the car, Leroy sat still before starting the engine.

'Coincidence?' he asked Quinn. 'Not. We talk to Mets, then he disappears. Either he knows something and has gone to ground; or he knows something and somebody wants him out of the way.'

'Or he could just be like his wife said, and visiting another woman.'

'He didn't look like a Casanova to me.' Leroy tapped the steering wheel. 'We'll give the MPU his details anyway. They can contact her; that might motivate her to file a report.'

'She didn't seem that concerned; did you notice that?'

Leroy agreed. 'Seems like you and I are more interested in finding him than his wife is.' He turned on the ignition. 'Until Mets shows up, we need to focus on that pick-up. We desperately need to get our John Doe identified.'

'Another thing, Sam,' Quinn said as Leroy pulled out into the traffic. 'Did you see what those kids were watching on TV?'

'Cartoons, yes?'

'Yes, Tom and Jerry. But did you notice the station?'

'No, what's your point?' They turned right into Reseda, heading for the freeway.

'That little logo top right hand corner of the screen. KVEA.'

'Okay.'

'That's a Spanish language station. Mets and his family are from Eastern Europe, supposedly. So why would they be watching television in Spanish?'

CHAPTER TWENTY-FOUR

THEY ARRIVED BACK at Police HQ early afternoon. On the way down, while stuck in freeway traffic, Quinn called the MPU and gave them Mr and Mrs Mets' details. As expected, the MPU officer advised Quinn that there was only so much they could do, as to want some privacy was not a crime. Quinn told them he and Leroy understood all that and thank you very much for taking the call.

Back at the Desk, they bought a sandwich and coffee from the vending machine and returned to the screen. As Quinn booted up the PC, Leroy went back in search of Sudeep Khan.

He was lucky this time, and returned after a few minutes with Khan.

Leroy and Khan both grabbed a chair and wheeled it to sit in front of the screen, either side of Quinn. Quinn went back to the time the camera was facing the dumpsters.

Khan pushed his glasses further up his nose. 'Hm. It looks like a Ram.'

'We thought a Dodge, yes,' Leroy said.

'Dark… black, maybe dark blue. Maybe dark red,' Khan added. 'The Ram has three pick-up models: the 1500, 2500 and 3500.'

'Can you tell which?' Quinn asked.

Leroy got up and fetched Khan a paper cup of lemon tea. 'It's a dead end on the tyres, Sudeep; I'm thinking the licence plate is the only way of getting a make.'

Khan looked closer. 'It's a California plate,' he said. 'Dark blue on white. Have you tried enhancing?'

'We've tried zooming closer and enhancing,' replied Quinn, 'but it's still too fuzzy and out of focus to read the plate.'

'Where did you do that?' Khan asked.

'On here.'

Khan tutted and shook his head. 'You're using the wrong program, guys.' He went to the Home screen and clicked on an icon.

'You can do it, then?' Leroy asked.

'Don't hold your breath, guys,' Khan replied. 'I can't get something out of nothing.'

It is a common misconception, fed by movies and television, that government agencies have magic software to create faces from blurry pixels. All imaging technologies, whether digital or analogue, work in roughly the same way. All cameras create an image when light interacts with an image creating medium. In a film camera it is a chemically treated light sensitive strip of celluloid. In a digital camera, it is a photoelectric sensor. Any picture, especially a screenshot from a moving camera, is taken over a finite period of time, usually a fraction of a second; therefore, there is an upper limit to the detail of any captured image. In digital imaging, the upper limit often has to do with the ceiling the camera or device has – the number of pixels the sensor inside the camera is capable of detecting, for instance. This is all about the limits of the device itself. In other words, as Khan had explained to Leroy many times, no camera, however advanced, has an infinite capacity for resolution. In basic terms, garbage in, garbage out.

So-called enhanced images are a function of the original image. When you start with a blurry or pixelated image, no amount of filters or computer trickery can coax data out of a place where there isn't any.

In the case of a person's face, it may be possible to create some face-like image from garbage data, but that doesn't mean that what comes out will look like the person that was actually there. You would more likely get a mass of pixels that kind of look like a different version of that face.

Leroy had heard all this before. 'Just do your best, Sudeep.'

In the new program, Khan called up the screenshot. The three of them looked closely at the screen.

'California plate, you said that,' Leroy said. 'Blue on white, number in State format. Number, three letters, three numbers.'

'The first number has to be a four,' Quinn observed.

'And the other numbers are zeroes,' added Leroy.

'Or eights.'

'Can you get it any clearer?' Leroy asked.

'Sorry, Sam. Best I can get it.'

'So it's 000, 888, 808 or 080.'

'Or 800, 880, 008…'

'Okay, I get the picture.'

Khan took off his glasses and held the lenses next to the screen. 'The first and last numbers,' he said, 'each have detail in the centre which a zero wouldn't.'

'So they're both eights.'

'More than likely.'

'And the middle one a zero?' Quinn asked.

'More than likely,' Khan repeated. 'Unless there's a sticker, or a mark, or even a splash of mud on the plate, corrupting the image.'

Leroy pointed to the very bottom of the plate. 'What's that?'

'That'll be the DMV website address. In red.'

'Of course, yes.' Leroy paused. 'So it looks like 4, three letters, then 808.'

'Most likely. Now we need to figure out the letters, Sam.'

Quinn said, 'The first. It looks like a two.'

'Which it can't be,' said Leroy, 'so it has to be a Z.'

Khan looked at each in turn. 'Good job, guys. You seem to be getting the hang of it. What about the next letter?'

Leroy suggested, 'What about either a C or a G?'

Khan nodded. 'I agree. C or G.'

'And the third letter,' said Quinn, 'is either U or V.'

'I concur,' smiled Khan. 'The letter's not wide enough to be a W, so: yes, U or V.'

Leroy sat on the desk behind. 'So we have a licence plate that reads 4Z; C or V or G or U; then 808.'

Khan sat back, arms folded. 'Yup.'

'So that means,' – Leroy made a quick calculation – 'four possible combinations to check with DMV.'

'Easy peasy Japanesey,' Khan said as he stood up. 'I'll let you guys get on.'

Leroy and Quinn thanked Sudeep and he walked to the door.

'We just need a pick-up, probably a Ram, with one of those combinations,' Leroy said. 'At last, we might be getting somewhere. Sudeep,hold on.'

Khan stopped in the doorway and swivelled around.

Leroy asked, 'We also need to identify our DB. The ME has sent over a mugshot of the guy, but because the head was lying in open country for a while, there's been some decay and some, er – animal intervention, it's not the best mugshot in the world.'

'You need some help with that?' Khan asked.

'If you can, thanks.'

Khan checked his watch. 'Sure, no problem.'

Leroy called up the face. Khan grimaced.

'Can you do anything with that?' Leroy asked.

Khan shook his head. 'Like I always say, garbage in, garbage out. You're just going to have to do it the old fashioned way.'

'That's what I was afraid of,' said Leroy. 'Trawling through thousands of mugshots.'

'You can save yourselves some time, though.' Khan leaned on the wall as he spoke. 'Even though your guy's not looking his best, you can make certain assumptions - no, deductions – in respect of your search criteria.'

'Say what?' Leroy asked.

'Look,' Khan explained. 'He's male?'

'U-huh.'

'Caucasian; I'm guessing under 40, over 25, so you have a range of years of birth; dark hair; you said it was a head: have you found the rest of him?'

'Yes, about twenty miles away.'

'So, approximately how tall was he?'

'Five-nine.'

'So filter your requests.'

Leroy nodded. 'You got time to help out?'

'No, but I'll show you what to do.'

Khan sat down again and clicked on a different icon. He looked up at Leroy, occasionally glancing over to Quinn. 'Facial recognition technology uses an algorithm to analyse the relative positions and sizes and shapes of the eyes, the nose, the cheekbones, jaws. Now, just like that licence plate, the image is corrupted, but whereas before the corruption was within the image, here, it's the subject itself. Now, broadly speaking, the human face is symmetrical, yes?'

Quinn and Leroy nodded.

'So, where *here...* part of this side is missing – using the detail of the other side of his face, we can extrapolate the missing piece.'

'I see.' Leroy sat back on the desk.

'The LAPD use the DigiKam application for this,' Khan said, 'but as always, garbage in...'

Leroy finished the sentence. 'Garbage out. Yes, Sudeep, I get -'

'The picture. Yes, very good, Sam.'

'No pun intended. So once we've got a satisfactory extrapolation of his face, we can compare that to other databases. Is that right?'

'Yes, but that'll be where your work begins. As you know, there's still no national database for this. The LA County Sheriff's Office uses a mugshot database, but that's only of use to you if your John Doe's been picked up in LA County.' He checked his watch. 'Sorry, Sam; I need to go. Hope I've been of help.'

For the second time, Leroy and Quinn told Khan he had and that they owed him.

Once Khan had gone, Leroy turned to his partner. 'Let's get started. Ray: you begin checking databases using those parameters Sudeep talked about: age, race, and like that. I'll finish working on the mugshot so we have a likeness to verify to if we get a match.'

'We're bound to get several matches.'

'I know, so that's where as complete a face as possible will come in. Check California records first, then go out of State. I think we should pan out once California's done: Arizona, Nevada, not Oregon yet - his skin colour suggests to me not from a northern State - New Mexico, Utah. He doesn't look Hispanic, but check with INS: he could have arrived over the border or through LAX.'

Quinn nodded. 'Once you've got a completed face, Sam, we could try social media as well. That DeepFace technology Facebook runs is apparently ninety-seven percent accurate.'

Leroy raised his eyebrows. 'Really. The stuff the Feds use is only about eighty. Good call, Ray. Yes, and I'll give the MPU a call back, see if they have anything for us, in exchange for Evald Mets.'

'Okay.' Quinn straightened up and turned to face the screen.

Leroy said, 'I'll go get us a coffee and pastry. Let's hope for a break.' On the way to the vending machine he paused. 'Our John Doe is in there somewhere,' he said, pointing to Quinn's screen. 'You wanna know something, Ray? Whoever finds him first, the other one buys the drinks.'

CHAPTER TWENTY-FIVE

IT WAS 11PM. Leroy and Quinn were still searching and had found nothing.

To be more precise, they had found plenty of possibles, using the search parameters Sudeep Khan suggested, but none of the mugshots matched the picture of their victim. Some were close, but not close enough.

Leroy leaned on his elbows and rubbed his eyes. 'This is hopeless,' he said.

Quinn spoke as he examined a mugshot on the screen. 'We're going to be here all night.'

Leroy sat back. 'No, we're not.'

Quinn paused and looked over.

'We've been here long enough today. Leave it for now.'

'You sure?'

'I'm sure. It's so late we're in danger of missing something. Go home to your wife.'

Quinn did not need telling twice. Switching off his computer, he stood up and picked up his car keys. 'You not going home to Joanna?'

Leroy shook his head. 'To tell you the truth, Ray, I don't think there is a Joanna anymore.'

Quinn seemed surprised. 'Hey, man: what's up? Is that what you were talking about before?'

Leroy continued studying his screen as he replied. 'Yeah.'

Quinn sat back down again. 'So…?'

'I don't know. We seem to be kind of drifting apart the last few months. Not finding so much in common, you know. Not being so interested in each other, that's all.'

'There's nobody else, is there?'

'Only this job. As far as I'm concerned, anyway.'

'When'd you last see each other?'

'The other night. I got back to my place, bushed. She had let herself in, to cook dinner. She started to talk about somebody she had worked with - another teacher - who'd just died of cancer. I seemed more interested in my day.'

'That went well, then.'

'Tell me about it. Then I fell asleep on the couch. When I woke later, she'd just gone home. No note, no nothing. She was clearly pissed.'

'And you've not heard from her since?'

Leroy shook his head.

'You tried to contact her?'

Leroy shook his head.

'How do you feel about all this, then? About her?'

'I'm still fond of her, I guess. But I'm not sure where things were headed. I don't want a repeat of last time.'

'But Sam, that was a long time ago.'

'I know.' Leroy paused. 'Ray, you get off to your wife. Tell her I said hi.'

Quinn picked up his keys again. 'I will. Don't work too late, Sam.'

'I won't. Just another half hour or so.'

Quinn paused as he was leaving. 'Why don't you give her a call now? Or a text? Just say you're sorry about the other night. Couldn't hurt, could it?'

'Yeah, I may do. Night, Ray.'

Leroy watched Quinn leave the room. Looked back at his screen. Then picked up his phone. Stared at it a few seconds, holding it in his hand as if he was checking its weight. Then shook his head and put it back on his desk.

He needed more coffee. Stretching, he stood up and wandered out to the vending machine. Got another strong black coffee, extra sugar, took a sip, and began to wander back to his desk.

He had got no more than twelve feet when he heard his name being called out. It was Quinn's voice. He looked around and saw his partner hurrying back to Homicide Room. A uniformed officer was a few feet behind him.

'What's up?' Leroy asked. 'You forget something?'

Quinn shook his head. He was slightly breathless. 'Sam,' he gasped, 'I think I've found our man.'

CHAPTER TWENTY-SIX

LEROY NOTICED OFFICER Ross coming up behind Quinn. 'He's the killer?' he asked.

Quinn shook his head. 'Come listen to this,' he said, leading Leroy back to their desks. Ross followed. He perched on the edge of his desk. 'Tell Detective Leroy what you told me.'

Leroy perched on his own desk, clutching his paper cup.

Ross took a deep breath. He was holding a letter-sized brown envelope. 'You see, Detectives, I was over at the

Stocker Hotel, Downtown. I don't know if you guys know the place.'

'Vaguely,' said Leroy. 'Was this on your own time, or on patrol?'

'Kind of both. I used to be working out of that Division before I got transferred here. While I was over there I kind of made a contact with one of the clerks there; you know the kind of thing: she'd tip me off if there was anything not kosher going on. Drugs, disorder, if any faces checked in that we might be interested in.'

Leroy nodded. 'And you kept up this contact when you moved over here. On duty or off duty? Just out of interest.'

Ross blushed and glanced down at his feet. 'Mainly off duty now.'

Quinn said, 'Harry, just tell Detective Leroy what you told me.'

Ross coughed. 'I was over there earlier today, just chatting over a coffee. Kirstine - that's her name – was telling me what they do when somebody fails to check out.'

'How do you mean fails to check out?' Leroy asked.

'It's like this,' Ross explained. 'These days, apparently seventy-five percent of bookings are made online, using a credit card. Especially a place like the Stocker, which caters almost exclusively for people visiting the Convention Center, folks in town on business, so the rooms are paid for in advance. The hotel retains the card details which they use to charge for incidentals, like the minibar, room service and so on. When the guest leaves, they hand their key in, the hotel says there's these extras, please sign here, have a nice day, thank you for staying and be on your way. Or, the guest can check out online or via the TV in the room, or just drop their card in a slot on the reception desk. Housekeeping knows when a guest is due to check out, so they know when to change the sheets and towels and stuff.'

'I get all that,' said Leroy. 'So what do you mean by fails to check out?

'That's what I'm coming to. If the maid lets herself into the room on the day the guest is due to leave - and she'll wait until after noon and the guy's stuff is still there, she'll tell reception and they'll call the guest to ask what the hell's going on, we thought you were leaving today. Now, nine times out of ten the guest will give them some bullshit excuse and say I can't leave yet and the hotel will say no problem, we'll just charge you another night. The problem comes if they can't get hold of the guest, but the room's booked for another guest that night. In a case like that, the maid packs up all the guest's stuff and the case is stored with the concierge. The bill's already been settled as the guest's card's been charged. They'll try to contact the guest a few times more, to say come get your stuff, it's taking up space. If they get no answer after a week or so, the case goes out with the trash.'

Leroy finished his coffee. 'I think I kind of know all this, Harry; what did your friend have for you? Any particular guest?'

Ross nodded his head vigorously. He was a career patrolman: fifty years old if he was a day, grey, receding hair, no more than five feet tall, no less than four feet around the waist. 'She was telling me that they were storing the bags from some guy who'd checked in a couple of days earlier. When they went through his stuff they found this in a drawer.' He passed Leroy the brown envelope.

Leroy took the envelope and pulled out the contents. Took one look, said, 'Ah,' and passed it to Quinn.

'He had those in his room?'

'He did. Kirstine's manager told her to shred them, said there's no way she was going to keep filth like that lying about.'

'Obviously, she hadn't gotten round to shredding it.'

Ross shook his head. 'She told me, "Harry, take a look at these before they go in the trash." I said, "No, let me take them off your hands. The guys in the squad room might like them."'

'To brighten up the locker room?' Quinn asked.

Sheepishly, Ross replied, 'Yes, kind of. Off the record.'

'"Off the record"?' Leroy asked, shaking his head.

Quinn took over. 'This is the clincher, Sam. As I was leaving before, I passed by the squad room. I heard all the laughter and went in to see what the guys were so amused by. Look.' He passed the contents, five or six letter-sized glossy colour photographs, back to Leroy, who flicked through them, more slowly than before. The photographs were of a man, early middle age, with two much younger girls. All three were naked and on a large bed. 'Locker room?' Leroy muttered, browsing the pictures.

'Sam,' said Quinn, 'look at the guy's face.'

Leroy flicked though until he came to a picture where the man's face was showing. He studied it for a few seconds, then sat down at his desk. Called up the mugshot Hobson had emailed over. He looked up at Quinn.

'It's him.'

CHAPTER TWENTY-SEVEN

'I'VE NOT BEEN Downtown in a while,' Leroy said as they left the freeway. 'No reason to come here.'

Quinn looked around as they took the exit ramp. 'My first call as a rookie was down here. A mugging in Olvera Street.'

'Nothing so exciting. I think it was when Joanna and I went to something at the Staples Center.'

'By the way,' Quinn asked. 'Did you get the chance -?'

'No. Here we are.'

It was the following morning. It was quite clear that the man in the photographs, or at least those where his face could be seen, was the same man whose head had later found itself yards away from the Hollywood Sign. As Leroy had commented before they went home, the guy certainly went out with a bang.

Pulling up outside the front entrance, and badging a bemused doorman, they walked through the lobby to the reception desk. A young man behind the desk greeted them, his less than genuine smile vanishing when they identified themselves and asked for the hotel manager.

After a few moments, they were met by a woman in black matching pants and vest, under which was a crisp white shirt. Her dark hair was intricately plaited in a ponytail. She introduced herself as Katherine Huth, the Duty Manager, and invited them to follow her to her office.

Once in the office, Leroy asked, 'I understand that a guest failed to check out on his allotted day, and you are storing his bags.'

She said nothing, but was clearly surprised by his question.

Leroy continued, 'We need to know who he is, and to check his belongings, and his room.'

She frowned. 'Don't you need a warrant for that?'

Leroy bristled. 'No, we don't. We're interested in the previous occupier of the room, not the current. Our authority doesn't extend to the current occupant. For example, if we found a hundred grams of cocaine and charged the owner, it would be deemed as inadmissible evidence as the search was illegal in respect of the present occupant. That doesn't apply to the guy we're interested in. And as far as the belongings and personal data are concerned, we have probable cause to believe him to be a murder victim. Are we okay with this? Or should I call somebody else?'

She blushed. 'Since you put it like that. I'll just check which room it was, and take you there. What was the guest's name?'

'That was my second question. Maybe you could print off his registration details.'

Ms Huth left them for a few moments and returned with a sheet of paper, which she thrust into Quinn's face. 'He was in Room 918,' she said, sniffily. 'Please come this way.'

She led them to the ninth floor and paused outside 918. She knocked on the door twice. There was no answer.

'Try again,' Leroy said.

She did so again.

'Can you let us in, please?' Leroy asked.

Reluctantly, she slid her master key through the slot. The LED flashed green and she opened the door.

As they entered, they heard the toilet flush and a man came out of the bathroom.

'What the hell?' he demanded.

Ms Huth was about to reply, but Leroy showed the man his badge. 'I'm sorry to disturb you, sir, but we did knock twice.'

'I was in the john. Couldn't have heard you. What is it?'

'We're conducting a murder investigation, and we would like to search the room. Nothing to do with you, sir; it relates to the previous occupant.'

The guest held his arms out. 'Be my guest. Liberty Hall. I was just about to go downstairs for breakfast.'

'I don't think we'll be long, sir,' said Quinn reassuringly.

Leroy and Quinn wandered about the room, giving the place no more than a cursory glance. The room seemed to match the one in the photographs, in particular the imitation painting on the wall, but then most hotel rooms do look the same. Quinn checked the bathroom.

'Sir,' Leroy asked, 'when you checked in, was there anything here, in the closet or the drawers, which didn't belong to you?'

The guest shook his head. 'No.'

Leroy examined the replica canvas hanging on the wall behind the bed, then the ceiling light fitting. 'Ms Huth,' he asked, 'is there any possibility of there being a miniature camera being hidden in the room?'

'What?' the guest asked.

'There certainly is not!' she replied, indignantly. 'Definitely not, no way,' she said to the guest.

Quinn allowed himself a smile as he knelt to look under the bed. He noticed a short strip of black duct tape stuck to the bed slats, for no reason. He took a small, clear plastic envelope out of his pocket, reached under the bed and pulled the tape off, carefully slotting it in the container. Leroy watched him, and said to the guest and Ms Huth, 'Thank you very much for your co-operation, sir. We'll leave you in peace now.'

As they took the elevator down to the lobby, Leroy told Ms Huth they needed to see the bags. She led them to the concierge's room, where the black case lay in a corner.

Leroy turned to her. 'Thank you, ma'am. If I need anything else, I'll let you know.'

Barely disguising her anger, she swung round on her heels and stormed out, almost knocking the concierge over on her way out. Leroy and Quinn put the bag on a table, unzipped it and checked through the contents. There was only two or three days' worth of clothes.

'Nothing jumps out,' Leroy said, 'but I think we'll take it back with us to check more thoroughly. We'll give you a receipt,' he said to the concierge.

'Not my worry,' the old man replied. 'Come the weekend, that's going in the trash, anyway.'

They zipped up the bag, gave out the receipt, and wheeled it back to their car. Once inside the car, Quinn took out the hotel printout. 'Our guy has a name now.'

Leroy looked over and read out the name. 'William Kirk, 18553 16th Street, Birmingham, Alabama 35223. Alabama? Christ, what was he doing here?'

'There's nothing to indicate why,' Quinn said. 'No business paperwork, laptop, anything. No cell phone, no airline paperwork. The section about licence plate number is blank. He must have flown here, though.'

'Let's try those numbers.' Leroy dialled both numbers; both went to voicemail, but he left no message. 'One's a cell phone; the other's bound to be a landline. I wonder: work or office?'

'Trip to Alabama?' Quinn asked.

'Might have to be. Let's get his stuff back to HQ. While we're headed back, Ray, see if you can get onto an airline website; see how much a round trip to Birmingham is.'

'Onto it,' replied Quinn, as they pulled away. By the time they hit the freeway, Quinn had a price. 'Here, with Delta. Round trip via Atlanta is $997.'

'What? Jesus, Perez will never agree to that.'

CHAPTER TWENTY-EIGHT

LEROY WAS RIGHT.

'Are you kidding me? A grand for a round trip to Birmingham, Alabama? Per person? No way.'

Leroy and Quinn were back at the Desk. Quinn was checking through William Kirk's bag again, and Leroy had gone to see Lieutenant Perez. 'We've no choice, Lieutenant. He's not picking up on either his landline or cell.'

'I can give the local station a call. They can send somebody round to check the address out,' Perez said.

Leroy shook his head. 'I need to go myself. Surely you understand, Roman?'

Perez looked up. 'Two grand's a lot of money. How long would you be there for?

'No more than a couple of nights.'

'Which means hotel accommodation. I'm guessing you'd want separate rooms.' He held his hand up. 'Don't answer that.' He paused. 'Can't you drive?'

'Phew, that's a long way. A lot of gas.'

'Hold on.' Perez took out his phone and ran his finger over the screen. 'I have this app here,' he said. 'Uploaded it a week or so ago, never needed it yet. It figures out the cost of a journey, cost of fares, cost of gas.'

'Oh, yes?' said Leroy, thinking *here we go*.

Perez tapped in the details of the journey, reading out loud as he did so. 'Los Angeles to Birmingham. What? Shit, no – that's Birmingham, England. Birmingham, Alabama. That's it. Here you go, Sam.' He looked up at Leroy as he read from his phone. 'Los Angeles to Birmingham, Alabama, will take you 30 hours 5 minutes, fuel cost $200.40. Stopping points Prescot, Arizona; Albuquerque, New Mexico; Amarillo, Texas and so on.'

'Thirty hours? That's a sixty hour round trip.'

'And would cost just shy of four hundred bucks. For both of you. Plus accommodation. You could get a Best Western somewhere.'

Leroy shook his head. 'But that would take too long. If we flew we'd be back in a couple of days.'

Perez and Leroy had once been partners, and Leroy had long learned what buttons to press. He said, 'Look, if two thousand dollars is above your pay grade, Lieutenant…'

The Lieutenant's head shot up. 'I didn't say that, Detective.' He paused, mulling something over. Standing up, he said, 'Wait here.'

Leroy remained in the chair while the Lieutenant left. As he sat waiting, Leroy looked around the office. Looking at all the stuff Perez had accumulated since his promotion. Except those damned silly executive balls he took with him. Leroy always hated them: always irritated by the click click click as the little silver sons of bitches swung to and fro, to and fro. One of these days…

Perez returned and went straight to his desk and sat down. 'The captain has authorised the expense,' he said, emotionlessly.

'Great,' said Leroy, sitting up in his chair.

'I sold it to him,' Perez continued, 'that as he and the Chief specifically instructed that you be assigned this case, then he was kind of obliged to agree the trip. The question of whose budget the cost comes out of is yet to be decided, he told me.'

Leroy passed on that one. Rising from his chair, he said, 'I'll let Ray know.'

'Hold on, Sam. Only you can go. Yes, I know you'll need back up, but he's going to call one of the captains down there to let you have someone. Down there, over there, wherever the hell Birmingham, Alabama is. Two days maximum, then you're flying home. Give Quinn something to do while you're away. Checking out some other leads, or has he any vacation days to take?'

'I don't know right now. I'll check.'

Perez scribbled down a website address and a number on a scrap of paper. 'Here,' he said as he passed it over. 'Book your flight through this site. When you're asked for a coupon number, enter that. That will give you a discount the Office of the Chief of Police has negotiated with the airlines. Then destroy that note. The Chief doesn't want detectives getting cheap vacation flights.'

'Will do, Lieutenant.' Leroy slipped the note into his shirt pocket and tapped it. 'Thanks.'

'Now go book your flights. And remember, Sam: two days. You have just two days.'

CHAPTER TWENTY-NINE

IT IS SAID that only forty percent of US citizens own a passport, and only fifteen percent have travelled overseas, Hawaii and Canada not included. It is also said that over fifty percent have never been outside of their own State.

Ray Quinn, born and raised in Southern California, was one of those statistics; in fact, Leroy would often tease him about the fact that he had never left his home state, not even a weekend in Vegas, or a trip to Tijuana.

Leroy himself, on the other hand, whilst not exactly describing himself as a globe-trotter, had travelled. To begin with, he was not a Californian. Born and raised in

New York City, he had been to Europe, and many places in his home country.

But not Birmingham, Alabama. In fact, Alabama was one of the thirty-odd states he had never been to, and deep down, he was looking forward to this brief trip.

The previous day, after booking his flights and accommodation, he did some research on his destination. He had heard and read things about the city in the context of the civil rights movement, but all of that was a lifetime ago.

He read that the city was incorporated on 19th December 1871, and was named for the city of the same name in England. He read that the airport was named after Fred Shuttlesworth, a preacher who became famous for leading the civil rights local activists. Nowadays, Downtown Birmingham, where Leroy had booked his hotel, was a 24-hour mixed use district, comprising loft apartments and condominiums and restaurant, retail and cultural centres.

As his McDonnell Douglas MD-88 began its descent into Birmingham, Leroy stared out at the tailing ends of the Appalachian foothills running to the south-west of the city. There was still a trace of snow on the peaks; Leroy had not seen snow since he was last in New York, visiting family.

They say that any landing is one you can walk away from; however, he had experienced smoother landings than the one here. He was sure the airplane bounced a foot back in the air when the tyres touched the tarmac, and he had to press against the seat in front when the deceleration started. Once they had left the runway and began taxiing to the gate, he closed his eyes momentarily. He was weary from the last few days, and this journey had not helped; neither had the stopover in Atlanta: he had hoped for a direct flight.

Once deplaned, Leroy headed for the street. He was carrying only a small case, so could bypass the baggage reclaim area. As he wheeled the case down the long corridor to the exit, he studied the mural the length of the corridor: it appeared to be portraits of famous people from Birmingham. He could pick out the gospel singer Inez Andrews; Piney Brown, the R&B and blues singer and songwriter; the country singer Tammy Wynette. Many other faces he kind of recognised, but could not name.

The airport terminal is shaped like half a giant donut, the buildings on the outside, then two lanes of street, then the parking structures in the centre. Leroy had considered renting a car for the two, maybe three, days he would be there, but the captain had arranged for him to be escorted around by a local officer. Leroy would have rather had Quinn with him, but as Lieutenant Perez had reminded him, out here, he was in reality a private citizen: his LAPD badge meant nothing. He even had to leave his service weapon behind.

Through the wide glass doors of the terminal, Leroy could see a row of taxis. He quickened his pace, only to notice a female police officer standing outside on the street. She was holding a piece of card on which was printed LEROY. He grinned and walked over to her.

'You were expecting me? I'm Leroy.'

She quickly looked him up and down, head to foot. 'You got ID?'

'Okay,' he said quietly. He put his case down and took out his badge. Showed it to her.

'You wanna see mine?' she asked, after checking out his identification.

'That won't be necessary,' he replied, studying her name badge, 'Officer Duvall.'

She nodded and held out her hand. 'Sally Duvall.'

They shook hands. 'Sam Leroy. Good to meet you, Sally. And thanks for meeting me.'

'You're welcome. My car's over here.' She led him the thirty yards or so down to where she had left her patrol car. Painted white with a blue band, its livery was not dissimilar to the LAPD's. 'Let me take your bag, Detective.'

'No, I'm okay, thanks. Call me Sam.'

'Sam,' she said, non-commitally as they reached the car.

'Where's your partner?' Leroy asked as they got inside.

'He's taking some sick leave,' she replied as they drove away with a squeal from the tyres. 'Not exactly sick; he's taking a few days to recover from an injury.'

'What happened?'

'Oh, we were answering a 911 and there were two dogs in the property. German Shepherds, I think. We effected entry, and both dogs went for his arm.'

'Shit, what happened?'

'I shot one of them, and the second backed away, and we were able to restrain it.'

'And your partner? How is his arm?'

'Some muscle damage and torn ligaments. Nothing too serious.'

'Thank God for that.'

'You bet. So I was kicking my heels while he's off the streets. Then my sergeant told me you were coming for a couple of days and needed backup.'

'I shouldn't need any backup, really. I'm just here to find and talk to a couple of people. Did they tell you about the case I'm working on?'

'Only that you guys have a John Doe who came from these parts and you're trying to figure out what he was doing in LA.'

'Not a John Doe. We have a name, and I got his address. Here it is: we can go straight there.'

'I'll take you to your hotel first. Where are you staying?'

'The Westin. It's on Richard Arrington -'

'Richard Arrington Junior Boulevard. Yes, I know it.'

'We'll go to the address first.'

'Best go to your hotel first.'

'No.'

She sniffed. 'I think you'd better go to your hotel first. Take a shower.'

Leroy lifted an arm and sniffed. 'Yeah, see what you mean. My hotel, then.'

The hotel was less than three miles from the airport, and the journey took only twenty minutes. Leroy looked out at it as she pulled up outside.

'Oh, shit.'

'What's up?' she asked.

'It's a bit... upmarket. My Lieutenant's expecting me to be in a Days Inn or Best Western.'

'No, no, this place is cool. It's not as fancy inside as it looks. Unless you booked yourself the Presidential Suite.'

'No, not the Presidential Suite.' Leroy opened his door. 'Give me an hour?'

Duvall shook her head. 'Sorry, Detective. Sam. I'm off duty then. Pick you up here eight-thirty tomorrow.'

'Tomorrow?'

'Sure. You have plenty of time here. Look, enjoy your evening. Long shower, or bath. Catch up with some sleep. Try some fried steak and butter beans. See you in the morning.'

'Okay. See you tomorrow.'

As he was about to shut the door, she called out, 'One thing, Sam. They said you wouldn't be carrying. That is right, isn't it?'

He bent down to look at her. 'No. I was ordered to leave my weapon in LA.'

'Good. As you must know already, you're -'

'I know, I know. I'm not a cop here; just a private citizen.'

'Cool.' She nodded and started the car.

'You'll just have to look after me, Sally.'

She gave him a wry smile as he closed the door and watched her drive away. Leroy picked up his bag and wheeled it into the hotel. It was almost 5PM, over two more hours of daylight. He had planned on going to Kirk's address direct from the airport, but Officer Duvall - Sally – was probably right. He decided to take her advice.

CHAPTER THIRTY

A TEXT MESSAGE came through from Officer Duvall at 7:15 the next morning to the effect that she would be waiting in the hotel lobby at 8:30. Leroy was in the shower at the time; wrapped in his towel, he sent an acknowledgement and continued dressing.

He arrived in the lobby seventy-five minutes later, and saw her standing by the doors, browsing a revolving stand containing leaflets about local attractions. She looked up at him and smiled.

'Morning, Detective,' she said, slipping a leaflet back into its slot.

'Hey,' Leroy replied. 'You parked out front?'

'This way,' she said, leading him outside. She was again wearing the BPD uniform of black pants and shirt and blue tie. Her blonde hair was again tied back in a ponytail; as he followed in her wake, Leroy took in the sweet but understated fragrance of her perfume.

'So, your guy's address?' she asked as they got into the car.

'Here.' Leroy showed her the copy of the booking details he had obtained from the Stocker in Los Angeles.

'I don't think that's far,' she said as she keyed the address into the vehicle's GPS. 'No - about five or six minutes.'

'The street looks quite residential.'

'You already been there?' she asked, looking over her shoulder as she pulled into the traffic.

'Kind of. I checked out on a street view app last night.' He paused. 'During my room service fried steak and butter beans.'

'You enjoyed one of our local dishes? Don't tell me you had grits for breakfast as well.'

'Jesus, no. Eggs and coffee.'

'Don't tell me: you can take the boy out of California, but you can't take California out -'

'But I'm not from California. I'm a New Yorker at heart.'

'Oh yeah?'

'U-huh. Born and raised in Queens. Started with the NYPD.'

'What made you move west?'

Leroy sighed. 'Long story. What about you?'

She laughed. 'Born and raised in Birmingham, Alabama.'

They had left the elevated highway and were now in a residential street. 'This is 16th Street,' she said, tapping the GPS screen with her index finger. 'Now we need the 18,000 block.'

Leroy was surprised how rural the street was, being so near to Downtown Birmingham and the I-59. It was a quiet thoroughfare: there were no yellow centre lines and it looked as if it had not been blacktopped in years, so numerous were the cracks, gullies and potholes. The sidewalks were mainly grass, with a single row of paving slabs along each side of the street.

The dwellings were mainly single storey places of wood construction. As they passed a cross street, Leroy noticed that the house on the corner was devoid of roof tiles in places, exposing the bare timber to the elements. It was quiet too: a handful of vehicles parked here and there and a couple passing them by. No pedestrians.

Neglect was a word that came to mind for Leroy, but he kept the thought to himself; after all, this was Sally's home town.

This neglect seemed not to apply on the next block. Here the grass had been regularly watered, mown and strimmed. It bordered onto a large, empty, parking lot, freshly surfaced with white lines neatly painted. In the centre of the lot stood a church. It was on clean red brick construction; from the architecture, it did not look new, just very well maintained. Small bushes had been planted in the centre of the grass verges, and either side of the entrance was a smart raised flowerbed containing green and red heathers. Once they had hit the next block, however, it was business as usual.

'It's all so green,' Leroy observed. 'Compared with this, it's like a desert in LA.'

'Yup. It's a whole nother world outside of Southern California.'

'I told you: I'm from New York originally.'

'I went to New York once. Hated it.'

He looked over at her. 'Why?'

'It was so cold.'

'When did you go?'

'December. It was kind of a Holiday shopping trip.'

'If it was December, it would have been winter, therefore cold.'

'Hm.'

'It's a two-storey building,' Leroy said.

'Is it? Oh, yeah; I forgot you've already googled it. What number?'

'18553.'

Duvall slowed down and checked a house number. '18800. So, three blocks away. Or have we already passed it? I didn't check the street sign.'

'That's it up there,' Leroy pointed out. 'I recognize the cell phone antenna next to it.'

Duvall slowly came to a halt outside the townhouse. 'This is clearly his home address.'

Leroy concurred. 'Looks that way. It's the only one we have, though.'

'You can always check his social security records to get a business address.'

'I know, yes,' Leroy replied as he climbed out of the car. 'Let's take a look here first.' He wandered up the path to the front of the house.

The place had seen better days: the mustard-coloured paint was flaking in various parts of the fascia; some wood had rotted just above an upstairs window. There were two square windows upstairs and a matching one downstairs. The ground floor window was behind a black metal set of bars, the front door behind a matching metal gate. Adjacent to the door, a wooden sign was screwed to the wall. A couple of letters were missing, but Leroy could get the gist.

WILL AM F. KIRK

PRIVATE INVES IGATOR

Leroy turned back to Duvall, who was still standing by the car. 'This might explain it. He was a private eye. He must have been in LA working for a client.'

'I hope they paid him well,' she said, walking round the front of the car to join him.

'Yeah, and in advance.' Leroy tried the lock on the gate protecting the door, but it was locked firm. 'I'll check round back.' The back of the house was a mirror image of the front: same two square windows upstairs, and one below, next to a back door; only here the door was on the left, whereas out front it was on the right. Again, the window and door downstairs were barred. The back yard was mainly grass, but had not seen a mower in months. The yard was bordered by a three foot high chain-link fence. Leroy vaulted over the fence, and after peering in through the square window, tried the lock on the gate.

Duvall joined him out back. 'So this must have been where he worked from,' she said, looking up at the top floor. 'Maybe he lived on the second floor, also.'

Leroy looked up and down the house. 'Maybe. Now we need to look inside.'

'Sam, you can't just break in.'

'Why not? It doesn't look occupied, and he's dead. And as well as finding who killed him, we need to find someone who can make the formal identification.' He leapt back over the fence and went back round the front of the house, reaching into his pocket.

A typical lock is made up of two parts: the barrel and the pins. The barrel is the chamber you put the key into. The pins are the small metal cylinders that sink into the barrel, holding it in place until a key, or a pick, pushes them up and out of the way. The pins are cut in half, and when the halfway mark lines up with the barrel you can turn the lock. To pick a lock, you have to manually push up each of the pins into the correct position, slowly turning the barrel so that they can't slot back into place. Once all the pins are out of the way, the barrel will turn freely and the door will be open. A key is basically a complex pick. The grooves are tuned so that, once inserted, all the pins are perfectly aligned and you can turn the knob.

What Leroy took out of his pocket was a keyring, but also attached to the ring was what looked like a slightly bent bobby pin. Crouching in front of the gate, he carefully inserted the pin into the lock. Turning the pick slightly in the direction he would have turned the key, he jiggled it around until he found the first pin. That moved easily. The second not so, so he gently pushed up with the pick until he felt and heard a slight click. Then he went on to the next pin. After the final pin and five minutes of crouching, he could open the gate.

Grinning at Duvall, he stepped over to the door. This took only two minutes to open. They both stepped inside.

CHAPTER THIRTY-ONE

FOR SOME REASON, probably the state of the outside of the house, Leroy had expected the interior to smell musty, to feel damp. Neither was the case; it must have been empty only a few days.

They checked upstairs first: a bathroom, and two bedrooms. One bedroom was being used as a storeroom: a couple of filing cabinets stood up against one wall, and some large cardboard boxes lay on the floor. One empty box had a picture of a PC printer on its side. The second bedroom was more functional. It has a single bed - a cot, almost - with a pillow and sheets, and a small closet.

Downstairs, there was a small but functional kitchen. There was a small toilet under the stairs. The main room was divided in half by a wooden partition, containing a glass door. One side had been configured as a waiting room with an old couch and a couple of chairs around a low table. Behind the partition was Kirk's office. A couple of chairs in front of a desk the other side of which was Kirk's own chair. Except for empty in and out wire trays and a telephone, the desk was clear. There was a small table behind Kirk's chair: on the table sat a PC monitor and keyboard. A printer, the box for which lay upstairs, sat next to the monitor. The computer must have been twenty years old if it was a day, and apart from the telephone, there was no sign of any technology in the office.

Leroy sat in Kirk's chair and tried the six desk drawers. All were locked: he took a letter opener from the tube-shaped pen rack and forced open the top one. Duvall gave a sharp intake of breath.

A letter-sized desk diary was the only item in the drawer. Leroy took it out and opened it.

'Anything there?' Duvall asked.

'Well,' Leroy said as he read the open pages, 'he was due to see his doctor next Tuesday…'

'He won't be making that.'

'No. And last week - and these are the last entries - he saw three clients. A Dennis Anderson, a Mrs Smith – not very original…'

'Smith is actually the most common surname in Alabama,' Duvall pointed out.

'Both have addresses here in Birmingham,' he continued. 'Then we have a John Hightower. His address is in Jasper.' He looked up. 'Where's that?'

She shook her head. 'Not far. About forty miles along the 78.'

'Okay.' Leroy pushed the chair back. Stared at the other drawers a moment. 'I'll take just this for now.'

'What about that?' she asked, pointing at the computer.

Leroy turned and looked it over. 'Not right now. If we need it we can always come back.' He picked up the diary, took one more look around the office and left. As he sat in the car reading through the diary, Duvall put a call in to get the house secured. 'I think we'll work backwards,' he said as they pulled away. 'If these three don't have anything for us, we'll have to look at the week before.'

'How long do you have?' she asked.

'Unless I come up with the mother lode, I fly back to LA tomorrow evening.'

'What's the first address, Sam?'

'That would be Dennis Anderson. Here's the address. Could be home, could be work. No way of telling from this.'

It was Dennis Anderson's home address. There was no answer, but a neighbour said he would be at work, running a hardware store ten blocks away. Dennis Anderson told them he had engaged Kirk as he suspected his wife was having an affair. Kirk had said he would take on the case, but could not start until the following week. Obviously, as Duvall said to Leroy afterwards, he was expecting to be back from Los Angeles by then.

Mrs Smith lived in a townhouse not too dissimilar to Kirk's, only without the flaky paintwork. Again, there was no answer at the door, and no neighbours to talk to.

'Rather than kick our heels here,' Leroy had said, 'let's head on over to Jasper. We can try here again when we get back, or this evening.'

So they headed up to Jasper, Alabama.

As they entered the city limits, they passed a sign declaring *Welcome To The City Of Jasper. Working People, Working Together.* The population was apparently 14855, and it is the county seat of Walker County.

Duvall soon found the street and the house. It was a two story brick residence, much larger than the other houses they had visited today. Set back some hundred feet from the street, a curved driveway took them through the neat and tidy front yard to the house and double garage.

'This is his home address, of course,' Leroy sighed.

'Yes, but look.' Duvall pointed over to the double garage, the door of which was open. A gleaming black sedan stood outside the garage, and a tall and heavy figure was polishing the roof. 'Is that him?'

As they pulled up, the man stopped polishing and stepped over to them. 'Can I help you, Officer?' he asked Duvall, giving Leroy a brief glance.

'Yes, sir,' she replied, introducing herself, and showing him her badge. 'And this is Detective Leroy from the LAPD. We're working on an enquiry together. Are you John Hightower?'

'I am. John Hightower. How can I help y'all?' He looked at Leroy. 'LAPD. You're off the beaten track, aren't you, boy?'

Leroy let Duvall do the talking.

'Sir,' she asked, 'do you know a man by the name of William Kirk?'

Hightower froze a second. He was about to reply when a woman appeared at the house door.

'Who is it, J.T.?'

Hightower turned to her and called back, 'Nothing, Maybeline. Just giving some folks directions, that's all.'

The woman went back indoors. Hightower said, 'She always gets nervous around the police.' He pronounced the word *pol*ice. Turning back to Duval, he said, 'What was that name again?'

This time Leroy answered. 'William Kirk. A private investigator from Birmingham.'

Hightower closed his eyes in thought. 'Kirk,' he said. 'Kirk. No; I'm sorry, I've not heard the name.'

'Can you explain why your name and address should be in his appointments diary?' Leroy asked.

Hightower shrugged. 'I have no idea. I'm truly sorry, Officers. Is there anything else?'

'One more thing,' Leroy said. 'Were you in Los Angeles recently?'

Hightower shook his head. 'No.'

'Have you ever been to Los Angeles?'

'A few times, I guess.'

'When was the last time?'

'Er – two, maybe three years ago.'

Duvall glanced over at Leroy, then back to Hightower. 'I want to thank you for your time, sir.'

'No problem, Officers. I'm sorry I wasn't able to help you.'

Leroy and Duvall thanked Hightower again and walked back to their car. As he got in, Leroy could see Hightower back polishing his sedan. Once back in the passenger seat, Leroy took out his phone and began texting. Within seconds of his sending the message, a reply came back.

Duvall slammed her door and buckled up. 'Back to Birmingham, then?' she asked, firing up the ignition.

'Not yet,' Leroy said quietly as they backed off Hightower's drive. 'Park over there for a moment.'

'Okey dokey,' she said with a puzzled look on her face. Once off the drive, she drove forward a few yards and parked. 'What are we doing?'

'I'm just waiting for a call.'

'A call?'

'Yup. Might be nothing. It won't take long.' They sat in silence. After a minute or so he asked, 'So what's your story then, Sally? Career policewoman? Future Chief?'

She laughed. 'Not thought that far. I've been working for the Department five years now; I haven't really thought that far in the future.'

'You always done this?'

She nodded. 'Right after I left High School. Always wanted to wear the uniform.'

'And what about Sally off duty? Is there a Mr Sally?'

She made a hand gesture. 'There may be. I'm not sure right now. This job's hard on personal relationships.'

'You're not wrong there.'

'What about you, Sam? Is there a Mrs Leroy? I don't see a wedding band.'

'No, there's no Mrs Leroy. Apart from my mother. There is somebody back home - I think - but I'm not sure how much longer we have. We seem to be looking for different things; I don't know. Even when things were at their best, I was seeing more of my partner than of her.' He looked over at her. 'We seem to be in a similar place.'

She was about to reply when Leroy's phone bleeped. He snatched it off the dashboard. 'I knew it!' he exclaimed, tossing the phone back.

'Knew what?'

'I sent Ray - my partner – a message asking him to call back the hotel where the John Doe - where Kirk - had stayed. He just texted me back to say that they confirmed that a John Thomas Hightower from Jasper, Alabama stayed there three weeks back.'

'So why did he lie?'

'You tell me. Two men, and there may be more, from this locale stay at an LA hotel. One is murdered, and has the other listed as a client, more or less. Or some relationship.'

Sally chuckled.

'What is it?'

She grinned. 'J.T. Hightower. John Thomas Hightower. While I was at High School, I had a boyfriend. He was English - his father was working over here or something.'

'And?'

'And he told me once that the name John Thomas is used in England as a euphemism for… you know.' She nodded her head down to Leroy's lap.

He looked at her blankly, then it sank in. 'You mean, like Johnson?'

'That's right.'

Leroy turned in his seat and looked back at Hightower's house. 'Dick by name, dick by nature, then.' He paused a beat. 'Come on; we need to get some answers.'

Duvall reversed to Hightower's house, and, allowing the tyres to protest against the road, turned back into his driveway.

CHAPTER THIRTY-TWO

HIGHTOWER WAS STILL polishing his car when Leroy and Duvall walked up to the house. He did not seem surprised at seeing them return. As they approached, he looked nervously to the house and walked towards them.

'Mr Hightower,' Leroy said.

'Could we talk in here?' Hightower asked, opening one of the sedan doors, moistening his lips as he did so.

'Surely,' Leroy nodded.

They all climbed into Hightower's car, Leroy in the front passenger seat; Hightower and Duvall in the back. The car smelt new, even though it was not. Inside, the seats, the upholstery, the dashboard were all highly polished. The aroma of leather was everywhere. The chrome parts of the interior were gleaming. Leroy wondered if the vehicle ever moved anywhere, if Hightower ever drove it anywhere. Maybe he kept it here as a kind of status symbol, remaining stationary on the drive for the neighbours to see him polish it.

Leroy turned around to face Hightower. 'This hotel in Los Angeles you've never been to,' he said, 'has told us you stayed there two weeks ago.'

Hightower buried his face in his hands. 'All right, all right; I admit it. I was in Los Angeles.' He oddly pronounced *Angeles* with a hard *g*. 'And yes, I was in that hotel.' He looked around, through the car windows. 'My wife…'

'Tell us what happened in Los Angeles,' Duvall said quietly.

Hightower looked over to her. 'I was there on a business trip. And I *sinned* there.'

Leroy frowned. 'What do you mean, you sinned there?'

'What I did there, it was so sinful. I asked the Lord to forgive me; I know he has, but Maybeline, my children, my family, my church… Will they ever?'

'Just slowly,' Leroy said quietly, 'and in your own time, tell us what happened. Why were you in LA? You said it was a business trip. What kind of business?'

'I deal in rare books. You know, first editions, manuscripts. I was at a convention at the… the...'

'The LACC. I know it. Is that why you were staying at the Stocker? Its proximity to the Center?'

Hightower nodded.

'Who made the booking; or rather, who chose the hotel?'

'I did it myself. The Convention Center has a list of nearby hotels, and I picked that one.'

'Online, or person to person?'

'Online.'

'Fine. So tell me what happened.'

'I don't recall much. After the convention, I went back to the hotel. It was still fairly early - too early to eat - so I decided to go up to the pool for a swim. And then… I recall being in my hotel room with a headache the next morning. I realised I needed to check out, so I started packing my bags. Then this fella knocked on my door. I answered, on account that I'd ordered breakfast. But this guy hadn't - he showed me a pile of pictures. Of *me*.'

'What kind of pictures?' asked Duvall.

Hightower spoke in a hushed voice. '*Dirty* pictures. Of me in sexual congress with two young girls.'

'Do you still have them?' Leroy asked.

'I do.'

'Can I see them, please?'

'Sure.' Hightower scrambled out of the car, looked around and went over to a tool cabinet at the other end of the garage. Glancing about once more, he pulled open a drawer and took out a brown envelope. Then hurried back to the car.

Leroy took the envelope and leafed through the contents. They were more or less the same as the pictures of William Kirk, although where Kirk was slightly younger and was slimmer meaning his pictures were aesthetically easier on the eye, Hightower was bigger and paunchy and not so easy on the eye when naked.

'B-but,' Hightower stammered, 'I don't recall any of that. I don't remember being with those girls. But I must have been; I'm there, *fornicating* for all the world to see. Oh, God.' He buried his face in his hands again.

Leroy put the pictures back in the envelope. 'Do you remember meeting the girls?'

He shook his head. 'No, I don't.'

'Nothing at all?'

Hightower screwed up his face and rubbed his forehead. 'I do have a vague recollection of rubbing some cream - sun lotion - onto some gal's back…'

'One of the girls in the pictures?'

Hightower shook his head. 'Sorry, I don't recall a face.'

'Do you remember drinking anything at the pool?'

'No. If I did, it would be water, may have been root beer. I don't touch the booze.'

'Tell us about the man with the photographs. Describe him.'

Hightower closed his eyes as he recalled. 'Younger, maybe thirty. Asian, he was Asian. Chinese, maybe. Shorter than me, about five six. Black hair. Very smartly dressed, suit and tie.'

'Did he give you his name?'

'Yes, Lee. Mr Lee, he said. He knew my name.'

'What did he say to you?'

'He said he was sure Maybeline wouldn't want to see these pictures, so he could arrange it that she never did. Called it insurance. That's it: he said he was selling insurance.'

'And how much were the premiums?'

'He asked for two thousand dollars before I flew home, and another two every month.'

Duvall asked, 'How did he want you to pay him?'

'Cash at the hotel, then he gave me an address to send the other payments.'

'An LA address?'

'Yes, but it's a box number. I have it somewhere.'

'So, what next?'

'He said I could keep those, as he had many other copies. He told me to meet him in the lobby that afternoon with the cash. I went directly to the bank, and paid him. Then flew home here.'

'Why didn't you destroy the pictures?' Duvall asked.

He shook his head. 'I thought about it, but never got round to it. I just didn't know what to do.'

'I'll keep these,' Leroy said. 'Is that all right with you?'

'I'd be glad if you did.'

'Do you recall anything else?'

Hightower shook his head.

'And have you told anybody else? Not your wife, I'm guessing?'

'I can never tell Maybeline. She'd never forgive me.'

'So nobody?'

'Only Pastor Martyn.'

'Pastor Martyn?'

'He's the pastor at our church. I had to confess my sins to someone, don't you see?'

'What did you tell him?'

'I just confessed about my fornicating with those two gals. With *two* of them! It's so… so… wicked.'

'And what did the pastor say?'

'He just said that if I was truly repentant - which I am - then I would have the Lord's forgiveness.'

'That's it?'

'He kind of asked where I stayed in Los Angeles. Said he would see if he could do anything to help. Said if the Lord was willing to forgive a sin of the flesh, then I should not be paying for it for ever.'

'And?'

'Then we prayed. Prayed to the Lord to wash my soul free from any sin.'

Leroy and Duvall exchanged glances. 'And where is Pastor Martyn?'

'At our church. The Church of the Holy Gospel. It's on Sycamore.'

'We'll find it,' said Duvall.

Hightower looked at Leroy. 'Will Maybeline have to find out?'

'Only if it's relevant to the enquiry. Otherwise, I won't be telling her. It might make it to the newspapers, but just to Southern California ones. Unless the story gets syndicated. Look, here's my cell number. Call me if you recall anything else; things might come back to you over time.'

'Is that it?' Hightower asked. 'Are you done with me?'

'I think so, for now. We may need you to make a formal statement, but we will endeavour to protect your privacy if we do.'

Leroy and Duvall got out of the car, leaving a stunned Hightower in the back. As they left, Duvall leaned back in. 'Sir, you may like to know that it looks as if you were drugged with the sole purpose of taking those pictures and blackmailing you. They didn't steal anything, did they?'

Silently, Hightower shook his head.

'Okay. It looks like you were drugged, that's why you don't recall anything. And if you were drugged, then you wouldn't have been physically capable of fornicating, as you put it. If that makes you feel any better.'

He looked up at her, nodded, but staring into space.

Leroy and Duvall walked back to their car. She took one more look back up to Hightower's house. It looked as if he was still sitting in the back of his gleaming black sedan.

'Poor guy,' she said, opening her door. 'Pastor Martyn?'

Leroy nodded. 'It's time we went to church.'

CHAPTER THIRTY-THREE

THE CHURCH OF the Holy Gospel was a rather grand affair, its traditional Gothic building standing out amongst the eclectic mix of homes on the street. A massive parking lot, again well blacktopped with neat white lines painted on the surface, lay the other side of an immaculately maintained grass verge. A large, freshly painted white notice board proclaimed the name of the church, and that Pastor Martyn West was the Rector.

The church building itself was set back some way from the street; a *porte-cochere* in matching brownstone brick stood in front of the building. Entry to the church appeared to be through two large dark-stained wooden doors, set in an alcove which was decorated with three ornate pillars.

About a dozen vehicles were in the parking lot; Duvall parked next to one of them. There was nobody about as they walked over to the heavy oak doors. Duvall pulled at the shiny brass handle and opened the door. The doorway led directly into the nave of the church, onto the thick purple carpet which ran from the door between the rows of pews to the three steps leading up to the chancel, and the altar.

They took a few steps along the carpet, looking around for someone. Leroy could hear muffled voices coming from somewhere, but could not make out where from. Eventually, the sound of a vacuum cleaner started. They crossed through the pews to the direction of the sound, and came across a tiny lady vacuuming the carpet. She switched off the machine when she saw them coming.

'Can I help you?' she asked.

Duvall did not feel it necessary at this stage to show identification. She merely asked where Pastor Martyn was.

The lady looked up at the large clock over the entrance doors. 'Right now, he'll be in the Bible Study Group.'

'And where would that be?'

The lady pointed over to the other side of the church. 'In that room there. The South Room.'

Leroy and Duvall thanked her and walked along the edge of the chancel to a large brown closed door. Sure enough, the room had SOUTH stencilled in gold on it. Leroy knocked twice on the door and opened it.

Inside, a dozen or so chairs were arranged in a circle. Woman of varying ages were occupying the chairs; each had a book - a Bible - open on their lap. One of the women was reading aloud from it. There was one man in the room: dressed in a suit and clerical collar, he was obviously Pastor Martyn. He looked up at Leroy and Duvall. 'Please, come and join us.'

'Pastor Martyn?' Leroy asked.

'I'm Pastor Martyn,' came the confirmation. 'Let me get you good people a chair,' he said as he got up.

'We just need to speak with you for a few moments.'

Pastor Martyn frowned and glanced back at the group. Duvall was in uniform so there was no hiding the fact that they were police. 'Very well,' he said. Turning back to the woman who was reading from the Bible, he gestured for her to carry on. Leroy and Duvall backed out of the room as the pastor followed. Back in the nave, he gestured at the empty pews. 'Please, take a seat.' He nodded over to the now closed South Room door. 'Our weekly Women's Bible Study Group. Studying the Second Book of Timothy.' He paused and took a deep breath. 'Now, how can I help you?'

Duvall introduced herself and then Leroy. She explained he was from the LAPD and they were working together on a case. The expression on the pastor's face changed slightly when LA was mentioned.

Leroy began the conversation. 'John Thomas Hightower. He's one of your… your church?'

Pastor Martyn nodded. 'J.T? Yes, he is one of our flock. As are his wife and family.'

'We've just come from Mr Hightower. I'm interested in a conversation you and he had a couple of weeks back.'

'A conversation?'

'Yes, concerning a trip he made to Los Angeles.'

'Officers, the conversations I have with my flock are private and confidential.'

'Sir,' said Leroy, 'Mr Hightower has already told us about his visit to LA, about the photographs, about the blackmail, and about going to you to confess.'

Martyn coughed. He looked around then spoke in hushed tones. 'J.T. came to me because he needed to confess and be forgiven. He had had sexual relations with those two girls. He confessed, we prayed together a while, read the Holy Bible a while, and he asked the Lord for forgiveness.'

'Okay,' Leroy said. 'It looks like Mr Hightower had nothing to be forgiven for. The most likely scenario is that he was drugged. Something like Rohypnol.'

'Is that what they call roofies?' the pastor asked. 'The date rape drug?'

'Something like it. Probably not Rohypnol itself. He told us he was probably drinking only mineral water. For the last few years, Rohypnol has contained a blue dye, which would obviously show in a glass of water. But there are other sedative-type drugs out there which could have been used. In fact, the most commonly-used date rape drug is alcohol.'

'J.T. is teetotal. He doesn't touch it.'

'And, as we told Mr Hightower, assuming he was drugged he wouldn't have been capable of anything, if you get my drift.'

'Mm... mm; yes, I see.' The pastor looked uncomfortable.

'Now, according to Mr Hightower, after you had both prayed for forgiveness -'

'Prayed for forgiveness for him,' Pastor Martyn corrected.

'Prayed for him to receive forgiveness, you asked where he had been staying in LA, and that you would see if you could do anything to help. You said if God was willing to forgive a sin of the flesh, then he should not be paying for it for ever. What did you mean by that?'

The pastor looked even more uncomfortable.

Leroy asked, 'Do you know a private investigator called William Kirk?'

Pastor Martyn frowned. 'William Kirk?' he said vaguely.

Leroy was starting to lose patience. 'Sir, I am leading a murder enquiry. William Kirk was found dead in Los Angeles. Shot in the head and decapitated. Hightower's name is in his diary. Kirk appears to have retraced Hightower's steps.' He paused a beat. 'So, over to you.'

The pastor's face blanched at the word *dead*. He ran both hands through his hair. 'Oh my God, my God. I had no idea. What..? Tell me what happened.'

'That's what I'm trying to establish. Now, tell me about you, Hightower and Kirk.'

Pastor Martyn swallowed and took another deep breath. 'J.T. told me about the pictures and the blackmail plot. I know... knew William - Bill - Kirk as a private investigator, have done for several years. I asked if Bill could help somehow. He suggested as you rightly surmised retracing J.T.'s steps as exactly as possible in the hope that the miscreants who so wronged J.T. would approach him.'

'That would be a risky strategy,' said Duvall. 'It would mean allowing himself to be drugged and not recalling the event.'

'We discussed that, but Bill said he would be going into it forewarned. If he was unable to avoid taking the drug, then at least the next morning he would know what had happened the night before, even if he couldn't remember it. Do you understand what I mean?'

'I get it,' said Leroy. 'So the three of you set up this venture. I guess none of you thought of going to the police?'

'J.T. was adamant not to. He said they had told him if he did, the pictures would go on the internet.'

'I see. So, the following morning, how was Kirk going to confront them?'

'J.T. said a young man - Chinese, he said - called on him in his hotel room, showed him the pictures, and made his demands. A large sum of cash that day, then instalments monthly afterwards.'

'So what was Kirk going to do?'

'He was going to challenge the man, and demand the return of J.T.'s money.'

Leroy rubbed his face. 'Jesus.'

Pastor Martyn sat up. 'Detective, please.'

Leroy held up his hand. 'I apologise.' He paused a beat. 'How was Kirk expecting to do this? Would he have been armed?'

'That is something we discussed. I know he carried a weapon here. If he had driven, he said he would have taken his own gun.'

'Over several state lines? That would have been risky if he had been stopped.'

'Possibly. We didn't get that far. J.T. flew to LA, so Bill booked the same flight, same airline, therefore couldn't take his gun.'

'So he was unarmed?'

'No, in our discussion about this, he said he had somebody out there whom he could contact to get a weapon once he had arrived.'

'Okay. It's still out there,' Leroy said more to Duvall than the pastor. 'It was never recovered.' He turned back. 'And when was the last time you heard from Kirk?'

'He called me the morning he left here. He said he would call to update me once the matter had been settled. He anticipated two or three days.'

They all turned as the South Room door opened and the women filed out into the church. The Bible Study Group meeting had clearly finished. The pastor looked even more uncomfortable.

'Is there anything else you need to tell me, sir?' Leroy asked.

'No.' The pastor shook his head slowly. He was clearly in a state of shock.

'If anything comes to mind,' Leroy said, handing him his card, 'my cell phone's on there.'

Silently, Pastor Martyn nodded and took the card. 'I need to pray now for Bill's soul,' he said, sadly. 'And for forgiveness for myself. I sent him there.'

'No, he chose to go there. And you didn't kill him. If that helps,' Duvall said.

'Not really.' He looked up at Leroy. 'What about his body? He was single, no family...'

'That's for the Coroner's office to arrange. There is also the question of formally identifying his body, so I'm afraid they may be in touch with you, or Mr Hightower.'

Leroy and Duvall left the pastor sitting silently in the pew. They joined the throng of Bible students leaving the church, and walked back to their car.

'Oh. My. God,' said Duvall once they were out of earshot of the others. 'Is that guy serious? He sends a private dick to LA to say "please can I have J.T.'s money back? Please?"'

'Looks like it. So naïve. The guy obviously doesn't live in the real world. Or on the same planet as the rest of us.'

'But what about Kirk? What was he thinking?'

'He was probably thinking I'm being paid by the hour so the end result doesn't matter. Of course, it did for him.'

They got back into the car. 'So what now?' she asked.

Leroy checked his watch. 'I think I have all I came here for. Thanks for all your help, Sally. I'm booked on a 4PM flight tomorrow. While we're driving back to Birmingham, I'll see if I can change it to this evening, head back then.'

Duvall looked over to him. 'That's such a rush. Why not rebook on a morning flight? It'll be mid-afternoon when we get to the City. Let me show you some of Birmingham; we can have dinner, maybe.'

Leroy didn't need much convincing. 'You're on, Officer Duvall.'

'Sweet.' Duvall started the engine and pulled away.

Back inside the church, Pastor Martyn was kneeling in front of the altar, sobbing.

CHAPTER THIRTY-FOUR

LEROY GOT BACK to his hotel room just after three. His first job was to call the airline, and managed to rebook himself onto the next day's 9AM flight. Then he called Ray Quinn. Quinn was at home.

'I was at the Desk going over the case notes, then the Lieutenant came out and told me to take some of my hundred or so hours I was owed. Said not much was going to happen with the case while you were out there, so he could save the department a few dollars. Sorry, Sam.'

'Jesus. Not your bad, Ray. I'm not surprised, though: he hinted at that when he agreed the this trip. He probably waited till I was in the air, too. You at home now, then?'

'Yeah, but I took the case notes with me. Looking through them now.'

'Good man, Ray. Come up with anything?'

'Not really. There's one thing, though. It might not be anything, but apparently, a patrol car from Hollywood Division picked up a kid the other night, suspicion of possession. He was on his bike coming down from the Hollywood Hills. While they were interrogating him down at the station, he blurted out that he had been up near the sign, when another vehicle fetched up. He said he hid as he had a bad feeling about things. Said he didn't see much, but there were a lot of sounds like carrying - something being dragged along the ground - then they left.'

'Interesting. What was he doing up there?'

'Says taking in the view, but they found three cans of paint in his backpack.'

'Up there tagging. Where's the kid now?'

'He's been booked, but is out at present. We have his address. You still flying back tomorrow night? How you getting on?'

'I'm done. I have all I need. I'm booked on the 9AM tomorrow, again via Atlanta. I get into LAX 2:10 tomorrow afternoon, so you can meet me there.'

'Sure. So what did you find?'

'Hightower was bullshitting me, until you called with the hotel confirmation. It looks like he picked up, or was picked up by, those two girls in the pictures. They must have drugged him, and a third party took those shots. Next morning, possibly the same guy, Asian by all account, visits him, shows him the shots and asks for money. Two grand in cash that day, and then another two each month.'

'Only two, Sam?'

'Come on, Ray. You know what's gonna happen. After a month or two, it goes up to three. Then four. All with the threat of the pictures turning up on YouTube, or somewhere. Well, Hightower paid the first two grand, then went back home. He's big in his local church, so went to the pastor there to confess.'

'Confess?'

'Yeah, he was more worried that he's been screwing those two hookers, if that's what they were, than the money. Then the pastor gets hold of a private eye down here, who flies to LA, retracing Hightower's movements exactly, in the hope that the same thing happens to him.'

'Which it did. So this private dick was going to get himself drugged?'

'He considered it a calculated risk, apparently. Charged Hightower appropriately, I guess. He had a contact in LA get him a weapon as he was flying in; planned to confront them.'

'Then it all went wrong.'

'As wrong as it could get.'

'I was looking at the pictures again, Sam, and there's something about them.'

'I'm sure you were. Just joking. What did you see?'

'The one where one of the girls is kneeling on the bed.'

'The doggy one?'

Quinn chuckled. 'Yeah, that one. Well, for the guy, it takes quite a bit of balance, you know what I mean?'

'You seem the expert, Detective. Go on.'

'Where it looks like his right hand is holding her thigh, the other girl has her hand on his arm. Like she's holding it. And her chin is resting on his left shoulder, so she could be propping his head up.'

'And he's sandwiched between her body and the other girl's ass,' Leroy added. 'What a way to go.'

'And he had no idea what was going on?'

'No. I think, Ray, that just adds to the theory that both men were drugged. I'm not sure about Rohypnol itself: Hightower didn't touch the booze so only drank mineral water, according to his pastor. If that's so, the drink would have turned blue, unless these guys were using an old batch, or another drug. There's plenty on the market.'

'Or even from over the border.' Rohypnol, whilst banned in the United States, is legal in Mexico, and is legitimately prescribed by doctors to combat insomnia.

'When we're done here,' said Leroy, 'I'll call Hobson, get him to do a blood test on Kirk. Maybe there's something left in his system. No point checking Hightower; it's too long past now. Any sign of Mets yet, by the way?'

'No, nothing yet. The APB's still out on him, though.'

Leroy and Quinn said their goodbyes. Leroy immediately messaged Russell Hobson, asking him to carry out the tests on Kirk's body, giving the reasons why. He then took a shower and while he was in the shower, Hobson replied, saying okay, but it would be four or five days before any results came back.

Par for the course, thought Leroy.

Leroy and Duvall had arranged to meet outside his hotel at 5PM. He was there promptly, only to find her already there. She had been waiting ten minutes, she said.

'Just got here early. Guess I could have gone up to your room,' she said, looking up at him.

'Could have done. Where shall we go?'

There were still at least two hours of daylight left, so Duvall said she would take him to one of her favourite places. The Railroad Park is in Downtown Birmingham, sandwiched between 14th and 18th Streets. Celebrating the city's industrial and artistic heritage, it comprises woods, green open space, and man-made lakes. It was spring, and the landscaping was filled with masses of flowers, all in full bloom. Even Sam Leroy could appreciate the aesthetic beauty of it, and could understand why she liked it here so much.

They wandered through the park, taking an ice cream, and talking about themselves, both work related, and out of work. They seemed to have much in common; 'kindred spirits', as Sally put it. He was glad he had showered, shaved and changed, as she had obviously put in a lot of effort; her shiny blonde hair was no longer in a ponytail, but cascading down her back. She was wearing a white tee-shirt which stopped just short of her waist, giving Leroy a tantalising glimpse of two inches of tanned skin before a pair of tightly-fitting blue jeans.

Come seven o'clock, she took him to a fish restaurant Downtown.

'You want to try a traditional Alabama dish?' she asked.

'Sure. Go for it.'

They started off with Pickled Citrus Shrimp, followed by Flounder with Lady Pea Succotash, with Fried Baklava Ice Cream for dessert. They shared a bottle or two of Pino Grigiot.

'I enjoyed that,' Leroy said after the meal. 'My first experience of Southern cuisine.'

'And your last?'

'I don't think so.'

She nodded, and rested her chin on her hand, her elbow on the table. 'So what now, Sam?'

He looked at his watch. 'It's almost eleven now. I have to be up early for my 9AM flight.'

'I could give you a wakeup call.'

'You'll call me?'

'No, I mean person to person.' She brushed his hand with her finger.

Leroy kept his hand where it was. 'Sally… I'm not sure…'

'Hey, Sam,' she said quietly. 'Your work here's finished. You fly home tomorrow. We're both kind of single, both kindred spirits.'

He nodded slowly, saying nothing.

'So why not, Sam? Who's going to know? After all, it's only a fuck.'

He looked at her for a moment. 'Yes, that's true.'

CHAPTER THIRTY-FIVE

LEROY CHANGED POSITION. He could just not get comfortable. He tried on his back, then foetal, then on his back once more. He groaned. He was not usually this restless. Perhaps it was because there was a lot on his mind.

The truth was, he was metaphorically kicking himself. Three hours earlier, he was sitting in a restaurant with Sally Duvall. He could visualise her now: the blonde hair, the short tee, the tight jeans, and the great ass.

'Come on, Sam,' she had said. 'It's only a fuck.'

'That's true,' he had said. He had never been so tempted. Even now he could still smell her perfume. 'That's true, but I don't think it's what I need right now.'

'How so?' she asked, disappointed.

'I told you about Joanna and me. I'm not sure how things are between us, and I think… I think sleeping with you would just cloud things between the two of us right now.'

Duvall said nothing.

'And you? The guy you've been seeing: what about him?'

She shrugged her shoulders. 'I don't know about him.' She paused. 'Okay, I get where you're coming from. But can we keep in touch?'

'Sure. I'd like that.'

'Maybe I'll come visit you in LA.'

'I'd like that also. I'll take you to Disneyland.'

She smiled and nodded.

They parted outside the restaurant with a kiss, a few notches up from a peck. Leroy hailed her a cab home, then walked the five or six blocks back to his hotel. Back in his room, he flopped down on the bed. He was glad to be flying back the next morning, for personal as well as professional reasons.

But had he made the right decision? She was quite right: only the two of them would have known. It would have only been a physical thing, kind of jogging while horizontal. And what had Joanna been doing all this time back home? Was he being sensible, doing the right thing, or just being a damn fool? Whichever, it was too late now: he could hardly call her up and say, 'Hey Sally, I've changed my mind. Do you want to get a cab back here?'

He would have to settle for sleeping alone, just dreaming of Sally Duvall. And of her great ass.

*****

When he had eventually gotten off to sleep, his slumber did not last for long. With a jolt he sat up in bed as his phone trilled.

It was Quinn.

'Sorry to call so late, Sam. Are you in bed?'

'It's okay, Ray. What do you need?'

'It's just I thought you'd want to know. They've found Mets.'

'Hey, that's fantastic. About time. Look: while I'm flying back tomorrow, can you get a hold of that translator: Charlie Miller, wasn't it? See if you can get her to the station late afternoon, and we can talk to Mets then.'

'No, Sam. That's not possible. He's not at the station.'

'Where the hell is he then?'

'They found him in Hollywood.'

'In Hollywood? What was he doing there?'

'Lying face down in a dumpster.'

CHAPTER THIRTY-SIX

'YOU MUST GO away more often, Sam. That seems to kick-start the case,' joked Quinn as they left LAX.

Sitting in the front passenger seat, Leroy was checking his service weapon. Quinn had brought it with him when he collected Leroy from the airport.

'It looks that way,' he agreed, checking the number of rounds and flicking the barrel shut. 'After all that time goofing around the 101, we finally have not one break, but three.'

'Where do you want to go first? Back to the Desk?'

'No, no. We've wasted enough time already. I think we'll talk to that kid first. I know the Hollywood Division guys have already done that, but I want to hear it direct from him.'

'What about Mets?'

'He's not going anywhere. He can wait. Where is he?'

'LA County Morgue, waiting on the PM last we heard.'

'Cause of death?'

'Waiting on that, but the body was intact.'

'As opposed to being here and there,' Leroy said grimly. 'And you heard from DMV?'

'Yup, and only one of the plate combinations is a pick-up, reported stolen three days ago.'

'There's a newsflash. Where does the owner live?'

'Down there.'

Leroy looked down at the notepad. 'Marlin Place, Van Nuys. Mm.' He tapped his knee with the notepad.

'What is it?'

'Nothing. Let's go see this kid.'

'I could have called,' Quinn said. 'Have them pick him up again. We could have headed direct to there.'

'No.' Leroy scratched the back of his neck. 'I don't want to piss him off even more than he must be right now. If he's just been busted, then he's hardly going to volunteer information to us. Unless he wants to cop a plea.'

'No plea to cop. Oh, shit.' As Quinn spoke the traffic began to slow down rapidly. There was a long line of red tail and brake lights heading up Sepulveda Boulevard as far as the eye could see.

'Cut across,' Leroy said. 'Get onto La Brea or La Cienega; either will take us up into Hollywood. I'm guessing that's where the kid lives.'

'Not quite. Beverly Hills.'

'Beverly Hills? No way.'

'Way. His address is down there.' Quinn nodded to the notebook he had left on the dashboard. Leroy picked it up and read the address.

'It's just off Melrose,' Quinn added, making a sharp left into La Cienega Boulevard. 'Arguably West Hollywood. Just on the border.'

'Let's head there, then. What were you saying about no cop to plea? He wasn't carrying?'

'He was, but only 27 grams of Mary Jane.'

In the mid-1990s, the State of California decriminalized the possession of marijuana, or cannabis: this means that a first-time possession offence no longer means prison time or a criminal record for a small amount for personal consumption. Being in possession of 28.5g or less is a misdemeanour with a $100 fine; over this amount could lead to 6 months' jail time. Selling or cultivating is still a felony.

'Lucky him,' said Leroy.

'U-huh. They let him go with a warning.'

Leroy chuckled. 'After taking the stuff off him, of course.'

'I guess so. His name's Delroy Wilson.'

'Delroy Wilson. It's ten of four now. Let's hope Delroy's home.'

'School will be out by now, anyway.'

The address was in fact in West Hollywood, but was so close to the more upmarket Beverly Hills that there was little in it, particularly for a realtor. A quiet street off the busy Doheny Drive, it boasted a line of precisely manicured lawns fronting large but not palatial houses. Some of the houses were of colonial-style construction, but this, number 9070, was a more contemporary, box-like house, with large, rectangular windows. There was no gate, but to get to the front door meant driving up a modest slope. Over the flat roof of the house Leroy could see the top floors of the Cedars Sinai Medical Center, down on Wilshire.

'You sure we have the right address?' Leroy asked, as Quinn turned into the drive.

'That's what Hollywood Division gave us.'

The front door opened as they pulled up at the top of the inclined drive. A tall, elegantly dressed black woman stood on the step, watching them as they got out of the car. She did not look welcoming.

'Mrs Wilson?' Quinn asked, holding out his identification. Leroy did the same.

'My God,' she exclaimed, 'can't you people leave him alone?'

'Excuse me?' asked Leroy, putting his badge away.

'You're going to tell me you've come to harass Delroy.'

Leroy glanced at Quinn, then back to Mrs Wilson. 'We'd like to speak with him for a few moments, not harass him.'

'I'm going to call my husband. He will be furious. He will be calling our attorney. This is nothing more than harassment.' She paused a beat, looking them up and down. 'Racial harassment.'

Leroy tried to calm her down. 'Please, Mrs Wilson; we just want to ask your son a couple of questions. There's nothing to be worried about.'

'Damn right there's nothing to be worried about. Because you're not doing to see him. It's bad enough him being held in a cell with those... those people down in Hollywood, but you not leaving him alone. I won't have it!'

'Mrs Wilson, I'm not here to talk to Delroy about the possession. I understand it was only a tiny amount, and he was never charged.'

'What do you want with him then? Search him some more?'

Leroy shook his head. 'Ma'am, we're from the Homicide Division.'

'You have to be kidding me! What are you saying now?'

'We're investigating a homicide which took place near the Hollywood Sign a few days back. You might have read it in the newspapers or seen it on TV.'

'The one without the...?' As she spoke she tapped the top of her head.

'That's the one. Now, while Delroy was talking to the officers from the Hollywood Station, it came to light that he has invaluable information which could help that enquiry.'

'He didn't do it, if that's what you're trying to say.'

'I'm not saying he did, but he, without being aware, may have been a witness. He's already said what he saw, but I'd just like to get it from him first hand, myself.'

'I see.' Mrs Wilson was thawing.

'So, is Delroy at home? Could we talk to him?'

Still not a hundred percent convinced, she acquiesced. 'Come this way.' She stepped back inside and allowed them to follow.

Inside, they stood in the large hall. Lobby would be a more appropriate word. On each side, three doors led off the hall to various rooms; the centrepiece was a wide, sweeping staircase. Mrs Wilson stood at the bottom of the staircase and called out for Delroy. After a few moments he appeared at the top.

'What is it, Mom?'

'Honey, there are two men from the LAPD -'

'LAPD? No, Mom...'

'It's cool, Delroy. They're not here about that. They want to ask you a favour.' She stared at Leroy, almost daring him to contradict. He said nothing. 'I think you should come down, honey.'

Delroy slowly came down the stairs. He was well over six feet tall, thin, with short curly hair. He was barefoot, and wore a pair of lime green shorts and dark blue football shirt.

Leroy looked up at him and said, 'Delroy, I work for the LAPD Homicide Division. I'm given to understand that the other night you told the officer in Hollywood that you might have witnessed something up by the sign. Is that correct?'

Still suspicious, Delroy nodded.

'You want to tell me about it, in your own words?'

Delroy nodded again. 'Well, I was up there, just by the sign. I was…'

'Delroy, I'm not interested in what you were doing up there, or what you had with you. I just want to know what you saw, or heard.'

Delroy took one more step down. He was three steps above the others. 'I was up there on my own. It was so quiet and peaceful, man. Then I heard the sound of a car or something. Then the lights. My bike was already by the side of the road, so I ran and hid, behind some bushes.'

'What did you hide? Did you see who it was?'

'I hid in case it was a pi -'

'Delroy!' Mrs Wilson admonished. She looked at Leroy and Quinn. 'I apologise.'

'No need. Go on, Delroy.'

'Nothing much else. I heard a lot of doors banging and talking. They were too far away for me to hear what they were saying.

'I hit the deck when they got closer, and it seemed like they were dragging something heavy along the ground. Then one of the guys said something like, "I know somewhere else"; no, it was "I know another place", then they drove off.'

'"I know another place"?' Leroy asked. 'Yes?'

Delroy nodded.

'A man's voice?'

'Yup.'

'Accent? Did he have an accent?'

Delroy frowned. 'Don't reckon so. But he was white.'

'White?'

'Yes, he had a white man's voice.'

'Okay,' said Leroy, slowly. 'And that's all you heard, or saw?'

'That's what I'm telling you. I was scared, man; I hid behind some bushes till they'd gone. It was dark up there, man; no street lamps.'

'Was it a car?' asked Quinn. 'A sedan? Or something bigger?'

Delroy pondered. 'Bigger than a car. Smaller than a truck.'

'A van?' Mrs Wilson suggested.

'Maybe. Maybe a pick-up,' Delroy replied.

'Anything else?' Leroy asked.

Delroy shook his head. 'No.'

'No problem,' said Leroy. 'I want to thank you for your help here. Here's my cell number. Give me a call if you remember anything else, deal?'

Delroy took the card and gave a large, toothy grin. 'No problem.'

Leroy and Quinn thanked Delroy and his mother and left.

'That proves what I've always told you about being stereotypical,' Leroy said, 'and making assumptions.'

'How so?'

'Black kid, caught in possession. Plus the three cans of paint he was carrying. He wasn't about to decorate his Granny's garage, was he?'

'No. What's your point?'

'Where would you expect to find him? Compton? South Central?'

'I get you. Not here. Was what he told us any use?' asked Quinn as he turned and went back down the drive.

'Maybe. White man in a pick-up. Not exactly a case buster. At least it confirms what we'd already figured out. Come on: let's go see the guy who had his pick-up stolen.'

CHAPTER THIRTY-SEVEN

THE 9 SEATER Piaggio Aero Avanti P180 lifted off from the runway, the buzz from the twin Pratt & Witney PT6A66 engines filling the cloudless skies as it gracefully banked left over the Van Nuys Golf Course and headed north north east, slowly climbing, to reach its cruise speed of 425mph.

It would have been a private aircraft, perhaps an executive in his private airplane headed away from LA for the weekend. The airport at Van Nuys specializes in non-commercial aircraft, its big sister to the west being the main commercial destination.

Quinn had always been interested in aviation: not just the huge commercial airplanes, but smaller craft; in fact it was here, at Van Nuys Airport, that Raymond Quinn Senior would take his six-year old son on a Sunday morning to watch the planes taxiing, taking off and landing. Quinn's pipe dream since then had been to own a small plane and get himself a pilot's licence, but it was the day job, or rather the pay for the day job which killed that ambition. One day, maybe.

'You ready?' Leroy asked.

Quinn took his gaze off the Turboprop and turned back to his partner. 'Sure.'

They were at the house of one Rudi Johansson, the registered owner of the Chevrolet Milverado, which was the only match to the four possible licence plate numbers that was not a sedan.

The houses in the street were typical Southern California homes: one floor, large front yard. Johansson's house was no exception: the yard had no grass, just earth with weeds dotted around. The skeleton of what they recognized as a British Mini stood on the earth, its doors and hood a mixture of primer, dirt and rust. It had no tyres: the naked wheels rested on piles of cinder blocks.

The risk of calling on somebody during the day is that there is a good chance they are out, at work, normally. Today, Leroy and Quinn were lucky, as Johansson answered the door himself.

Johansson confirmed he was the owner of the pick-up, but explained what had happened.

'It was the other night. I had parked it on the street. I normally use the drive, or on the yard there, but my girl had already parked hers there, so I put it on the street.'

'What time was that?' Quinn asked.

'About eleven. Then we went to bed. Wasn't until six, six-thirty next morning when I looked out of the window and saw it gone. You guys found it, then?'

Leroy ignored the question. 'So it was taken, then, sometime between eleven and six-thirty. You didn't hear anything?'

'Nothing, nothing.'

'You guys sleep at the front of the house?'

'We do, yes…'

'Window open at night?'

'No way. Not in this neighbourhood.'

'And of course you locked it, and there was no key in the ignition?'

'What do you take me for? Of course I locked it, and of course the key wasn't there.'

'It's in the house?'

'Sure.'

'You want to get it?'

'You want the key?'

Leroy nodded.

Johansson looked at the ground. He shuffled his feet slightly. Mumbled something.

'Sir?' Leroy prompted.

'All right, all right. I left the key in the truck. Stupid, I know. I don't normally.'

'Did you tell the insurance company that?'

Johansson shook his head and swallowed.

'I don't care about them,' Leroy said. 'When you filed the police report, what did you tell them about the keys?'

'Er... I might not have said the keys were in there.'

'And that's all you can tell me? You left it there, went to bed, and next morning it was gone?'

'It's the truth, I swear. Have you found it?'

'No, we haven't found it. And to be truthful, I'm not expecting to.'

'Hmm?'

Leroy sighed. 'If it is found, it'll be lying somewhere torched, seats gone, tyres gone. Any valuables in there?'

Johansson said no.

'Do you work, sir?' Quinn asked.

He shook his head. 'Not at the moment. I used to work in a local store, filling shelves and driving deliveries, but I got laid off.'

'You're on welfare, then?'

He shrugged. 'My girl, she works. I am looking for something, though.'

Leroy nodded. 'Thanks for your time, Mr Johansson.' As he turned to leave, he asked, 'Chevrolet Milverado? I've heard of a Silverado.'

'It's the same, more or less. It was ex-US Army. Military green, but I sprayed it white. It was a good runner.'

'I'm sure it was a good runner,' said Leroy as they got back into their car. As Quinn drove away, Leroy looked back at Johansson's house. 'What do you think of that guy?'

'He's an idiot. Who else would leave their vehicle unlocked, keys in the ignition outside their house overnight? Or anywhere for that matter?'

'Unless you wanted it taken.'

'That's what I was thinking. But why?'

'Insurance scam, has to be. Nobody can be that dumb.'

'Do we need to call anyone?'

'Nothing to do with us. It's no surprise Kirk's body was dumped with a stolen vehicle. I'd just like to see what he says to the insurance company when they asked about the keys.'

'What about the report he filed with us? He said they keys were in the house.'

'Forget it. How much time are they going to waste looking for it? We need it more than he does.'

'And like you said, that's not going to happen.'

'No, so the truck's a dead end. Let's get back to the station. See if there's any news from them on Mets.' As Quinn headed away from Van Nuys, Leroy asked, 'Johansson: have we come across him before?'

Quinn pondered. 'No; I don't think so. Why do you ask?'

'I don't know. He just seems familiar, that's all.'

'How can he be, Sam?'

'He can't. Maybe I'm thinking of another case, someone like him. Even dumber. Maybe it's just the jetlag talking.'

CHAPTER THIRTY-EIGHT

BACK AT THE station, there was the inevitable discussion about jurisdiction.

Lieutenant Perez leaned across his desk and flicked one of his silver executive balls. It swung and hit the next, and the click, click, click began. Leroy winced. The lieutenant sat back in his chair.

'I've already spoken to the captain,' he said, 'and to the Chief. They're both agreed, much to the annoyance of Hollywood Division, that you can have first dibs on this one.' They were talking about Evald Mets.

Leroy stood behind one of the chairs in front of the lieutenant's desk, both hands on the chair back. 'Lieutenant, it has to be linked to Kirk's murder. Otherwise, it's one mother of a coincidence.'

Perez nodded. 'One unlucky son of a bitch. What about the COD, though? That was different here.'

'Yes, William Kirk was shot and decapitated; Evald Mets appears to have been strangled.'

'Weapon?'

'From the marks on his neck, a rope. One around an inch or so in circumference. Apparently, there are some slighter burn marks on the tips of his fingers, which suggest that he put up a fight. I'm thinking someone got behind him, rope around his neck, pulled it tight, and *sayonara* Evald Mets.'

'He was found in a dumpster - a dumpster again - up in Hollywood. Have you been up there yet?'

'No, not yet. It's no longer a crime scene now: forensic have already finished there.'

'Where in Hollywood was it?'

'Up at the Bowl. There's a refreshment counter and the Bowl Shop in one building.'

'Yes, I know it.'

Leroy said, 'Well, behind that building, there's a row of dumpsters, apparently. Needed for food trash. He was in there. Two kids found him while they were dumpster diving. Not quite what they were expecting to find.' He checked his watch. 'It'll be dark before we get up there. I don't know if there's anything on there tonight, but if forensics are done with the scene, I can't see any value in racing up there tonight. Ray and I'll head up there first thing.'

'What are you expecting to find up there?' Perez asked.

'I'll let you know when I find it. Then my focus is going to have to be following up on what I learned in Birmingham.'

'I was wondering when you were going to get around to that. Sam, you know how much that trip of yours cost the Department?'

'Money well spent, Lieutenant. I think I've finally figured out what's been going on.'

'Quinn told me it started as some kind of scam, yes?'

Leroy nodded.

'So fill in the blanks for me.' Perez flicked another silver ball and leaned back. His phone chirped: he checked the screen and put it back down again, looking at Leroy.

'It all seems to centre around the Stocker Hotel. It's Downtown, across the street from Union Station, but more importantly, it's used by folks - mainly men - attending events at the Convention Center.'

'Men away from home, away from the wife and kids.'

'Correct. We only know of two - Kirk and Hightower - but you can bet your ass there have been others.

'The way I figure it, the guy's alone in the hotel, he gets approached by one or both of those girls in the photographs.'

'You guessing they're hookers?'

'Possibly, possibly not. While I was away, Ray let Vice take a look, but came up with nothing. Their faces aren't that clear on the pictures.'

'Probably deliberate.'

'Right. So I'm figuring the girls start flirting with the guys, getting them merry, although apparently Hightower didn't drink. I'm figuring then the girls somehow, maybe while he was distracted with the other, slipped something in a drink. Not sure if it was Rohypnol itself – Hightower said he was on mineral water and would have noticed if his Evian turned blue.'

'Anything in Kirk's system?'

'I asked Hobson to check, but he tells me it will be a few days, and there's no guarantee anything's still there. So once the guy's under the influence, they hit his hotel room and do what they do. Ray and I are convinced the pictures are staged: on one of them it looks as if one of the girls is holding Kirk up.'

'If they're not hookers, they might also be reluctant to get intimate with the guy,' Perez observed.

'Possibly, yes. Or they're wearing crotch pads; you know, like they do in the movies. You can't *see* anything in the shots.

'The next morning, the guy wakes up, can't remember what happened the night before, and gets a tap on the door. The guy at the door - Hightower says maybe Chinese in his thirties – shows him the pictures and demands a couple of grand that day, and the same every month.'

'So how did Kirk end up dead?'

'Hightower is big in his local church. He went to his pastor to ask for forgiveness for fornicating - his words - and the pastor hired a private eye - William Kirk - to retrace his steps and confront them.'

'Which got him killed. Why cut his head off?'

Leroy shook his head, stifled a yawn. 'No idea yet. Maybe they were planning on dismembering the whole body to make it easier to hide. From what a witness up by the sign said, the killers were out looking for a place to dump the body.'

Perez rubbed his chin. 'How is he supposed to pay the next month? Mail a cheque?'

'No, mail the cash to a box number, here in LA.'

'Are you going to stake that out?'

'Yes, but in time. I want first to get someone into the hotel, pretending to be a business traveller, and hoping the girls will make contact.'

'That's risky, Sam. For one thing, there's the question of entrapment; and whoever you put in will end up being drugged.'

'I know. As far as the entrapment is concerned, I'm not looking to book anyone on the strength of maybe drugging our man; I just want to get a hold of the two girls. And as far as the drugging is concerned: yes, there is that risk.' Leroy walked round the front of the chair and sat down.

'The thing is, Lieutenant, if somebody at the hotel is involved - identifying likely guests, I mean – then if either Ray or I pose as a guest, then we're going to be spotted. It has to be another officer.'

'I'm not happy about that, Sam. The drug could have all kinds of side-effects.'

'I'm aware of that. I know there's a risk, but when isn't there?'

Perez closed his eyes and rubbed his forehead. 'I'll give it some thought, Sam. I'll have a word with downstairs, see if anyone's prepared to volunteer.'

'Swell, thanks.' Leroy got up. 'I'm going to call it a day here now. First thing tomorrow, Ray and I'll head up to the Bowl, take a look at the scene. Then we'll come back here and set things up for the hotel.' He paused on the way out of the Lieutenant's office. 'It just won't work if Ray or I do it. We'll be recognised.'

'I get that, Sam. But as you yourself said, whoever volunteers, and whatever they volunteer for, there's always a risk.'

CHAPTER THIRTY-NINE

THEY ARRIVED AT the Bowl just after 9AM. The parking lot was almost deserted: Leroy parked in the nearest set of spaces to the pathway leading up to the amphitheatre, next to three other cars. As they got out and looked around, another car drew up next to theirs. A man in a green tee got out, gave Leroy and Quinn a glance, and then walked over to the building containing the men's room. Sunglasses on, Leroy and Quinn walked in the same direction. As they passed the men's room, the man came out, and headed over to the box office. They could hear the sound of a hand drier coming from the restroom. A white van was parked on the corner, and a man in grey overalls was carrying out some work on an electrical junction box.

'Where is it?' Leroy asked.

Quinn pointed up the inclined path. 'Up there, behind the concession stand.'

They walked up the slope, past the still closed Bowl Store; Leroy glanced over to the flyer hanging from the streetlamp advertising a Diana Krall concert the following Sunday. A white Johnston CN101 street cleaning truck with the Hollywood Bowl logo on its doors trundled down the slope, its twin brushes at the front spinning round, collecting the trash from the previous night. At the top of the slope, just before the concession stand, the road bends round to the left and on the bend a man this time in green overalls and matching baseball cap was tending the bushes.

'Behind here?' Leroy pointed to the stand, which was a long structure, painted olive green and with white shutters which were closed at that time of the morning.

'Yeah, round the back.'

As they walked round the back of the stand, a woman in grey shirt and darker grey pants came out of one of the doors in the adjacent building. 'Can I help?'

Leroy and Quinn flashed their badges. 'Just following up on the other day,' Quinn told her.

'Oh, sure,' she said, holding the clipboard she was carrying to her chest. 'I wasn't on duty then, but they told me about the other day.'

With Quinn following, Leroy stepped round the rear of the stand. Sure enough, there were dumpsters, one green with a black lid and one black with a white lid. The green one had FOOD TRASH stencilled in white onto the front. Leroy lifted the lid, sniffed and pulled a face.

'Food trash?' Quinn asked. Leroy nodded. He peered inside the black container and wandered up and down the back of the stand.

'It's a bit narrow back here,' he said. 'How would whoever dumped Mets in there know the dumpsters were here?'

'It says refreshments out front. Maybe they guessed. They didn't have to actually put him in one of those: they could have just left him back here.'

'Mm.' Leroy rubbed his eye, taking out a fleck of dirt.

'Maybe he was killed here,' Quinn suggested. Somehow lured here, strangled and dumped.'

Leroy sniffed and shook his head. 'I don't buy that. For one thing, are you saying Mets voluntarily came back here with somebody else? And why was he at the Hollywood Bowl? Just to hang around the back of the concession stand? And the other thing: the ME says he had been dead around twelve hours.' As Leroy spoke, they made their way back to the front of the stand. 'Something just doesn't feel right, Ray. And if he was killed somewhere else, like Kirk was, how would they get the body there without somebody noticing?'

Quinn gestured back down the slope to the parking lot. 'You wouldn't get a car up here. Unless they used the pick-up, and everybody guessed it was a Bowl vehicle.'

'You got it, Ray. No, you couldn't get a car up here, could you? And you certainly couldn't get a garbage truck up here.' Leroy looked around. Down by the box office there was a figure in the grey uniform the woman earlier was wearing. He ran down to the man. Holding out his badge, he asked where the garbage is collected.

'Three times a week, sir,' came the reply. The guy appeared Hispanic, no more than five feet tall, with black hair long but in a ponytail. He wore a matching grey baseball cap. 'Around one, maybe two in the AM.'

'And how are the dumpsters up there collected? Does the truck make it up the hill?'

The man laughed. 'Oh no, sir. It would never fit up there. The road's too narrow.'

'So how's the trash collected?'

He pushed his baseball cap back an inch. 'Those nights, once we're done here, which is about twelve, we have to wheel the larger containers down the hill to over there.' He pointed to a corner of the parking lot, where two containers were still standing. 'The garbage truck empties them down there. Then next morning, we wheel them back up the hill. 'Course, they're not heavy then, on account them being emptied already.'

'So, you're telling me that, between midnight and…?'

'Around 8AM.'

'Midnight and 8AM, the dumpsters would be standing over there. Is that right?'

'That's correct, sir.'

By now, Quinn had caught up and had heard the conversation. 'What about CCTV?' he asked. Is the parking lot covered by CCTV?'

'Er, no. I don't believe it is,' the man said apologetically.

'No problem,' Leroy told him. 'Thanks for your time.'

Quinn was already walking down to the lot. He turned round and called out, 'No cameras.'

Leroy joined him. 'Pity, but I'll bet you a pound of sugar to a bag of shit that it was the same pick-up that dropped Kirk off.'

'Which was stolen?'

'Apparently so.' Leroy's phone bleeped: he quickly checked the message and turned back to Quinn. 'I think we're done here.'

'That would figure,' Quinn said. 'Mets's body was found by some kids dumpster diving, remember? They wouldn't have been able to get up there, behind the concession stand, would they?'

'No,' said Leroy who was wandering over to a *Forthcoming Events* board. 'They'd have the pick of the lot over there.'

Quinn joined his partner as they both read the board. Events for that summer began with fireworks second week of June, followed by more fireworks on the July 4th weekend. Coming soon was *Smooth Summer Jazz*, and a New Kids on the Block concert, neither of which they found appealing.

Then Quinn spotted something. 'Hey – the Rolling Stones in September. I might see if Holly wants to go. Why don't you take Joanna to something here? You know, make a real effort.'

Leroy glared at him.

'You guys still not…?'

'No. Come on.' Leroy walked quickly back to the car, Quinn saying nothing. Once back in the car, Leroy turned to Quinn. 'That message I got before, it was from the lieutenant. He says we have our volunteer.'

CHAPTER FORTY

'YOU?'

Leroy looked to Quinn, who said nothing, then back to Lieutenant Perez.

'What's your problem?' asked the lieutenant.

Leroy was lost for words. 'It's just that I… I just wasn't…'

'You weren't expecting your volunteer to be me?'

'No, to be honest. Why?'

'Weren't there any volunteers, Lieutenant?' Quinn asked.

Perez walked round the side of his desk. 'Think about it, guys. Sam: how long have I been behind this desk?'

Leroy shrugged. 'Around three years, I guess.'

'Three years seven months. And one week two days if you want to be *pedante*. And how much action have I seen in that time? Very little; I've been stuck behind that desk shuffling papers, worrying about budgets, figuring out rosters.'

'So you're missing the action?' Leroy was unsure where this conversation would end up.

'Some times. In a fashion. There's no reason why I shouldn't keep my hand in, as it were, is there?'

Leroy said nothing.

'You have a problem, Sam?'

'No problem, no. Just surprised.'

'Also, I need every available man or woman on what they're doing right now. So do downstairs. The captain's happy with this: he says he'll provide cover for me while I'm on this.'

A little less time on the golf course, Leroy thought, but did not say.

'The other point is, Sam,' the lieutenant went on, 'is this. We talked about the risk whoever volunteers takes regarding whatever drugs these people are using, but it doesn't need to go that far. If, for argument's sake, I allow them to slip me something so the next morning I'm presented with some of my own dirty pictures, then we can't book them for that. It would be entrapment. All we need to do is to flush these girls out, maybe the Chinese guy also. Or use the girls to get the Chinese and lead us to whoever else is in this.'

Leroy nodded. 'Yeah. All that's true.' He pointed to some wiring lying on the lieutenant's desk. 'Is this what all that's for?'

Perez picked the wiring up and unwound it. 'I drew it out earlier. Take a look.' He tossed it over to Leroy.

It was small: a junction box, no more than two inches long and the same in circumference. From one end led a single wire, coiled, which led to a small black box inside which was room for two small batteries. From the other end came three uncoiled wires. One led to an earpiece, one to a signet ring, the other to a miniature microphone.

'Motorola Stealth,' Perez explained while Leroy was checking over it. 'The ring is actually the Push To Talk button.'

'I know. I've used them a few times before.'

'The wire to the earpiece is quite discreet, but I have no problem not using it. Each attachment is detachable. This one would be for you.' He gave Leroy a smaller version, with two wires: earpiece and microphone. 'As long as you're listening in.'

Leroy dropped the wires back down on the desk. 'Okay,' he said quietly. 'Let's do it. But we still have the question of Evald Mets.'

Perez returned to the other side of his desk. 'Yes, Evald Mets. Do you feel his murder's connected to all this?'

'The COD is slightly different. Strangled, not shot, not dismembered, but found in a dumpster, just like Kirk.'

'Sam, you got any idea how many dead bodies are fished out of dumpsters in a year?'

'No, but I can imagine. But it's one hell of a coincidence.'

'It is, yes; but he could have been involved in something else which got him killed and just happened to be at that mall at that time.'

'Then why not just leave it?' Quinn asked. 'What's that expression? "Discretion is the better part of valour"? And why was he looking in the dumpster at that time of night, anyway?'

Perez looked over to Leroy. 'What do you think, Sam? What do you want to do about him?'

Leroy replied slowly. 'I think Mets was somehow mixed up in all this. I don't know how or why, but my gut tells me he was. But I also think that the key to all this is those girls, and we need to flush them out. They've been very clever: their faces aren't really shown on the pictures, and they don't have any distinguishing marks – tattoos, that sort of stuff. Ray's checked with Vice, and come up with nothing there. We need to get them.'

'But we can't put investigating Mets's murder on ice,' Perez said.

Leroy nodded. 'I know. But I want Ray and I to focus on this, for the next day or two.' He paused, then asked the lieutenant, 'I'm assuming somebody has called on his widow?'

'Of course. A patrol car called to give her the news. She has to identify the body, after all.'

'When we last spoke to her, she'd not seen her husband, and said she had no idea where he had gone. Was that still the case when they called?'

'I'm not sure; we'll need to check.'

'What about where he worked? He worked in the kitchen in some Eastern European Restaurant a few blocks from where he lived.'

Perez shook his head. 'I don't believe so. I think they were waiting to decide on who was taking his case. I can get a patrol car to call, see if anybody had heard from him. I'm guessing we'll need to call on that interpreter again.'

'You may not need to. The restaurant's owner is a prick by the name of Andrew Dudley. Told us he was originally from Sacramento, now has a house in Burbank. In fact, that's where Mets had apparently been the night Kirk's body turned up. For the purposes of his restaurant, he calls himself Dudinsky, Andrey Dudinsky.'

'I'll arrange for a patrol car to call on the restaurant, ask this Dudinsky - Dudley - if he can tell us anything, talk to some of the staff also.'

'And tell him Mets won't be showing up for work anymore,' added Quinn.

'Do me a favour, Lieutenant,' Leroy said. 'Get the patrol car to park in plain sight outside the restaurant. Dudley's too arrogant, brash, cocksure, for my liking.'

'You think he had something to do with Mets's murder?'

'I'd like him to, but there's no evidence.'

'You just don't like the guy?' Perez asked.

Leroy said nothing.

'I'll do that now, then.' Perez sat down and picked up his desk phone. You two go do what you need to do. Sam, can you get me booked into the Stocker for tonight, and tomorrow night. We'll take a view if nothing happens after two nights.'

'What alias?' Leroy asked.

'Better use my real name; they might ask for ID. Nobody knows me there, in any case. Once I'm booked in, I can get down there late afternoon and check in. I have next month's rosters and overtime projections to work through while I'm there.'

Leroy and Quinn turned to go. 'Hightower was at the LACC so would have gotten back to the hotel around five, five-thirty. Kirk would have done the same. What say we touch base here around four, then head off? We can't arrive there together, of course.'

'Of course not. We can leave here together; you can give me a ride as far as Pershing Square, maybe. I'll get the subway the rest of the way.'

Plan agreed, Leroy and Quinn returned to their own desks.

'I didn't see that coming,' Quinn said as they stood by the coffee machine.

Leroy grinned. 'No, neither did I.'

'What's funny?'

Leroy shook his head. 'You've never met *la senora* Perez, have you?'

'No.'

'Our lieutenant's going to have to spend the next few hours convincing her why he's booked himself two nights alone at the Stocker.'

Still grinning, Leroy took his coffee back to his desk.

CHAPTER FORTY-ONE

LEROY AND QUINN left the Station at just after four, with Lieutenant Perez in the back seat. Somehow, during the day, he had gotten himself an overnight bag. Maybe he kept one in his office in case of an emergency; maybe he had always intended to volunteer himself. They dropped the lieutenant off at Pershing Square and headed straight for the hotel, remaining in the underground parking garage. Perez himself headed for the Red Line and took the two stops to Union Station and walked across to the hotel, overnight bag over his shoulder and attaché case in his hand. As agreed, they did not inform the hotel management of their presence.

'We're not going to tell the hotel manager about this, are we?' Perez had asked on the way there.

'No,' Leroy replied. 'These girls may just be bar-hopping on the look-out for men on their own, men who look like family men. Or, there's also the possibility that somebody working at the hotel is looking at who's booked in, and if they fit the profile, passing their details on. Which is why I didn't want Ray or me to be staying here; we'd be recognised.'

Quinn looked over to his partner. 'So Hightower, and Kirk, were marked men even before they arrived.'

'I reckon so,' Leroy replied. 'They must have fitted the profile these people were after, so - yes, maybe even before they took off from Alabama.'

Perez adjusted his position in the back of the car. 'I've come up here from La Mesa. I'm here for two nights. I have a wife and five children back home.'

'Yup, that seems to be the right profile. Let's hope you get lucky tonight. Here's Pershing Square, Lieutenant.'

Perez checked in, and went up to his room, Room 922. It was almost 5PM. 'Can you guys hear me?' he asked as he walked round the room. He had decided to retain the earpiece as it was very discreet, the wire being almost invisible except at a close distance. To activate the microphone, all he had to do was press the top of the dummy signet ring.

'Yes, Lieutenant, loud and clear,' answered Leroy, relieved that they had an excellent reception, even though they were parked in the hotel's basement garage.

'I'm going to go downstairs, take a look around. Make myself visible. See if I can spot either of those two girls. Get this over with tonight.'

'Ten-four, Lieutenant.' Leroy released his microphone and said to Quinn, 'I just hope he doesn't screw things up by jumping the gun. Ten to one he's up there worrying about how much overtime this operation's incurring.'

Quinn grinned. He watched as two cars entered the garage, drove around and found a space. The drivers both locked their vehicles: one waited for the elevator which went direct to the lobby; the other headed for the emergency staircase. 'Last night,' he said, 'you made some crack about the lieutenant's wife. What was all that about?'

Leroy chuckled. 'You never met Rosanne Perez?'

'No.'

'She's Hispanic, like him, but has a real hot temper. He can get a bit fiery at times - always has – but she can get off the Richter scale. When I moved out here, his previous partner had retired early or something, so I was with Roman literally from Day One. Well, we were about a week into things when he let it slip that he had been banging some traffic cop.'

'A woman cop?'

'Oh, for sure. This was all before your time, I think. Anyway, Rosanne found out somehow - she didn't get it from me – and for weeks he had to sleep in hotels, in the squad room, in his car. He even spent a few nights on my couch.'

'She forgave him, though?'

'Eventually. I guess she did: they had two more kids after that. But he's always had to give her a minute by minute account of what he was doing, where he had been, after then. Things might have changed since he got the lieutenant's job, but I can imagine her reaction when he told her he would be staying here for two nights.'

'To pick up two girls.'

'Oh, he won't have told her that. He would have said it's some kind of undercover operation, given her some kind of bullshit. Oh Christ, I hope she doesn't show up.'

'Is she likely to?'

'Unlikely. Jesus, what a thought.'

As if on cue, Perez came through on the radio. 'I'm headed for the bar. Just bought three or four newspapers. I'll sit in the bar with them, see who comes in.'

Perez took his four newspapers to the bar, read all of them front page to back, twice. He ate alone in one of the hotel restaurants, checked out the other, and returned to the bar, where he remained until midnight.

While they waited downstairs, Leroy called the patrol team who were going to visit the restaurant where Mets worked. They had not been there yet: they were on their way but were diverted to a shooting. Now they were about to go off shift: did Leroy want them to pass the details onto another car?

'No, don't do that. Go tomorrow, not at the crack of dawn. Sometime after 11AM, when everybody's there. It's a restaurant, remember? And remember to park out front, in plain sight. I want everybody eating there, in fact everybody on that block, to know the police are visiting.'

Midnight, and Perez told them he was going to bed. 'Wasted evening. Let's hope we have more success tomorrow; otherwise we 're going to have to try another approach.'

After Perez had signed off, Leroy said, 'I told you he'd be bothered about the cost of all this. Look: here's our relief.' The patrol car pulled up alongside: Leroy handed over the radio and briefed the officers one more time. It was very unlikely that anything was going to happen tonight, but if it did, he told them how to respond and then to call him. He and Quinn would relieve them by seven the next morning.

It was actually 6:30 the next morning when Leroy and Quinn arrived back in the parking garage. The officers reported that it had been a quiet night: Perez had called a half hour ago, and was getting up. Once back in the car, Leroy called Perez and told him they were back.

'Fine,' the lieutenant said. 'I'm out of the shower, and will head downstairs for breakfast around seven. You never know, they might be around then.'

Leroy shook his head. Unlikely, but the lieutenant might get himself spotted.

Perez had himself a plate of *heuevos rancheros,* while Leroy and Quinn settled for a breakfast burrito from a stand at the end of Olvera Street. At 8:15 Perez went down to Reception and asked them to call him a cab to the Convention Center. The receptionist told him there was no need, as there was a taxi stand at the front of the hotel. Now the reception team knew he was headed for the LACC, Perez took his cab there, Leroy and Quinn following.

CHAPTER FORTY-TWO

THERE WERE TWO events on at the Convention Center that day: a naturalization ceremony in the south hall, and a convention held by the American Society of Cataract and Refractive Surgery in the west hall. The next week the Center was due to host auditions for the television show *America's Got Talent*.

Perez had arranged to meet Leroy and Quinn at the cafeteria on the mezzanine level: his taxi dropped him off out front, while the others headed for the parking lot. To park outside and have to go through the ritual of showing identification may have attracted unwanted attention. They arrived some fifteen minutes after the lieutenant; taking the escalator up one level, they found him sitting at one of the tables with three cups of coffee.

'We need to be careful, even here,' Leroy said as he sat down and looked over the balcony to the huge lobby below. 'It's possible that Hightower and the others were picked out here. Most of the guys down there would be in the same situation: here on business, away from home, staying alone in a hotel. Not too difficult to follow someone back to where they're staying.'

'Others?' asked Quinn.

'Think about it. It's too slick for them to be just starting out. No way were Hightower and Kirk the only ones. No way, man.'

'Kirk followed Hightower's route exactly, didn't he?' said Perez.

Leroy agreed. 'Yup, even down to catching the same flight.'

'So it could be somebody here, or at the hotel, or even the cab driver.'

'Or even the airline,' said Quinn.

'Or even the airline.' Leroy looked around. 'What do you plan to do here all day, Lieutenant?'

Perez snorted. 'No way am I sitting on my ass drinking coffee all day. I'll have to make it look as if I have business here. There's lots of guys in suits just wandering about. Look.'

Leroy and Quinn looked down at the lobby. The place was full of business men: most in suits, most on their cell phones, some sitting on chairs working on laptops.

'There are two events on here: a naturalization ceremony and something about eyes - an opticians' convention, or something. I'm sure they're both closed to the public, but I have my badge with me.' He drank more coffee. 'I didn't notice any girls hanging around in either bar last night, or the restaurant. If I did, I'd've called you guys.'

Leroy raised himself in his chair and looked down at the lobby again. 'Well, while you're spending your day with eyes and naturalization, Ray and I will keep our eyes open for either one of those girls. We can separate for that, Ray: it's a huge place here.'

'There are a lot of hotels Downtown,' Quinn said. 'Maybe they're working out of there now.'

'That's possible,' Leroy replied. 'But remember both Hightower and Kirk were taken at the Stocker. That hotel is the common denominator.'

'If nothing happens tonight,' Perez said, 'I'll have to take a view on where we go next.'

'Stay for a few more nights?' Quinn asked.

'Not with me. I can't be away too long. We'll have to find a volunteer.' Perez checked his watch. '9:25. I'd best start hanging around here playing with myself. You two go look for those girls.'

'Hightower told me he left here around four. Got back to the hotel 4:30.'

Perez spluttered over his coffee. 'What? That's seven hours here.'

'Have a nice day, Lieutenant,' Leroy grinned as he and Quinn got up. Perez muttered something in Spanish and picked up his attaché case. Back down in the lobby, Leroy and Quinn split up, leaving the lieutenant to descend the escalator alone and look business-like.

Quinn was assigned to the upper level, and spent the next few hours looking busy, and watching. He called his wife Holly a couple of times, just to relieve the boredom, and to look authentic.

'Jeez, Ray; that must be so boring,' she had said.

'It is, but I keep telling you police work is mostly boring and routine.'

Leroy stayed on the lower level, doing the same. He wanted somebody to call on his cell phone, just to blend in more: he was on the verge of calling Joanna, when his phone rang. It was the driver of the patrol car which had stopped by the *Europa* restaurant.

'Who did you get to speak to?' Leroy asked. 'Was the owner there?'

'Guy called Dudley? Yes, he was there. We talked to him.'

'How did he react when you told him Mets had been murdered?'

'You know, Detective, he didn't seem concerned. Said something like, "he wasn't a good worker, easily replaced."'

'All heart.'

'Did he seem surprised?'

'I can't be sure. A tad, maybe.'

'What about the rest of the staff?'

'We told them, and asked when they had seen him last. Those who could, said they hadn't seen him for a few days.'

'How do you mean those who could?'

A lot of the guys there are European, Detective. Didn't understand English. One of the waiters had to translate. A couple of guys in the kitchen seemed to get upset at the news.'

'Okay. Anything else?'

'No, that's pretty much it. I dropped a report into your station, left it on your desk. Just a list of who we saw and spoke to, and what they told us. Like I've just told you.'

Meanwhile, Lieutenant Perez was occupying himself with blending in with the surroundings. He had several work calls to make, and so spent a lot of time on his phone, as were many of the other suits around. His police badge gained him access into the naturalization ceremony before he lunched alone, and also into the American Society of Cataract and Refractive Surgery convention.

At just after 4PM, he left the Center and took a cab back to the Stocker. Not having spotted anybody remotely like either of the two girls, Leroy and Quinn followed him back, heading directly for the parking garage.

Perez was aware that Hightower met up with one of the girls at the hotel swimming pool, so headed up there at

5:30. Being wired up, he was unable to actually swim, but got himself a Pepsi and sat on one of the loungers with a newspaper. He remained there until 6:45, having made no contact.

As he sat in the restaurant for dinner, he continually looked around. The restaurant was half full, all with men and woman obviously in town on business. He was sure he recognised two men from the opticians' convention.

After dinner, he headed into the bar. Ordering another Pepsi, he found himself a table and sat with his notepad and tablet, pretending to be working.

The bar was not particularly busy, just a steady procession of men and women arriving, having a drink or two, and leaving. Leaving with the person with whom they came in.

10:15, and only three other tables were occupied, all by men and one woman on laptops. Two men sat alone at the bar: one was chatting with the bartender. There was also a girl sitting alone at the bar. She had just arrived, coming in while Perez was in the men's room.

The man who had been talking with the bartender then took a call. As he spoke on his phone, he got up off his stool and began to pace up and down as he spoke. His pacing eventually took him out of the bar.

The girl then moved to sit next to the other man at the bar. She spoke to him briefly: Perez could see him say something to her, then the man's gaze returned to his phone. The girl sat up and spoke to the bartender. Then she was on her phone. As she made her call, the man got up and left.

Now the girl was pacing up and down a little as she made her call. Continuing with her call, she walked past the table where Perez was sitting and into the restroom. She was still talking as she passed him, but was talking too quietly for him to hear what she was saying.

Perez pressed the button on his signet ring. 'Stand by, guys,' he said quietly.

'Ten four,' came Leroy's voice in his ear.

A few moments later she came out of the restroom. The man from earlier had returned to the bar, having finished his call. Perez was scribbling nonsense on his notepad, but out of the corner of his eye he could see the girl pause ten feet away from him. He glanced quickly at her.

She was Caucasian, with dark shoulder-length hair. She was wearing a tight-fitting dress, the whiteness of its material accentuating her tanned face, arms and long legs. She was fumbling in the little white purse she was carrying.

After a few moments' fumbling, she stepped over to Perez.

'I'm sorry to bother you,' she said, 'but do you have a light? I think I've left mine in my room.'

Perez reached into his pocket. 'No problem,' he said, holding it out so she could light her cigarette. It was long and thin: one of those menthol brands, he thought.

She took a long drag and blew the smoke out. 'Thanks,' she said. 'I needed that.' She looked around. 'Though I don't think I'm allowed to smoke in here.'

'I don't think you are,' Perez smiled up at her.

She shook her head. There was an empty glass on the next table and she stubbed out the cigarette in it.

'Look,' she said. 'I know I can't smoke in here, but you gave me a light all the same. Let me get you a drink.'

'No, it's okay,' Perez said, hoping she would not take a refusal.

'No, I insist. What are you drinking?'

He laughed. 'All right. Jim Beam and Pepsi.'

'Cool, she said, and walked over to the bar. After a few minutes, she returned with his drink and a white wine for herself. 'Mind if I join you?' she asked. 'I hate drinking alone.'

Perez pulled out a chair. 'Be my guest.' She sat down. 'You in town on business?' he asked. 'LACC?'

She shook her head. 'Well, part business, part vacation. I'm here with a girlfriend.' She laughed. 'A girl *friend*, not a girlfriend, I mean. She's here for an audition.'

'Oh, not *America's Got Talent*?' he asked, recalling the poster at the Convention Center.

The girl laughed. 'No, nothing like that. For a TV pilot. She's auditioning somewhere off Santa Monica Boulevard.'

'Still? It's way past ten.'

She paused a beat. 'I think there's a lot of people being auditioned.'

'And she's joining you here when she's done?'

She nodded. 'U-huh.'

Perez sat upright, nodding and smiling. He held out his hand. 'My name's Roman, by the way.'

She shook his hand. 'Pleased to meet you, Roman. My name's Paula.' She looked around and moved closer to Perez. 'My friends call me Pinky.'

'Pinky?' asked Perez, casually pressing his ring. 'What an unusual name.'

CHAPTER FORTY-THREE

'THAT'S IT,' SAID Leroy. 'Let's go. He's made contact.' He and Quinn leapt out of the car and ran toward the stairs.

Meanwhile, up in the bar, Perez was engaged in deep conversation with Paula, aka Pinky.

'That *is* an unusual name,' he had said.

Moving slightly closer, she ran her index finger up and down his hand. He could smell her perfume: while not knowing the brand, he recognised it as something his wife kept, to use for special occasions.

'Would you like to know why they call me Pinky?' she purred. He sipped his drink and nodded.

Drawing a circle on his hand with her fingertip, she licked her lips. 'Maybe you'll find out later.'

He nodded eagerly. 'Will your friend be joining you here?'

Pinky ran one hand down the side of her body. 'She will. Soon.' She nodded down at his whisky and cola. 'You've not finished your drink yet.'

'No, I haven't.' Perez downed the drink he had bought himself - the straight Pepsi - then took a mouthful of the one she had bought. He could taste the Jim Beam: maybe there was another taste in there somewhere?

Leroy and Quinn had arrived in the lobby. There was no need to rush in guns blazing: the lieutenant would not be in any danger at this time. The lobby was quite busy. A group of tourists were in the process of checking in. Duty Manager Katherine Huth was clearly working tonight. She looked up from her screen as Leroy walked across the lobby. They made brief eye contact, then one of the tourists asked her something, so she turned her head away. Two small groups of people were gathered around the indoor plants in the centre: as Leroy and Quinn walked past them, both groups moved *en masse* towards one of the restaurants.

They paused in the entrance to the bar, easily able to see the lieutenant and the girl sitting at a table. She was sitting with her back to them; he casually made eye contact. They walked up to the table. As they approached, Perez reached into his pocket and took out his badge.

'Peek-a-boo, Pinky,' he said.

Her eyes wide open in astonishment, she stared up at Leroy and Quinn, who were by now standing over her. 'You're five-oh?' she mouthed.

'You got it in one,' Leroy replied as he and Quinn each pulled up a chair. 'Now, where's your friend?'

'What friend?'

'Don't bullshit me, honey. Your girlfriend.'

Pinky looked away. 'She's in the other bar.'

'Doing what? Looking for another john?'

'We're not hookers.'

'No, of course you're not. You packing?'

'No.'

'Show me your bag,' said Perez.

Pinky bit her lip and tossed the little black bag over to him. He looked inside. 'Shall we pat you down in here?'

'You can kiss my ass,' she muttered and reached down under her skirt, glaring at Leroy as he watched. Even though her legs were bare, she was wearing a black garter, holding a small handgun. Leroy reached down and took it.

'Glock 26?' he asked, discretely checking the weapon. It was about the size of Pinky's hand, metallic pink and titanium. There was an ornate monogram on the barrel. She shrugged as Leroy emptied the chamber and barrel and slipped it into his coat pocket.

'You stay here with me,' Perez said, 'while they go get your friend. No tricks. Or shall we cuff you here and now?'

Pinky said nothing; just shook her head and stared at the floor.

'What's your girlfriend wearing?' Leroy asked as he got up.

'Green dress,' came the reply. She remained staring at the floor.

'What's her name?'

'Roxy.'

'Back soon. Don't go away.' Leroy and Quinn headed over to the other bar. Standing in the doorway, they could see Roxy sitting at the bar, talking to a man.

Quinn looked around. 'That has to be her. Black girl, green dress. Nobody else matching that here.'

'The dude she's talking to: is he Asian?'

'No, Caucasian.'

'Come on, then.'

The walked up to the girl. The man she was talking to saw them approach and looked up. She turned round.

'Your name Roxy?' Leroy asked. He held out his badge.

'I thought I could smell bacon,' she spat. The man turned around and slid a couple of feet away from her.

'Watch yourself, honey,' said Leroy, 'or I'll book you for having an offensive mouth as well as extortion, accessory to murder *et cetera, et cetera.*'

'I didn't kill no one,' she protested.

Ignoring her, Leroy asked, 'You carrying as well as your friend?' as he pointed down to her thigh. Silently, she reached down and pulled out exactly the same handgun as Pinky. He emptied it and put it with the cartridges into his other pocket. 'Let's go meet Pinky,' he said as he took her by the arm.

'She's nothing to do with me,' the man spluttered. 'She just started talking to me.'

'Then you had a lucky escape,' said Leroy. 'My partner here will just take some details; I expect another officer will be along in due course to get a statement.'

While Quinn checked the man's ID and got confirmation that he was staying at the hotel, Leroy led Roxy to the other bar. 'And what do your friends call you?' he asked.

'Perky, 'she snapped.

She tried to pull away as he laughed, only for him to tighten his grip.

Back in the other bar, he told her to sit next to Pinky.

'Pinky, this is Perky; Perky, this is Pinky,' Leroy said as he sat down himself. 'Now, where's your friend? Your Chinese friend?'

Both said nothing.

Leroy sighed. 'So - you were planning on getting my lieutenant here high, then taking him up to his room when - let me guess: your friend arrived to take some pictures. Am I right?'

Perky just glared at the two men, then at Pinky as her friend replied, 'That's right.' Then she looked up at Leroy. 'Anyway, whataya talking about, accessory to murder? What murder?'

Perez gave her a wide smile. 'Or maybe murder one. You remember William Kirk?'

The expression on Pinky's face changed as it sunk in. 'He's dead?'

Perky looked at the floor. 'I know. Chong told me,' she muttered.

'I didn't know that!' Pinky exclaimed. 'I swear!'

'What's his name, and where is he now?' Leroy asked Pinky.

'He calls himself Chong Lee. He's over the street in his car, waiting to hear from us.'

'Over the street?'

'The lot out front of the train depot.'

'What's the plan, then?' asked Leroy as Quinn joined them.

Pinky looked over at Perky who reluctantly replied. 'Once the guy's totally passed out, we call him, and he comes to the room.'

'Then what?' Perez asked.

Perky looked at him as if to say *do I have to spell it out?* 'We pose for the pictures, then leave. Next morning, he goes back to the room, shows the scumbag the pictures, then puts the deal together.'

'Puts the deal together? You mean blackmail him?'

Perky shrugged, petulantly. 'Whatever.'

Perez said, 'Let's all go up to the room, get things moving.'

The officers stood, Leroy and Quinn taking Pinky and Perky by the arm. As she stood, Perky's arm shot out and she knocked Perez's drink on the floor. The glass smashed and the Jim Beam and cola began to soak into the carpet.

'Nice try,' Perez said, crouching down. He picked up the still intact bottom of the glass, a tiny amount of the brownish liquid swilling around in between the jagged edges.

'We only need a tiny sample,' Quinn explained as Perez produced a clear plastic evidence bag and slipped the remains of the glass inside.

The bartender watched as Perez led Leroy and Pinky and Quinn and Perky out of the bar and into the lobby. Leroy indicated over to him about the broken glass on the floor.

As the five of them walked over to the elevators Leroy gave Katherine Huth one more glance: she seemed to still be checking in guests.

'Nice view,' Perez said cheerily as the elevator headed up to the ninth floor.

Once inside 922, Leroy told them to sit on the bed. 'Don't try anything; otherwise we'll restrain you now.'

To Perky's annoyance, Pinky repeated that she had nothing to do with Kirk being killed.

'Save that for later,' Leroy told her. 'Now: who calls him?'

'I do,' Perky said.

'Call or text?'

'Usually text.'

'Text him now, then. Remember: *exactly* as he's expecting. No tricks; no attempts to warn him. Otherwise… Well, you know what otherwise. Show me the message before you send it.'

Fixing him with an angry stare, Roxy/Perky took out her phone. She quickly typed a message, then held the phone out to Leroy. He took it and read the message, then tabbed down the list of her sent messages. She tried to protest but he put out his hand to silence her. Eventually he found a previous message to Lee, the exact wording as the message she had just typed. 'Good girl,' he said and pressed *Send*. She snatched the phone back.

'How long?' Perez asked.

'Five minutes. Maybe ten.'

'Ray, you go wait down the corridor,' Leroy said. 'The lieutenant and I'll wait here.'

As Quinn left, Perez stepped into the bathroom. He called for back-up, then remained in the bathroom, waiting. Leroy pulled out his own Glock and sat on the chair, four feet away from the edge of the bed where the girls were perched.

The girls flinched as he cocked his weapon.

'Not long to wait,' he said.

CHAPTER FORTY-FOUR

'So, you two are hookers, right?'

Perky looked at Leroy with contempt, then returned her gaze to the floor.

It was Pinky who replied. 'We're actresses.'

From the confines of the bathroom, Perez laughed.

'Porn actresses?' suggested Leroy.

'Adult performers.'

'That why you don't mind humping dirty old scumbags?'

Now it was Perky who replied. 'We never humped anyone. You can't hump a limp dick.'

'Honey, that's what happens when you fill a guy full of R2. So you just staged the pictures?'

'Whatever,' Perky said, dismissively.

'And what about Chong Lee? He comes up here to shoot it all? What's his story, anyway? He Chinese?'

Pinky slowly nodded her head. 'I think he said he was from Singapore. That makes him Chinese, I guess.'

'No,' said Leroy. 'They're different.'

'Whatever,' repeated Perky.

Pinky was just about to answer when there were three taps on the door. Both girls looked at each other nervously.

Leroy stood up. 'Go answer the door, the same as you did before. And remember, no tricks, no warnings. *Capisce*?'

Nodding once, Perky got up and slowly walked over to the door. Leroy moved so he was out of sight from the doorway. Perky checked the spyhole and slowly opened the door.

Leroy heard a man's voice, slightly accented. 'Man, this guy was fast going under.'

As Chong Lee stepped into the room, Leroy stepped forward covering him. Perez did the same. 'Freeze. LAPD,' Leroy called out.

Panicked, Lee stepped back reaching inside his coat.

'Freeze!' Leroy repeated. 'Last warning.'

Lee took his hand away. He was almost backed out into the hotel corridor, but Quinn was now behind him, weapon poised. Quinn shoved Lee back into the room and shut the door.

'Assume the position,' Leroy instructed as Quinn manoeuvred Lee up against the wall and frisked him. He recovered a Glock, similar to the girls', but all-over titanium. Quinn unhooked his set of handcuffs and cuffed Lee. Perez was now doing the same to the girls. As they were being restrained, Leroy read them their Miranda warning, their rights.

'You have the right to remain silent and refuse to answer questions.

'Anything you say may be used against you in a court of law.

'You have the right to an attorney before speaking to the police and to have an attorney present during questioning now or in the future.

'If you cannot afford an attorney, one will be appointed for you before any questioning if you wish.

'If you decide to answer questions now without an attorney present, you will still have the right to stop answering at any time until you talk to an attorney.

'Knowing and understanding your rights as I have explained them to you, are you willing to answer my questions without an attorney present?'

Lee called out, still pressed against the wall, 'We got nothing to say to you pigs, do we girls?' The girls said nothing.

Leroy continued, 'If you are not a United States citizen, you may contact your country's consulate prior to any questioning.

'Do you understand each of these rights I have explained to you?'

The girls each showed a trace of confirmation; Lee remained defiant.

'Having these rights in mind, do you wish to talk to us now?'

Lee, Pinky and Perky each said nothing.

'Okay,' said Leroy. 'Let's get these beautiful people out of here.'

'The back-up car should be downstairs by now,' Perez said as they ushered the prisoners out of the room.

'Pay attention to the view, people,' Leroy said as the elevator took them down to the lobby. 'It's gonna be a while before you see it again.'

'Screw you, man,' Lee spat.

As the elevator doors slid open at the lobby level, a group of surprised guests parted to allow the six of them passage. Noticing Lee and the girls were handcuffed, some of the lobby guests began whispering; a couple took out their phones and began taking pictures.

Two patrol cars were waiting outside the hotel, their four officers waiting in the doorway.

'You guys take the girls,' Leroy said. 'We'll take him in ours.'

The uniformed officers took Pinky and Perky away, as Leroy took Lee's manacled arm. 'Come on, handsome; we're downstairs.'

'You two take him,' said Perez. 'I'll catch you up.'

'Where you going?' Leroy asked.

'Need to tell the hotel manager we've been here. Courtesy thing.'

Leroy and Quinn took Lee back down to their car. Perez arrived five minutes later, and sat in the back with Lee.

'Right. Let's go,' Leroy said.

'What about that bitch from the hotel?' Lee asked.

'What bitch from the hotel?' asked Leroy.

'The one who'd been passing on the names of likely johns.' The three detectives looked at him. 'Why? You don't think those dudes were lucky finds?'

'What bitch from the hotel?' Leroy asked again.

'The manager. Don't recall her name.'

'Katherine Huth? She's upstairs. I saw her when we got here.'

'Yeah, that's her name,' Lee said, matter-of-factly.

'She's gone,' Perez said. 'When I asked to speak to the manager, nobody could find them; then one of the porters said, "I think Katherine's gone home sick." So I spoke to somebody else.'

'I'll bet she's gone home sick,' Leroy said. 'Ray: can you call her in? Get them to put out an APB on her. Don't worry, Mr Lee. She won't get far.'

CHAPTER FORTY-FIVE

BY THE TIME they had returned to the station with Chong Lee, the two girls had already been processed and were in individual holding cells.

'Both were carrying driver's licences,' said the desk sergeant. 'Paula Martinez and Roxanne DuPrat. Both have form for possession of Mary Jane. DuPrat was the most recent - six months ago.'

'Here's one more for you.' Leroy pulled Lee over to the sergeant. 'This one's from Singapore, apparently, so he may not have a record here.'

'He had his Miranda warning also?'

'Yup. Plus the piece about his consulate. If you can get him processed as soon as you can, I'd be obliged. We need to talk with him like yesterday.'

'Sure thing, Sam.'

The sergeant was as good as his word, and after Leroy and Quinn had made a bathroom stop, checked their desks and emails and got more coffee, Chong Lee was ready for them. Leroy noticed on his desk the report left by the patrolmen who had visited the Europa restaurant. He carried it to the interrogation room, flicking through it as he walked.

'Has he asked for an attorney?' Leroy asked the duty officer.

The officer shook his head. 'He's said nothing, apart from using the bathroom.'

'Well, he's had the mandatory warnings. We're under no obligation to wait until he decides on an attorney; let's get started, Ray.' He looked back at the officer. 'Has Lieutenant Perez been down?' Then to Quinn. 'I wondered if he wanted to sit in, given his involvement.'

'He came down looking for you, Sam. Then said something about having to check out.'

Leroy chuckled. 'Sure, thanks.' Then to Quinn again. 'His hotel room. He can watch through the glass later if he wishes.'

Chong Lee was waiting in the interrogation room, sitting one side of the table. The officer with him left as Leroy and Quinn sat down. Leroy began recording, saying aloud their names, then the date and time.

'Let's cut to the chase, Mr Lee: did you kill William Kirk?'

Lee said nothing.

'William Kirk was shot, shot to the head; and I'll take book that the slug we took out of his head will match your little Glock. You guys get a discount on the Glocks? You know, your little blue one and the girls' little pink ones?'

Lee said nothing.

'So you shot him, then you cut his head off, for Christ's sake.'

Lee said nothing.

'You're from Singapore, right?'

Lee looked up at Leroy; he looked surprised.

'They have the death penalty for murder there, don't they? They must do: they have it for most other things, so I understand.' Leroy leaned forward. 'You want to know something? We have the death penalty here in California. There are seven hundred guys waiting on death row, and I'm going to make it my personal mission to get you fast-tracked.'

That was enough for Lee. 'All right, all right. But I didn't kill him.'

'Who did, then?'

'It was her from the hotel.'

'Katherine Huth? You telling me she killed William Kirk?'

Lee nodded.

'How did she do it? When? Why?'

As Leroy and Lee spoke, Quinn was casually flicking the report about the restaurant.

'When… Kirk?'

'William Kirk.'

'When Kirk told me he was a private investigator, I called my boss. He told me to get Kirk to that parking garage at Union Station, top level. We parked there, and she came up and shot him through the head.'

'You said your boss. So Huth's not working on her own?'

'No. There's a guy as well. She had him deal with the body.'

'Who is this guy? You got a name?'

Lee traced an invisible line around the table. 'Guy called Dudley.'

Leroy sat back and looked over at Quinn. 'Andrew Dudley?'

'Yeah, that's the guy.'

'How did you meet them?'

'Last Christmas, I tried to steal his car. He caught me, threatened to call you guys, have me deported, unless I did stuff for him. He said he wanted me to "sell insurance", so he said. He said he knew someone - Katherine – who worked in some hotel Downtown. Said she'd give me the names of guys who were likely subjects.'

'What about those girls? Did he or Huth provide them?'

'No, I had to find them.'

'Where did you find them?'

'On Craigslist.'

Leroy laughed. 'On Craigslist? Their listing, or you posted one?'

'Their posting.'

They *are* hookers, then?'

'I think they're escorts. They told me they were actresses.'

'Sure. Same listing for both of them?'

Lee nodded.

'So, you found the girls online, and explained what you wanted them to do?'

'Yes. They were to be well paid, but insisted there would be no actual sex with the guys.'

'Which there wouldn't be if they were full of roofies. It was rohypnol you used?'

Lee nodded.

'Where did it come from? Who was the supplier?'

'She provided it?'

'Huth?'

'Yes. She said it came from over the border.'

'The stuff's legal in Mexico. So once the guys were out of it, you showed up and took the pictures. Camera or on your cell?'

'iPad.'

'Which we have downstairs.'

'So next morning, you'd show up and begin the extortion process.'

Lee nodded. 'Usually a couple of grand that day, then I'd give them a box number for the next payments.'

'Or you'd put the stuff online.'

'Yeah, something like that.'

'Is any of it online nevertheless?'

Lee nodded. 'Yeah, some of it went on already. Porn sites.'

'Going back to William Kirk, why did you cut his head off?'

'I didn't do that. I didn't kill him, either; I told you that. His head was on when they took his body away.'

'Who took the body away?'

'Two guys in some kind of truck.'

'A pick-up?'

'Sure, it was a pick up. They were already waiting in the parking garage.'

At that point, Quinn tapped Leroy on the arm. 'Sam...'

'Hmm?'

'You got a second?'

Leroy said, for the benefit of the recording, that they would be taking a break. They gathered outside the room.

'What's up?' Leroy asked.

'The report the patrol car left us about the restaurant.' Quinn showed Leroy the second page. 'Look at the list of employees they spoke to. The kitchen staff.'

Leroy scanned the list. One name stood out like a bikini in a snowstorm.

Rudi Johansson.

'Son of a bitch,' Leroy whispered. 'His truck was never stolen. He'd just gotten rid of it.'

'And I'll bet Evald Mets was the other guy,' Quinn added.

'Has to be. Ray, we were searching for a connection, and now we've found it.' He turned back to the interrogation room. 'Let's get him back into his cell. He and the girls can wait. If Huth's gone missing, she has to be with Dudley. We need to go get him.'

'Restaurant or house?'

'If they've guessed we're on to them, the house is the best bet. I'll get the lieutenant to send somebody to the restaurant just in case, but we'll head up to his house. If the R2 came from Mexico he might have a contact there: we need to get to him - them - before they get over the border.'

CHAPTER FORTY-SIX

EVEN AT THAT late hour, traffic on the freeway was heavy, so Leroy had to make full use of the lights and siren.

'If we don't get there in time, we've lost him - both of them – for good,' Leroy said grimly. 'Ten to one they'll head for the border.' Lieutenant Perez said he would go to the restaurant with two others, but the smart money was on the house.

To the side of the road, Quinn could see the illuminated Capitol Records building, on the Hollywood and Vine intersection, its thirteen floors constructed to resemble a stack of 45rpm records and stylus. The blinking light on top of the tower spells out *Hollywood* in Morse code. 'This case was never about Hollywood,' he said.

Leroy agreed. 'No, it never was. Apart from the fact that one of the witnesses just happened to be a screenwriter, and not a very successful one at that, there's no connection whatsoever. If we hadn't chanced to be on the Kelton case, some other poor sucker would be doing this.'

They exited the freeway at Burbank Boulevard and sped east. At the intersection with Lankershim a patrol car joined them, its own lights flashing and siren wailing.

'Nearly there,' said Leroy, as they made a sharp left across westbound traffic, earning several blasts from drivers' horns, drivers who clearly did not understand what police lights and sirens meant. 'What the hell's that?' Leroy asked looking to his right.

To his right, on one of the cross streets was what looked like a beam of yellow flickering colour, lighting up the night sky. Their GPS told them the next street was Dudley's, and as soon as they made the right they could see that one of the houses was on fire.

Quinn squinted against the brightness of the flames. 'You have to be...'

'I don't believe this,' Leroy said, pulling up with a squeal of brakes. 'It's Dudley's house.' They both leapt out of the car, joined by the two uniformed officers from the patrol car.

The house was for the moment intact, but the fire was beginning to take hold. Half a dozen neighbours were out in the street, some fully dressed, some in dressing gowns.

Leroy turned to one of the uniformed officers. 'Call the Fire Department.'

'My husband's called 911 already,' one of the neighbours called out.

'How long?' Leroy asked. He had to raise his voice over the crackling sound from the fire.

'Ten minutes, maybe more,' came the reply.

'This was deliberate,' Quinn said. 'They've been here to destroy any evidence. Oh, shit – Sam, look up there!'

They looked up and saw a figure in an upstairs window. The window was open, smoke pouring out. It was dark and the air filled with smoke, but from the flames below, they could see it was not Andrew Dudley or Katherine Huth, but Rudi Johansson.

'Why doesn't he jump?' asked Leroy. 'It's only one floor. Jump!' he called out.

'I can't, I can't,' Johansson screamed back.

Leroy looked at Quinn. 'We can't wait for the fire department to get here. I'm going in to get him.'

'Sam…?'

'I have to, Ray.'

'I'm coming too.'

'No way, Ray. It doesn't need two of us.'

'Way, Sam. Come on, before it gets worse.'

The onlookers gasped as Sam Leroy and Ray Quinn both inhaled as much as they could and ran into the house.

Had they looked the other way, they would have seen the red flashing lights of the two fire appliances halfway down the street.

CHAPTER FORTY-SEVEN

IN THE MOVIES, or on television, when a scene is taking place in a burning building, you will see a chair on fire, maybe a couch. Curtains will be burning, maybe stairs. The protagonists will parry against each other, neatly skirting the burning items. Visibility will be excellent.

The reality is very different. Visibility is poor, almost zero. Most people who die in house fires rarely get the chance to burn to death: the smoke gets them before long before the flames do. Once ignited, the flames will quickly consume wooden furniture, shelves, chairs. More and more heat is generated. The temperature just below the ceiling rises to 400 degrees Fahrenheit, which is hot enough to kill. This intense heat comes with very thick smoke which will rise to waist level. This smoke would be made up of arsenic, of lead, and of irritants such as nitrogen oxide, hydrogen chloride, and ammonia.

Fire can spread in two ways: by direct contact or by auto-ignition, which is the temperature at which objects will spontaneously combust without being touched by the fire. The type of wood used in house construction and furniture will auto-ignite at between 600 and 750 degrees.

When Leroy and Quinn entered the house, the fire had clearly been burning for some time, and there was not much time left before flashover. They both held handkerchiefs over their mouths and ran up the stairs, where they knew Johansson was trapped. The stairs were carpeted, and smoke was rising from the carpet. They did not have long.

At the top of the stairs, they had to make a one-eighty to get to the room at the front of the house where he was. Both jumped as a burning cabinet fell off the wall, breaking up and smashing whatever glass items were inside. The fire from there ignited the carpet.

The heat was becoming unbearable. Synthetic materials found in furniture, carpets, and bedding generate enormous heat, soon reaching five hundred degrees. The blaze must have started downstairs: now it had penetrated the walls and ceiling and was travelling through the shafts between the walls and between the floors.

The door to the room where Johansson was sheltering was already on fire and was hanging burning from its hinges. Through the smoke, they could see his figure moving anxiously from one foot to the other. Leroy lashed out with his foot and kicked the door off its hinges. Part of the door frame collapsed on the floor, also in flames.

All three men were coughing by now. Leroy beckoned to Johansson. 'Come on,' he cried through heavy coughing, 'we don't have long. The whole place is gonna go up!'

Johannson was frozen to the spot. Quinn grabbed him by the arm and both he and Leroy manhandled him out of the room and to the top of the stairs.

The carpet on the stairs was now beginning to ignite. The three men half ran, half slid down the stairs. As they got to the foot, Leroy realised something.

'What about the maid?' he asked Johansson. 'Is she here?'

Johansson stared blankly into Leroy's eyes.

'The maid, Godammit! The housekeeper! The little Mexican woman! Is she here?'

Johansson's mouth opened and shut a few times, but no sound came out.

'Get him out of here,' Leroy said to Quinn. 'I'll quickly check out back.' Quinn opened his mouth to protest, but Leroy pushed him and Johansson towards the door. 'Go; I'll just be a few seconds.'

Reluctantly, Quinn dragged the still paralysed Johansson to the door while Leroy ran through the smoke to the kitchen. The kitchen door was open and bizarrely the flames had not taken hold here as badly as other parts of the house. Clearly the fire had not started here.

'Hello?' he called out. 'Anybody here?' As if anyone could have heard him over the roar and crackle of the fire.

He turned and headed to the door, turning round briefly at the sound of a crash, as the kitchen ceiling caved in. Still coughing, he ran out into the cool night air. Two fire department trucks were now on the scene, and six or seven firefighters were tackling the blaze. He saw that Lieutenant Perez had arrived, and saw Rudi Johansson sprawled on the grass, coughing.

Leroy looked around.

No Ray Quinn.

'Where's Quinn?' he shouted at anybody who was listening. 'Where's Ray?'

Perez ran over to him. 'Sam, he went back in for you.'

Frantically, Leroy looked back at the burning house. The roof was almost destroyed, the cross beams showing against the flames, like a grotesque rib cage.

Leroy swung round to one of the firefighters. 'Douse me!' he yelled.

'Wha -?' asked the fireman, still looking up at the direction of water from his hose.

'Douse me, hose me!'

Knowing better than to argue, the firefighter turned his hose on Leroy. The fierce jet of water knocked Leroy over and back at least six feet. Now drenched, he ran back into the house.

'Sam, no!' Perez called out as the firefighter aimed his jet of water back at the burning roof.

Inside, the temperature was rapidly rising. Once it reaches 1100 degrees, you will have flashover. At that point, everything is now in flames. Oxygen is sucked out, consumed by the sudden combustion. Windows shatter. Flames shoot out of doors and windows. The whole place fills with hot, thick, deadly smoke and is by now impenetrable.

A helicopter was hovering overhead, making sure this blaze would make prime-time news, and the crowd on the street had grown.

The patrolwoman who had driven Perez to the scene began to cry.

'Sweet Jesus,' the lieutenant whispered, watching helplessly as the roof finally gave way, its burning beams crashing into the house below.

CHAPTER FORTY-EIGHT

ANDREW DUDLEY AND Katherine Huth high-fived each other as they passed the 905 intersection. In a few short minutes the freeway on which they were travelling, the I-805, would be merging with the I-5, which would take them to the border. Once through the checkpoint, the I-5 would become the MEX-1, and they would be home free.

'Here we are, baby,' he said. 'San Ysidro. Almost there. Then we head for my contact just outside of Tijuana, and we're history.'

There is, of course, an extradition treaty between Mexico and the United States, but the authorities would need to catch them first.

'You're sure about this?' she asked. 'About being history, I mean?'

'Listen,' Dudley said, oozing confidence and reassurance. 'The cops would have guessed we'd have gone to the house. By the time they and the Fire Department, whoever checks that stuff, realise we weren't in the fire, then we'll have gotten over the border, met up with my guy, gotten ourselves new identities, and be heading off.

'We won't stay in Mexico: it's too close, and the authorities will most likely be trying to kiss the President's ass, so we can head south, try somewhere like Guatemala, or Honduras. For the time being, the money's no object.'

'Okay,' she said, quietly.

'We can get ourselves a nice little *adobe* by the sea, and spend the next few years taking it easy. You okay with all this?'

'Yeah; sure I am. It's just sudden, that's all.'

'That got forced on us. That asshole from Alabama started that chain reaction. But it was always going to happen, eventually. Just sooner than I expected.'

'Will we get over the border okay?'

'Sure we will. It's always been much easier to go south than to come back; you know that.' He put his hand on hers. 'Speaking of going south…'

She took his hand away. 'Let's get over the border first. Andy - what's that?'

'Looks like… Shit!'

'They for us?'

'Maybe they are, maybe they're not. But they won't be looking for wheels like this.' When they set off from Burbank, Dudley had eschewed the Ford Mustang in the garage, and had taken a less conspicuous Roadtrek 210.

Dudley slowed down to fifty-five to pass the patrol car, which had in fact stopped in front of another vehicle which had broken down. In the distance, they could see the border: with a sense of anticipation and excitement, Dudley pressed down on the gas.

The row of booths had to be only a mile away.

Half a mile away, and five police vehicles appeared from a side road, lights flashing, sirens wailing. In the lead car, the officer in front was waving a flashlight for them to pull over.

Dudley pulled over and stopped. The lead car stopped in front and the driver got out.

They could see the border not five hundred yards away.

Dudley's foot hovered over the gas pedal.

'Well, my darling,' he asked. 'Is this our *Thelma and Louise* moment?'

CHAPTER FORTY-NINE

THE FIRE HAD taken hold.

Perez watched on helplessly as the roof collapsed, shooting flames and sparks high into the air. The Fire Chief had called the television network as he was concerned the draught from the helicopter blades might fan the flames.

He could hear some of the neighbours talking: one of the women was wailing that there were two cops in there. The patrolwoman with him fought hard to contain her tears.

He looked round as two ambulances arrived on the scene; then back at the house.

It would not be long before the second floor collapsed.

The lieutenant's radio crackled: still staring mesmerised into the conflagration, he answered. It was the news that Dudley and Huth had been apprehended just yards from the Mexican border. Now they were being brought back to Los Angeles. Perez took the call with no emotion in his voice, just staring with disbelief into the flames.

'Look!'

He was brought out of his trance by the cry of one of the neighbours.

In the burning house's doorway, amidst the black, acrid smoke billowing out of the inferno, and backlit by the flames inside, was a shape. It was moving. Its form was indistinct at first, then became clearer. One figure, limping, and carrying another on its back, fireman's lift style.

'*Gracias a Dios*,' Perez whispered, rushing forward with two of the firefighters.

The limping form was that of Sam Leroy, carrying his partner on his back.

Then, suddenly: flashpoint.

The temperature inside the house hit 1100 Fahrenheit. Those outside could hear the loud rush of air. The windows blew out and jets of fire shot out of the empty spaces. Leroy and Quinn were knocked to the ground by the backdraft: one of the firemen turned his hose on them, immediately extinguishing the flames on the back of Leroy's coat. Leroy yelled in pain as Perez dragged him away from the house; one of the firefighters did the same to the unconscious Quinn.

The Fire Department was beginning to gain control over the blaze, but not before the second floor collapsed with a deafening roar. More flames and smoke burst out of the windows.

The paramedics from one of the ambulances had already taken Johansson; now they rushed over to Quinn, turned him on his back and began CPR.

Leroy was conscious: black with soot and drenched with the water from the hose, he crawled over to his partner. Nodded to the paramedic who told him, 'He'll be okay.'

He sat up, rubbing his injured leg.

Then threw up.

CHAPTER FIFTY

WEST L.A. STATION was busy that night. For 2AM, at any rate.

As well as the normal clientele of pushers, drunks, hookers, a team of FBI investigators had been on an operation in the area, and had made five arrests. They had requested that the five be held at West L.A. while transportation could be arranged, and this was agreed. Plus, there were Chong Lee, Pinky, Perky, and now Katherine Huth and Andrew Dudley. Rudi Johansson had been taken to the Providence Saint Joseph Medical Center on South Buena Vista Street, as had Leroy and Quinn. All three were slightly more than 'walking wounded', but were no longer in the ER.

The hospital had not been able to tell yet when Leroy and Quinn would be able to be discharged: as it was not feasible to hold the five suspects until either had been released, Perez began the interrogation himself.

Huth and Dudley were of course being held separately, and would be interrogated separately. Unlike Chong Lee, they had both insisted on having an attorney present, and so Perez was forced to wait until Dudley's attorney had arrived. This attorney would be acting for both Dudley *and* Huth.

'No surprise there,' Perez remarked when told this.

The attorney, a supercilious, well-tailored twenty-something to whom Perez took an instant dislike, arrived at 9AM. He was, of course, refreshed having had a full night's sleep: Perez, on the other hand, had been up all night, only managing to grab a couple of hours on the couch in his office. His only consolation was that it was unlikely Dudley and Huth had gotten their full eight hours.

Andrew Dudley first.

The attorney sat next to his client, across the table from Perez. The lieutenant leaned forward. 'Let's cut to the chase, Dudley: did you kill William Kirk?'

Dudley looked to his attorney, who showed no reaction, then back to Perez. 'Who?'

'Did you decapitate him? Did you cut off his head?'

'Lieutenant,' the attorney cut in. 'My client knows the meaning of decapitation. With all due respect, I think my client has answered your question.'

'With all due respect,' Perez countered, 'your client hasn't answered my question. I asked if he killed William Kirk. The reply would be *yes* or *no.*'

Dudley looked to the attorney again and back to Perez. 'No, I did not.'

'Did Katherine Huth?'

'You'll need to ask her.'

'What about Evald Mets?'

Dudley said nothing.

'You know - knew - Evald Mets? You must have: he worked for you.'

'Yes, of course I knew Evald. His murder was a tragedy. Why aren't you out there looking for his killer, rather than asking me these ridiculous questions?'

The attorney put a restraining hand on Dudley's arm.

'Let's park those two murders for now,' Perez said quietly. 'First, tell me what you and Ms Huth were doing hurrying to the Mexican border in the middle of the night.'

Another glance to the attorney, who briefly closed his eyes. More subtle than a nod.

'Ms Huth and I... we are an item. We planned a trip there.'

'At midnight?'

'The freeways are quieter at that time.'

'With a trunk containing...' Perez glanced down at his notes. 'Four hundred and seventy-eight thousand dollars? In cash?'

Dudley leaned over and whispered in the attorney's ear; the attorney reciprocated, then spoke.

'My client wishes to invoke his constitutional right to plead the fifth amendment.'

Perez sat back. He was not surprised. 'So you were fleeing the country?'

'My client didn't say that.'

'What about the fire at your house?'

'A fire? At my house? When?'

'Which of course you knew nothing about.'

Dudley held up his hands. 'This is all news to me.'

'And Rudi Johansson? He died in the fire, you know.'

The arrogant expression left Dudley's face for a second, then returned.

'I told you, I have no knowledge of a fire at my house. I was not there, remember?'

Perez continued, 'You see, if it can be established that the fire was started deliberately, then it's murder. You know we have the death penalty in California?'

The attorney spoke. 'Lieutenant, please do not try to threaten my client. As you know, the State has not carried out an execution in over ten years.'

'That is true,' replied Perez, 'but as *you* know, Proposition 66, which California voters approved in 2016, seeks to speed up the process. So,' - as he spoke he leaned forward and looked Dudley in the eye - 'if you and Huth are found guilty of murder, I will make it my personal mission in life to fast-track you both so they lethally inject your ass with all due speed.'

Dudley was starting to look uncomfortable.

'Lieutenant, I must protest,' spluttered the attorney. 'This is absolutely -'

'Shut up,' Dudley said to the attorney, while still staring back at Perez. 'Look, Lieutenant: I want to tell you some things.'

CHAPTER FIFTY-ONE

ROOM 319 AT the Providence Saint Joseph Medical Center
was busy. In addition to the official occupant of the room,
Ray Quinn, who was lying in the bed, Sam Leroy, also
dressed in a hospital gown but with a brown walking cane,
was present. Also in the room were Lieutenant Perez,
Russell Hobson, the ME and one of Leroy's oldest friends,
and Holly Quinn with Joanna Moore. Quinn had been
affected by the partially burned particles in the smoke.
Some had gotten lodged in his lungs. Irritation to the lungs
and digestive system was a possibility, so the doctors
wanted to keep him in for a few more days. Leroy's

symptoms were less severe: he had inhaled some toxic gases which were causing itchy eyes and a sore throat. The doctor said this was caused by inhaling phosgene, which had been given off by burning vinyl. He had also torn ligaments in one leg, when he stumbled down the burning stairs, and by the impact of the flashover.

Alcohol was banned in the hospital, so any toasts had to be with mineral water. Perez held up his in a white plastic cup.

'Well, here's to the successful end to an investigation.'

Leroy held up his cup. 'Here's to you for getting the confessions. Back to behind your desk now?'

'Guess so, but it's a good experience being on the front line again. Like those managers at Wal-Mart who spend a day on the shop floor every so often.'

'Nice analogy, Lieutenant,' laughed Hobson. 'At this point, I need to head back. See you soon, guys.'

'Before you go, Doctor,' Perez said, 'I just need to say that by running back into a burning house not once, but *twice*, Detective Leroy here did one of the most reckless and foolhardy things I've ever seen a police officer do.' He paused for effect. 'And one of the bravest.'

'I think he deserves a medal,' Holly Quinn said, holding her husband's hand. 'Or some kind of commendation.'

'I wouldn't turn down a raise,' Leroy said.

Perez looked over at him. 'A commendation is better for the budget,' he replied with a huge grin on his face.

At that point Leroy's phone bleeped. He checked the screen and read the text message. It was from Sally Duvall: *glad 2 hear u ok. call if u need any tlc ;) xx*. He smiled and returned to the home screen.

'What was it?' Joanna asked.

Leroy slipped the phone back inside his gown. 'Nothing. Just good wishes from an old partner.'

'I think it's time I left as well,' Perez said, after Hobson departed.

'Before you go, Lieutenant,' Leroy asked, 'just how *did* you get the confessions?'

Perez sat at the foot of Quinn's bed and folded his arms.

'Well, it started with Johansson. The poor bastard was so traumatized by the experience of being in the fire: may have been some gratitude to you for saving his life; being pissed at Dudley and Huth for leaving him there. When Huth saw Lee being arrested, she called Dudley and Johansson and they arranged to meet up at Dudley's house. They began to burn all the hard copies of photographs they had – when they were picked up at the border, Dudley had a thumb drive with copies on. Nice piece of evidence. There was an argument about Johansson's share now that Evald Mets - who Dudley had ordered Johansson to kill - had gone. That's how the fire started: Johansson was knocked half-unconscious. By the time he had gotten it together, he was trapped in the blaze.

'Backtracking a tad, they had a nice little racket going on. Huth would identify any family men who had booked into the hotel on business. Those girls would set them up in a kind of honey trap, then Lee would set up the blackmail. Apparently, there are a dozen or so others we haven't looked at yet, but the details are on the thumb drive. So Hightower and Kirk were by no means the only ones.

'When Kirk pulled the gun on Lee, that set alarm bells ringing. Lee called Dudley, who arranged for Huth to pull the trigger; Mets and Johansson who both worked for Dudley at the restaurant, and were - are – illegals, turned up in Johansson's pick-up to get rid of the body.

'They took him up to Mount Lee - no relation - at first. Dudley had told them to dismember the body. That way, he told them, the body parts would be easier to dispose of. Smaller parts would be taken care of by wildlife.

'But when they cut off the head, they started to panic, Johansson said out of disgust, so in their panic, tossed the body in a dumpster.'

'Leaving the head on Mount Lee,' said Leroy.

'Yes. They had just gotten the body in the dumpster, when Harry Webb arrived. Apparently Mets went into panic overdrive at that point: rather than doing as Johansson told him and just quietly driving away, he thought he was getting himself in the clear by 'finding' the body.'

'And that cost him his life?' Quinn said.

'It did. Johansson said Dudley was concerned that Mets would go to us, so told him to deal with him.'

'And now he's turned State's Evidence,' said Leroy. 'Where is he, by the way?'

'He's here. Second floor, under guard. Wants to plea bargain.'

'I'm not surprised. What about Huth and Dudley?'

'They had Dudley's fancy attorney, and Dudley was pleading the fifth right from the start. But I told him Johansson had died in the fire and went down your *did you know we have the death penalty in California?* path.'

'Didn't his fancy attorney see through that?'

'To begin with, but I started talking about Prop 66, and Dudley told his attorney to shut up and confessed. Confessed that he had not actually killed anyone, it all being carried out by Huth and Johansson.'

'Nice guy. The loyal type.'

'Aren't they always? When I got to Huth, she had nowhere to run to.'

A nurse breezed into the room. 'Ladies and gentlemen, Mr Quinn needs to rest now.'

Perez shook hands with everybody else, and left. Holly gave Quinn a long hug and kissed him goodbye. Joanna reached up and kissed Leroy on the cheek. 'I'll call you,' she said. Leroy nodded.

Leroy was at the back of the line as they all filed out of the room.

'Sam?' Quinn called out. Leroy turned and limped back to his partner's bed.

'Yes?'

'Now everyone's gone, I just wanted to say thanks. You saved my life, you know that?'

Leroy waved his hand in a dismissive gesture. 'You ran in for me in the first place. Anyway, you know it's a pain in the ass breaking in a new partner.'

'Mr Leroy,' said the nurse, who had returned. 'Back to your room, *please.*'

Leroy high-fived Quinn and limped back to his own room. He was tired, too.

Later that night, he was still awake. He tossed aside the *Skiers Weekly* magazine and looked up at the clock. 11:25PM.

He pulled himself out of bed and slipped on the hospital dressing gown. Using the cane, he limped out into the corridor. Seeing the coast was clear, he walked slowly down to room 319. Quietly opening the door, he peered in. Quinn was asleep.

Leroy stepped in and closed the door as quietly as he had opened it. He stepped over to the bed and stood for a moment watching his partner sleep.

Then sat himself down in the armchair by the bed.

He watched Quinn until his own eyes became heavy and he finally drifted off to sleep himself.

THE END

INTRODUCING SAM LEROY
SOMETHING TO DIE FOR

Los Angeles, late September, and the hot Santa Ana winds are blowing, covering the city with a thin layer of dust from the Mojave and Sonoran deserts.

That night, there are three mysterious, unexplained deaths.

The official view is that they are all unrelated. The deceaseds had no connection, and all died in different parts of the city.

However, Police Detective Sam Leroy has other ideas, and begins to widen the investigation.

But he meets resistance from the most unexpected quarter, and when his life and that of his loved ones are threatened, he faces a choice: back off, or do what he knows he must do…

www.amazon.co.uk/dp/B00FNMWI28

www.amazon.com/dp/B00FNMWI28

WRONG TIME TO DIE

'I don't think I've ever seen so much blood.'

Los Angeles, California

When LAPD Detective Sam Leroy is called to a murder scene, even he is taken aback by the ferocity and savagery of the crime.

Furthermore, there seems to be no motive, which means no obvious suspects.

Believing the two victims themselves hold the key to their own murder, Leroy begins his investigations there, and before long the trail leads him to the island of Catalina, where a terrible secret has remained undiscovered for almost thirty years…

www.amazon.co.uk/dp/B00VPKN4TI

www.amazon.com/dp/B00VPKN4TI

ALSO BY PHILIP COX

AFTER THE RAIN

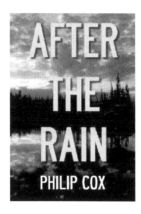

Young, wealthy, handsome - Adam Williams is sitting in a bar in a small town in Florida.

Nobody has seen him since.

With the local police unable to trace Adam, his brother Craig and a workmate, Ben Rook, fly out to find him.

However, nothing could have prepared them for the bizarre cat-and-mouse game into which they are drawn as they seek to pick up Adam's trail and discover what happened to him that night.

http://www.amazon.com/dp/B005FZ0RAI

http://www.amazon.co.uk/dp/B005FZ0RAI

DARK EYES OF LONDON

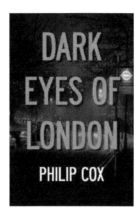

When Tom Raymond receives a call from his ex-wife asking to meet him, he is both surprised and intrigued – maybe she wants a reconciliation?

However, his world is turned upside down when she falls under a tube train on her way to meet him.

Refusing to accept that Lisa jumped, Tom sets out to investigate what happened to her that evening.

Soon, he finds he must get to the truth before some very dangerous people get to him…

www.amazon.com/dp/B007JMWBM2

www.amazon.co.uk/dp/B007JMWBM2

SHE'S NOT COMING HOME

EVERY MORNING
At 8.30 Ruth Gibbons kisses her husband and son
goodbye, and goes to work.

EVERY EVENING
At 5pm she finishes work, texts her husband leaving now,
and begins her walk home.

EVERY NIGHT
At 5.40 she arrives home, kisses her husband and son, and
has dinner with her family

EXCEPT TONIGHT

www.amazon.co.uk/dp/B009US94U0

www.amazon.com/dp/B009US94U0

DON'T GO OUT
IN THE DARK

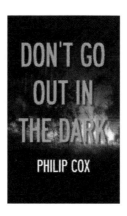

A WET AUTUMN NIGHT
Newspaper reporter Jack Richardson lends his coat and car
to a friend

AN ACCIDENT
Within thirty minutes, Jack's car lies in flames

The crash seems suspicious, and Jack wonders if it was an
accident, or murder.

But if it was murder,
Who was the intended victim?

www.amazon.co.uk/dp/B00LG005GM

www.amazon.com/dp/B00LG005GM

SHOULD HAVE LOOKED AWAY

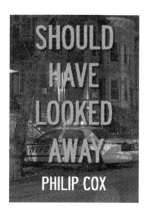

It began on a Sunday. An ordinary Sunday, and a family trip to the mall.

Will Carter takes his five-year old daughter to the bathroom, and there he is witness to a fatal assault on an innocent stranger.

Over the next few days, Will tries to put the experience behind him, but when he sees one of the killers outside his home, he becomes more and more involved, soon passing the point of no return.

Becoming drawn deeper and deeper into something he does not understand, Will feels increasingly out of his depth and is soon asking where this is going and was the victim as innocent as he first thought…

www.amazon.co.uk/dp/B01C4VVWUY

www.amazon.com/dp/B01C4VVWUY

THE ANGEL

Investigative reporter Jack Richardson is assigned to a story involving sleaze and a prominent Member of Parliament.

During the investigation, Jack receives a call relating to an old case, one involving the murder of a twenty-year-old girl, suggesting that the case might not be as closed as everybody thinks.

Torn between his assigned story, and one where there might have been a terrible miscarriage of justice, Jack must make a choice.

His decision leads him into a dark place he never knew existed, and which puts him in great personal danger…

www.amazon.co.uk/dp/B07BR2YQGG

www.amazon.com/dp/B07BR2YQGG

36355952R00167

Printed in Great Britain
by Amazon